Watching
Doctor Who

Watching Doctor Who

Fan Reception and Evaluation

**Paul Booth and
Craig Owen Jones**

BLOOMSBURY ACADEMIC
LONDON • NEW YORK • OXFORD • NEW DELHI • SYDNEY

BLOOMSBURY ACADEMIC
Bloomsbury Publishing Plc
50 Bedford Square, London, WC1B 3DP, UK
1385 Broadway, New York, NY 10018, USA
29 Earlsfort Terrace, Dublin 2, Ireland

BLOOMSBURY, BLOOMSBURY ACADEMIC and the Diana logo
are trademarks of Bloomsbury Publishing Plc

First published in Great Britain 2020

Paperback edition published 2021

Cover design: Andrew Orton

A catalogue record for this book is available from the British Library.

A catalog record for this book is available from the Library of Congress.

ISBN: HB: 978-1-3501-1676-4
        PB: 978-1-3501-8563-0
        ePDF: 978-1-3501-1673-3
        eBook: 978-1-3501-1674-0

Series: Who Watching

Typeset by Integra Software Services Pvt. Ltd.

To find out more about our authors and books visit www.bloomsbury.com
and sign up for our newsletters.

Paul dedicates this book to everyone in DePaul Doctor Who Club, and especially its founding members, Laura Buczynski, Katie Capparelli, Sophie Dixon, and Cate Morrow. You've given me so much more than just enjoyable evenings watching *Doctor Who* – thank you for opening my eyes to a new generation of Who fans.

Craig dedicates this book to his father, who thinks Daleks are rubbish.

Contents

List of Figures and Table

Figures

Table

Foreword

In the beginning, there was consensus. Primordial *Doctor Who* pro fan Jeremy Bentham, in his episode guide for Peter Haining's book *Doctor Who: A Celebration*, only expressed a negative opinion about one story, *The Gunfighters*, which he also mentioned as having the worst ratings ever, making its badness not just his opinion, but also, in passing, somehow an objective fact.

There was also, in fandom, an unspoken consensus that the Graham Williams era had been worse than the Philip Hinchcliffe era, and that John Nathan-Turner had now arrived to lead us back to greatness and old monsters.

And then, two years later, John Nathan-Turner got booed at a *Doctor Who* convention. It was an organized booing, the only one of those I've ever witnessed. I was startled. Were the things we all thought good now bad?

I think it was around that point that the weird consensus dissolved. That icebergs of first one alternative critique, then many, started to split from the un-considered mass of ancient fandom opinion. One new critique that was very important to me was the Anti-Pertwee movement: *The Daemons* was not the best story of all time, but was a bit rickety; Pertwee was not 'a dashing man of action in a sprightly yellow roadster' (these repeated phrases do so much of the job of solidifying fan opinion to the point where it's accepted rather than considered) but a paternalistic Tory; Graham Williams was not the shoddy despoiler of what had been a serious adult drama, but a genius of wit and character. In short, everything the old guard had put their feet up on was to be shot away, and here we came with our new paradigms.

In that moment it was glorious to be alive and a fan. Not only were there new critical perspectives to play with, to use as tools, to thump things with until they broke, but the whole notion of new critical perspectives on *Doctor Who* being possible was new!

Of course, there was a lot that was great about the Pertwee era. That same generation, after all, embraced Terrance Dicks as a hero, while seeing no contradiction. To merely hate was never the point. To say a lack of consensus, anti-consensus, isn't something scary but is in fact vital, that was far more important. (Of course, throughout this section, I've been speaking about *Who* fandom as if it was just the people who went to the Fitzroy Tavern in London, edited fanzines and just happened to control the means of production of everything but the TV show, and eventually the TV show. Seeing new critical perspectives also allows us to see that there were always other versions out there, of which I was unaware. The US experience of fandom led by women, for example, was completely different. UK fandom was very queer, vastly male and almost entirely white.)

I feel this battle has never been entirely won, that *Doctor Who* fandom is forever seeking to regain consensus, to have everyone think the same thing in its own, never-ending Operation Golden Age. Why, otherwise, would *Who* fans continually talk about canon, when the show clearly doesn't have one? If only, they think, everyone could at least agree on what constitutes *Doctor Who*, then we'd finally be getting something done! Who was a companion and who wasn't? How many actors have played the Doctor? Is he called Doctor Who? These questions are, as many local radio competition setters have discovered, unanswerable. And yet *Who* fans persist, like Light in *Ghost Light*, to try and make lists of what cannot be listed.

That central property of the series, to squirm out of the way of definition, is one of its most beautiful aspects. It means that, as in certain branches of mysticism, to study the texts of *Doctor Who* is to study only ourselves. We work them over, we find new perspectives, we work inward on ourselves. The *Doctor Who Magazine* story poll now, year by year, looks more like a pumping heart, cycling through ups and downs, than a dead iceberg.

I first suggested a panel on changing critical perspectives to Gallifrey One convention organizer Shaun Lyon for the 2016 event, but it went wrong. Author Andy Lane chaired the panel and made it about all sorts of things other than changing critical perspectives. It was fun, and I sat back and let it happen, but I'd really been after something meatier than that. So next year we had another go, and for that panel we were lucky enough to get fan academics onboard, including one of the authors of this volume. Paul and I started talking about pitching an academic track at the convention, Paul brought Joy Piedmont onboard, and suddenly we had recognition, at the biggest fan-run *Who* event, of many different critical perspectives on the show, of those perspectives changing all the time.

I feel sorry for people who've always liked *Four to Doomsday* (which is currently having a moment as part of the latest wave of rediscovery, as the Blu-ray season sets make their mark), much as I feel sorry for people who always liked Abba. The joy of fashion is the joy of obsession and loss. I look forward to reading this volume and having my perspectives shifted once again.

Paul Cornell.
Gloucestershire, January 2019.

Acknowledgements

This book started life during the Gallifrey One convention and a panel discussion led by Paul Cornell: we thank him for the talk on fans' changing feelings over time and for the foreword. The authors wish to acknowledge the following people, whose expertise and research help exceeded all expectations: Katharine Olson, for the reference to the devotional habits of pilgrims in the middle ages, Jef Burnham, William Staton, and Fatenah Issa. Thanks as well to the staff of the National Library of Wales, Aberystwyth, for their help in locating various materials relating to *Doctor Who* and Tom Hercock of the BBC's Written Archives Centre. We also wish to acknowledge Philippa Brewster at I.B. Tauris, who helped usher this project in its earliest days as well as the folks at Bloomsbury who oversaw it for publication. Chapter 3 was first published as Paul Booth, 'Periodizing Doctor Who', *Science Fiction Film and Television*, 7, no. 2 (2014): 195–216.

Finally, thanks to all the *Doctor Who* fans we've met and students we've taught over the years.

In addition, Paul wants to thank DePaul University and especially Scott Ozaroski in the Study Abroad office, who feed this madness by letting me teach the *Doctor Who* course every year. Thanks to Peyton Brunet, whose sharp editorial eye has improved the manuscript immensely. Thanks to my family: my soft and lovely Slinky, Rosie, Gizmo, and BK. Craig wants to thank Kate for the reference to pilgrimage, and for listening to (and tolerating) my lengthy perorations on a show she cares nothing about. (Except for the David Tennant period. And Paul McGann.)

Note on Titles

The nature of *Doctor Who* as both a contemporary and a historical document means that there have been numerous ways to identify the types of stories that exist. In short, the Classic *Doctor Who* stories (which we classify as the stories from 1963–96) are almost always told in multi-episode chunks: a single title story is usually made up of multiple (usually 4, sometimes 3, 6, 8, or 10) half-hour episodes put together in a story or serial (before 28 May 1966, all of these episodes also had a title; after 28 May 1966, the episodes were grouped under one blanket title for the story). New *Doctor Who* episodes (which we classify as stories from the revival of the show, from 2005–present) are usually forty-two minutes long (with some exceptions), single-titled episodes (even two-parters have individual titles). We have used the term 'episode' to refer to the single half-hour or hour-long television show and the term 'story' to refer to the larger grouping of episodes (or, in the case of New *Who*, we use the terms interchangeably).

Throughout the book, we italicize the titles of Classic *Doctor Who* stories (1963–89, 1996), and put New *Doctor Who* stories (2005–Present) in inverted commas. Furthermore, we retain the UK tradition of calling a full year of Classic *Doctor Who* stories a series (rather than the US season). In the case of New *Doctor Who*, we use the BBC-preferred nomenclature to identify New *Who* in seasons, and to begin numbering them anew (so the first David Tennant season is Season 2 not Series 28).

Introduction

Going Forward in All Our Beliefs: Regenerating and Re-Valuation in *Doctor Who* Fandom

There's a common joke about *Doctor Who* fans: 'What do you get if you put four *Doctor Who* fans in the same room with each other?' The answer: 'Five opinions'.

Fans are, famously, opinionated: from compiling lists about the best episodes, ranking films in sequence, or deriding particular plot points, fan discussion often becomes situated around notions of value. This book is about that value, and the way fan and official textual and extratextual discourse can shape both value and the evaluative processes for creating value. It's also about those fans: people who express strong emotion surrounding *Doctor Who*, and often in some ways act on that emotion (via textual or creative discourse). As fans expound on their particular favourites or least-favourites, they bring a sense of propriety to the media texts of which they are part. We're concentrating on *Doctor Who* fandom in particular in this book, not only because *Doctor Who* fans (nicknamed 'Whovians' by the *Doctor Who Fan Club of America* in the 1980s – a term that itself is devalued by many Classic *Doctor Who* fans) are notorious for rankings, best-of lists, worst-of lists, and polls about the most *fill-in-the-blank*-attribute of the series, but also because we ourselves are part of this fan culture, a positionality we interrogate in more detail in the conclusion. Both authors of this book are fans of *Doctor Who* (BBC, 1963–89, 1996, 2005–) and have been for many years; we are both part of *Doctor Who* fan communities and have first-hand experience observing (and even participating in) the construction of value through fandom. We come from different countries (Paul is from the United States and Craig from the UK) but both have relatives/experiences living in the other. At a moment when fan conversations and industry connections are merging, we believe it is important to be aware of our own participation in the making of meaning and value within fan, industry, and academic institutions.[1] For the process of value-making extends beyond *Doctor Who,* beyond fan/industry relations, beyond fan/academic relations: in today's converged environment, value becomes important in all responses to media. Quite simply, value is valuable, and understanding how value is constructive and constructed helps to reflect changing notions of mediation in the digital age.

For those who would not consider themselves fans of *Doctor Who,* perhaps a short introduction to the show and its fandom will itself be valuable (and to those who do consider themselves fans, apologies in advance for the condensed explanation). *Doctor Who* tells the story of the Doctor, an alien who can travel in time and space, whose curiosity leads them to explore the universe. The Doctor's people have the ability to change their body through a process called 'regeneration', which means that fourteen people so far have played this character over the past fifty-five years. The Doctor can travel anywhere in time and space in their time machine, the TARDIS – a small blue cabinet disguised as an old-fashioned police box that is bigger on the inside than on the outside. The Doctor is an adventurer and explorer but rarely a fighter (unless they have to be). The Doctor prefers to investigate and learn but does have some notable enemies whose plans they continually foil, including the Daleks, a race of mutated creatures that ride around in mobile tanks. The Doctor travels with a series of friends and companions, mostly from the Earth. First premiering on 23 November 1963 on the BBC, *Doctor Who* ran almost uninterrupted until 1989, when it was cancelled by the BBC. There were seven original Doctors, each with a unique look and personality. In the 1970s, *Doctor Who* was one of the most popular television shows in the UK, but in the 1980s the ratings went down. It was exported to more than thirty-five countries during its original run. From 1989 to 1996, the show was not on the air, but numerous books, magazines, comics, and other ancillary products were produced by fans, the BBC, and their offshoot companies. In 1996, the BBC teamed up with FOX to make a pilot episode of a new *Doctor Who* series with the Eighth Doctor. It was shot in Canada and took place in the United States. It did not get great ratings, so the planned show never appeared. From 1996 to 2005, *Doctor Who* was again off the air, but more products were being made, including a series of Eighth Doctor novels that continued his story and original audio dramas starring original Doctors made by an audio production company called Big Finish. In 2005 the show came back with a bigger budget and a changed format. It has been on the air since 2005 and six new Doctors have appeared. In all their incarnations, the Doctor is an iconoclast, an enemy of governments and establishment structures that oppress individuals. The Doctor champions the disenfranchised. *Doctor Who* fandom has waxed and waned over the last fifty-five years: three periods of intense fandom while the show was on the air (Dalekmania in the late 1960s, the 'golden era' of the 1970s, and the current revival [especially during Matt Smith's time on the series]) and highly charged fan activity during the hiatus years helped bolster the show during its downtimes (notably, the 1980s). Over all of this time, the way fans have interpreted different aspects of the series reflects changing norms and habits, and by examining the different ways fans have valued aspects of *Doctor Who* over the years, we can start to understand the importance of value for fan communities.

Value can also be measured differently depending on the source: in this book, we are largely not talking about monetary value, even though this is how industry analysts often frame notions of fan value. One tension, therefore, within the larger scope of the book is between the way fans position their own (non-commercial) notions of value alongside and askance industry notions of monetary value. What happens when the BBC, which places a price on a particular DVD or book about a *Doctor Who* text, is measuring value differently than the fans, who may value a *Doctor Who* episode for personal or idiosyncratic reasons? Thus, we use *Doctor Who* and its fandom as a key exemplar of changing cultural norms and mores, and this introduction reflects on these attributes to deepen scholarship on *Doctor Who* and fan values. In laying out aspects of value, fans are participating in a number of crucial activities: discussion, conversation, ordering of canon. But the formation of value within a corpus of texts risks reproducing stolid cultural hierarchies as well, and fans are often aware of their own position within these boundaries.

Lists of rankings populate message boards, social media sites such as Facebook, published books of fanfac (factual writing by fans), fan-scholar analyses, fan critical analyses, and inter-personal fan discussions.[2] Alan McKee's exploration of fans' evaluation of the best *Doctor Who* stories remains a powerful voice on studies of value in fan communities: 'Some texts are valued more than others, for a variety of reasons: and this happens without academics to police the canon and control what should be seen as good.'[3] It is through the lens of McKee's article that we can see some of the ways in which fans utilize and negotiate list-making within fan communities, and how fans *make value through formalization*.

Such exploration of best-of's and valuations of canonization and quality run the risk of eclipsing personal opinion, especially when those lists become public or formalized through official publications. For McKee, there are a number of places where fans can go both to assemble and to share their rankings, a prominent example of which is *Doctor Who Magazine* (*DWM*).[4] Because it is the official magazine of *Doctor Who*, licensed by the BBC, *DWM* serves as a marker of *Doctor Who*'s quality as well as its subcultural and social capital.[5] When *DWM* #413, therefore, held a definitive ranking of the Mighty 200 in 2009, which surveyed its readership and found 6,700 people ranking 200 stories of *Doctor Who*, it became a touchstone upon which fans could measure their own rankings. Does *Caves of Androzani* (1984) deserve the number one spot (readers of the magazine didn't think so: it fell to #4 in 2014)? Does *The Twin Dilemma* (1984) deserve last place? Why is *City of Death* (1979) the eighth best story of *Doctor Who* – or, as McKee notes, the best?[6] Comparisons are ubiquitous. Tensions develop upon the release of an authorized list.

Value goes beyond the individual episode, however, and can reflect particular viewpoints on different aspects of a series. *Doctor Who* is a show that relies on – and, in fact, is *about* – the notion of change. So too is its evaluative potential: McKee notes the importance of 'the *changing* nature of evaluations – stable but not static – and the ways in which they are challenged in public discussions about value'.[7] Since the earliest days of *Doctor Who*, fans, scholars, and producers have catalogued the series into eras based on production characteristics. The most obvious characteristics of value in *Doctor Who* reside in the Doctor themself, perhaps initially taking the cue from the shift in leading actor, the regeneration cycle and the resulting changes in characterizations of the titular hero. From a production standpoint, the shift in the lead actor often came with a shift in behind-the-scenes personnel, and each new producer or script editor might offer his (or her)[8] take on the show.[9] This is how James Chapman organizes his historical analysis of *Doctor Who*: 'While the character and performance of each "star" has done much to influence the nature of the series, the role of key production personnel, particularly the producer and script editor, is even more significant in shaping the content of the series.'[10] Beyond production staff, there are even more ways of characterizing the *Doctor Who* text: through technological changes (pre-colour and post-colour),[11] through audience viewership (from children to adult viewers),[12] through shifts in fandom,[13] through medium shifts (from television to books, from audio to multi-media),[14] through recording technology (film and videotape to digital),[15] or through the show's many intertextual connections.[16] Each one of these moments presents a 'crisis' point, a fracture against which some fans may judge or change the value of the show.

In 2017, *Doctor Who* introduced a female Doctor: Jodie Whittaker was announced as the thirteenth Doctor, taking over the role after a procession of (white) men had previously played the titular Time Lord. It is not rare for *Doctor Who* fans to reveal their highly charged opinions about new Doctors, but casting a woman in the role led some fans to proclaim the death of the show, and describe a corresponding loss in the value of the show reflexive of their own experiences. Value is intensely personal, and reflecting on that value can reflect on the fan themselves. Of course, the reverse is also true: the way a fan speaks about a series reflects the values of that fan. For example, noted fan-cum-professional continuity adviser Ian Levine had some choice words for the series when it was announced:

THIS IS REALLY SHIT – IT SUCKS – IT'S STUPID – KILLS THE SHOW. I want nothing more to do with it and I HATE [incoming showrunner] CHRIS CHIBNALL – HE CAN FUCK OFF.[17]

CHRIS CHIBNALL MAKES ME WANNA VOMIT He has put the final nail into Doctor Who.

RIP.[18]

Such pronouncements of value are commonplace in fan circles – although, perhaps not with as much vitriol as Levine had. An image created by Will Brooks, an artist and designer who designs official paratextual art for *Doctor Who*'s Titan Comics range and Big Finish's audio adventures, illustrates 'The Regeneration Cycle', for whenever a new actor playing the Doctor is announced (Figure 1).

Feelings change over time. Evaluative practices are intensely contextual. At what point does a series 'lose its way'? Levine's above quotations reflect one particular viewpoint (Chibnall…has put the final nail in *Doctor Who!*) of a moment when *Doctor Who* lost its way. Here's another:

'**Dr. Who**', the BBC's Saturday tea-time 'adventure in space and time', has quickly lost its way. The first installment promised much;

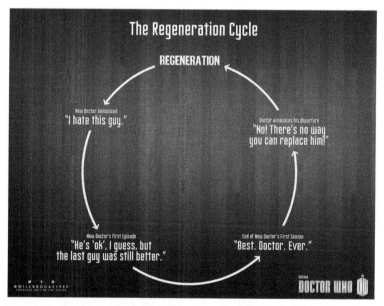

Figure 1 The Regeneration Cycle, @ willbrooks1989. *See Will Brooks' portfolio for more: https://willbrooks1989.myportfolio.com/.*

but in the second ... [the events] were so tedious that it encouraged our minds to wander – and to think; and thinking is the one thing that audiences should not be allowed to do when they are watching sci-fi ...[19]

We may expect such a pronouncement to occur well within a show's run. Perhaps this comment arrived in 1984, in between fan favourite *Caves of Androzani* and fan favourite-to-rip-on *The Twin Dilemma*.

Incorrect: this particular quotation comes from *December 1963*, written less than a week after the premiere episode of *Doctor Who*, *An Unearthly Child* (1963). The author, who wrote this letter to the *Huddersfield Daily Examiner,* went on to note that:

I was only too happy to accept the existence of the police box that could travel at will through space and time, but that rambling discussion group ... shattered the illusion. *I suspect that 'Dr. Who' is now lost and gone for ever.*[20] (Figure 2)

'"Dr. Who" is now lost and gone for ever' – how many times has that, or something like it, been uttered by *Doctor Who* fans? Here, it was written even before the introduction of the iconic Daleks. Going back to the second episode, it's hard to imagine a more long-standing notion of evaluation in *Doctor Who* fandom than this.

Serious examination of fandom has been the focus of a field in media and cultural studies for over thirty years, and *fan studies* has become a way of investigating the value that fans place on media texts (along with sports, music, celebrity, and so on) as well as the value that popular culture itself places on fans. Stemming from the canonical work of Henry Jenkins's *Textual Poachers* and Camile Bacon-Smith's *Enterprising Women*, fan studies has developed over the decades to encompass more than just the *Star Trek* fans Jenkins and Bacon-Smith described.[21] Indeed, *Doctor Who* has been the subject of a number of fan studies analyses, including many done by Matt Hills (*Triumph of a Time Lord* examined how fans of the Classic series of *Doctor Who* have become masterminds of the New series), Miles Booy (whose *Love and Monsters* describes the rise of organized *Doctor Who* fandom in the 1970s), and Henry Jenkins and John Tulloch (whose *Science Fiction Audiences,* which examined fans of *Star Trek* and *Doctor Who*, served

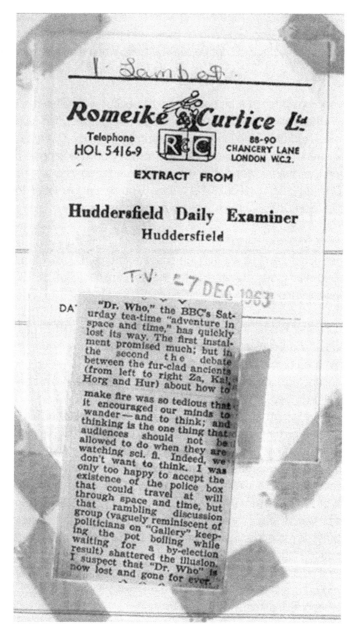

1. *Lambert*.

Romeike & Curtice Ltd

Telephone
HOL 5416-9

88-90
CHANCERY LANE
LONDON W.C.2.

EXTRACT FROM

Huddersfield Daily Examiner
Huddersfield

T.V. 27 DEC 1963

DA

"Dr. Who," the BBC's Saturday tea-time "adventure in space and time," has quickly lost its way. The first instalment promised much; but in the second the debate between the fur-clad ancients (from left to right Za, Kal, Horg and Hur) about how to make fire was so tedious that it encouraged our minds to wander — and to think; and thinking is the one thing that audiences should not be allowed to do when they are watching sci. fi. Indeed, we don't want to think. I was only too happy to accept the existence of the police box that could travel at will through space and time, but that rambling discussion group (vaguely reminiscent of politicians on "Gallery" keeping the pot boiling while waiting for a by-election result) shattered the illusion. I suspect that "Dr. Who" is now lost and gone for ever.

Figure 2 Letter to *Huddersfield Daily Examiner*, anonymous, from Graham Kibble-White Twitter.

as an inspiration for the format of this current volume).[22] Fan studies doesn't just examine fans of cult media, but also focuses on larger cultural issues in mainstream and popular societies; for instance, recent fan studies work has focused on cultural identity markers like race and gender, on the relationship between the media industry and fans, and on fandom as a political movement.[23]

This book examines not just the affective work that fans do to create value within a canon, but also the way the 'value' of *Doctor Who* changes over time. As a show with an over 55-year history, *Doctor Who* and its fandom can explore the *changing* nature of value and quality. There have been many *Doctor Who* guidebooks published,[24] as well as collections of information about the series[25] and there are a number of books that look at 'best' episodes and stories of *Doctor Who*,[26] but this volume explores the changing definitions of 'quality' as they apply to *Doctor Who* specifically, and to 'quality television' and fandom more generally.

But what is value? From a media studies perspective, this book revisits arguments about the value of value – or the way that valuation of particular aspects of television reveals underlying cultural mechanisms of canon, authorship, periodization, and fan-talk. Some previous work on what has been called 'Quality TV' highlights the way that any talk of value stems from 'the criteria used to define quality – taste, personal judgement, commercial success, industrial connections, aesthetic values, product differentiation'.[27] So-called quality TV is often articulated through auteurist language, or discourses that say that if *this* particular writer/director/producer/showrunner has created a programme, *it must be good.* Yet, many assertions of 'quality' within the television field are themselves based on stolid or culturally privileged positions. Thus, examining how value is constructed is a worthwhile exploration: as Beaty and Woo describe in their book *The Greatest Comic Book of All Time*:

[Fans and scholars] generally act as if something called excellence exists – it is the necessary assumption behind every review, best-of list, and word-of-mouth recommendation – but that assumption is wrong...we contend that excellence is not a property of works but a judgment asserted on their behalf. Comics [and, by extension, any form of media] are not self-evidently great; rather, they are claimed to be great by powerful actors within the field, and these judgments may be accepted – and consequentially reinforced – by certain reading communities.[28]

Value is not about favourites, as McKee describes: 'personal choices about "favourites" are not the same thing as decisions about which stories are "best", have the most "value". In some sense, the concept of "value" only really comes into play when interpersonal attempts to reach a consensus about stories are begun'.[29] Value has to do with consensus of quality, but it also has to do with the *lived experiences* of quality, or the phenomenology of quality. We examine the impact of fandom on notions of quality, specifically focusing on *Doctor Who* and how its reception changes perceptions of value through the affective nostalgia of fans – the 'behind the sofa' memories of *Doctor Who*.[30] Finally, from a fannish point of view, we re-visit the canon of *Doctor Who* to provide alternate readings of quality. Matt Hills argues that 'fans treat *Doctor Who*'s texts as "thick" creations', where moments of information mean more than just what is on screen.[31] Rather than a traditional 'best-of' book, which examines, say, the 'top 50 episodes' of *Doctor Who*,[32] we turn to the detritus, the discarded, the maligned, and the ignored moments of *Doctor Who* in order to tease out why fans may see the best of the worst (or, the worst of the best?) of the canon. Indeed, despite the popularity of *Doctor Who* from both a fan and an academic perspective – and despite the hundreds of books written about *Doctor Who* for the past fifty years – there has never been a book (let alone a monograph) written about the perceptions of *the worst* of the series (there are, however, humorous books intended to poke fun at the less good aspects of the series). Our underlying focus on both reclaiming these perceived bottom-of-the-barrel episodes and using them to re-examine the notion of quality and value in television and fan studies provides an important addition to studies of fandom.

Chapter outline

Watching Doctor Who features four main academic chapters that discuss the nature of reception history, including fannish perceptions of value, organization, and quality. These chapters are co-written by the authors. Each of these chapters is followed by two shorter pieces, each written by one of the authors, which offer case studies that fit within the academic analyses of that previous chapter. Finally, each of these case studies is followed by a dialogic provocation between the authors in which they debate some of the issues the other brought up in the case study. In this way, we hope to articulate both a glimpse of fannish perceptions and a more academic perspective to the analysis.

In Chapter 1, 'The Concept of Evaluation in *Doctor Who* Reception', we offer a typology of fannish evaluation that conceives of the evaluative process as a communal activity. This typology presents, as one of its main functions, Butler's imperative to perform one's fan identity – that is, the ability to pass judgment in a compelling (but not necessarily empirical) way on the merits of this or that story, implying as it does deep knowledge of the canon, becomes an important badge of fannishness. At the same time, fannish performance can take many forms, and this chapter will complicate Butler's imperative as a way of re-examining fan evaluation in the digital age.

Our first case study section examines the concept of evaluation in two different arenas. The first case study, 'The Mightiest Values', by Paul, interprets and analyses *DWM*'s Mighty 200 compilation. This list, compiled from votes by *Doctor Who* fans and subscribers to the magazine, attempted to hierarchically rank every episode/story of *Doctor Who*. As a mirror of what traditional *Doctor Who* fandom values in its stories, the Mighty 200 list records not just a list of 'must-watch' stories, but also a systematic method of evaluation. Comparing the Mighty 200 to other *DWM* best-of lists from 1998 to 2014 reveals how value begets more value: that engendering a 'best-of' elevates some stories while others fall. The second case study, 'Fan Reaction Videos', by Craig, examines these relatively recent developments in fandom. As the name suggests, the reaction video consists of a video of viewers watching a key story within a particular episode. These allow the makers to perform their identities, and also allow viewers to perform theirs; indeed, regular reaction video makers are themselves subjects of online fan communities. In these videos, emphasis is placed on emoting at pivotal 'moments', as is reflected in their editing; such moments provide validation for *their* fans' reactions. However, reaction videos represent a particular type of fan homage that is distinctly different from the fan-produced edits of episodes and scenes.[33] Rather, reaction videos allow for a sort of vicarious pilgrimage – the opening up of a space where fans can participate in the beholding of the show beyond the boundaries of what we might consider to be critical evaluation, reliving the moments when they had their first visceral experiences of this or that revelation free of the need to justify their responses. Following this, the first dialogue between Paul and Craig, 'Evolving Evaluation of *Doctor Who*', reflects both the physical and emotional elements of nostalgia as it manifests in fans' watching of *Doctor Who*.

The second chapter of the book, 'Reception History and Fan Perceptions of *Doctor Who*', explores fan culture and *Doctor Who* more specifically. We take a holistic approach to focus on the influence of fandom on interpretation of the programme itself. This draws on research from Chapman, Sandifer, and Wood and Miles, all of whom perform historiographic research into the programme – that is, they examine historical, cultural, and economic contexts to inform the development of the programme.[34] For this chapter, we apply their methodologies to an examination of the fandom of *Doctor Who*, as understood as a historical presence through *DWM*. The longest-running magazine based on a fictional text, *DWM* has a long history of evaluative elements. Not only does the magazine offer actual reviews, but it also focuses on evaluations of eras, rankings of episodes, and evaluative explorations of behind-the-scenes personnel. Using *DWM*, as well as a selection of fanzines from the Ray Hevelin collection at the University of Iowa, we contextualize *Doctor Who* fandom as a generator of the interpretation of value in the history of the programme.

This chapter is also accompanied by two case studies. In the first, 'Tegan: The Makers' Vision', Craig writes about the re-evaluation of companions over time, specifically focusing on Tegan Jovanka. Added to the cast in order to capitalize on reports of a burgeoning audience for *Doctor Who* in Australia and New Zealand, Australian actor Janet Fielding starred in the show as airline stewardess Tegan from 1981 to 1984. However, fan reaction to her arrival was initially lukewarm, especially in Australia, the very country in which she was expected to perform well, due to perceptions of her as embodying a negative national stereotype. Elsewhere, the characterization of Tegan alternately as a 'mouth on legs', as whiny, or as an ineffectual member of the TARDIS crew can be found in the fanzines and magazines of the period. However, contrary to expectations, Fielding's character went on to become one of the longest-serving companions in the show's history and is now so fondly remembered that she is one of the very few companions from the 1963–89 era of the show to be referred to during the new run. This case study will focus on Tegan's reception among various subsections of fandom, concentrating on how perceptions of the character have developed over time.

The second case study, Paul's 'Reception after the Fact', focuses on the audio universe of *Doctor Who*. In 2007, Matt Hills examined the influence of Big Finish Productions, a media production company that specializes in original audio productions of *Doctor Who* (and other cult television properties such as *The Prisoner* (ITV, 1967–68) and *Sapphire and Steel* (ITV, 1979–82)), as a way of preserving 'fans' memories and discourses of "golden age" *Doctor Who* on television'.[35] Indeed, much of Big Finish's output is focused on revisiting the Classic Doctors, especially the Fourth, Fifth, Sixth, Seventh, and Eighth incarnations. Piers Britton's *TARDISbound* also focuses on Big Finish, addressing the way it augments the narrative canon of the series.[36] In this study, Paul examines the more recent addition to the Big Finish catalogue of the New *Who* Doctors and, especially, the companions – focusing particularly on the *River Song* box sets (2015–), the *Jenny – The Doctor's Daughter* box set (2018), and the *Tenth Doctor Adventures* (2018). In attempting to preserve fans' memories of the golden era of *Doctor Who*, Big Finish may be shifting what that 'golden era' means in the age of multi-generational *Who*. Finally, the second discussion, 'The Ends of an Era', sees the authors discussing the rehabilitation of characters through fan discourse, focusing particularly on how Doctors and companions are re-evaluated over time.

The third chapter, 'The Error of Eras', critiques the common tendency to divide *Doctor Who* into discernible eras. It argues that, although a convenient shorthand for understanding changes in production staff, regenerations of the main character, or behind-the-scenes script editing, the meaningful articulation of ruptures in the continuity of television series also acts reductively on story interpretation. We call this 'periodization', and argue that it disciplines fan values about particular eras of the show. This chapter argues for a more nuanced understanding of the practice of periodization across television studies, focusing specifically on the archival principles of the *Doctor Who* text. Specifically, it argues for the joining of periodization with continuity and canon as two complementary organizational factors applicable to the understanding of the ontology of any television text.

The two case studies that accompany Chapter 3 explore the ontology of television. In the first, Paul uses *The Nightmare of Eden* (1979) as an exemplar story that doesn't 'fit' neatly into perceptions of value. One of the consequences of periodizing any television programme – that is, of artificially separating out 'eras' of the show's content – is that there will always be parts that don't quite fit. In addition, judging one era by the standards of another can create hierarchies within fan cultures. In contrast to the 'convivial evaluation' noted in Chapter 1, this case study examines antagonism around particular aberrations in *Doctor Who*'s periodization. It examines, most specifically, *The Nightmare of Eden* as a story that is not highly regarded among mainstream fandom, but has tended to be judged by criteria of an era rather than of the story itself. Craig furthers this in his case study of *The Time Meddler* (1965), which met with a muted response from viewers on its broadcast in 1965. Audience ratings for the serial were the lowest since the end of the show's first series, and contrast markedly with its near-contemporaries (of the episodes immediately following, only *The Myth Makers* (1965) and standalone episode *Mission to the Unknown* (1965) had such uniformly poor ratings). Yet its reputation has taken great strides since its rediscovery in the 1980s. Traditionally this has been ascribed to the story's pacing (which was relatively fast for the period), as well as excellent performances from William Hartnell and Peter Butterworth as the eponymous meddler, and the intriguing plot, which marks the beginning of exploration of the Doctor's origins. This case study, however, argues that another explanation requires scrutiny, positing that certain aspects of the serial's production, as well as directorial decisions and the interrogation – for the first time in the show's history – of the conceits behind the Doctor's travels combined with the aforementioned elements to elevate *The Time Meddler* to its exalted status today.

Finally, both Paul and Craig dialogue about the twenty-fourth series (broadcast in 1987) of *Doctor Who,* Sylvester McCoy's first, which consisted of four stories: *Time and the Rani* (1987), *Paradise Towers* (1987), *Delta and the Bannermen* (1987), and *Dragonfire* (1987). Rarely has a collection of stories engendered such strong feelings among fans, whose response to the series was almost uniformly negative at the time – poor production values, pedestrian directing, and the competent but uneven performances of a leading actor still coming to grips with the role of the Doctor all conspired to hobble the series, whose poor ratings reflected the lack of alacrity for the show among the general audience.

In our final academic chapter, 'Re-Evaluating Value in the Canon of *Doctor Who*', we examine the tension between quality and memory in *Doctor Who*'s cultural history, paying particular attention to the way specific moments in *Doctor Who*'s history are examined and re-examined due to fan and critical memory. Long-time producer John Nathan-Turner was said to comment that 'the memory cheats', meaning that fans often remember episodes as better and more resonant than they may have been. *Doctor Who* fan-scholars Tat Wood and Lawrence Miles note that there are many times in the history of *Doctor Who* when 'we remember moments when something happened' but tend to forget or ignore the 'bad' parts of an episode.[37] In this chapter, we explore these 'operational aesthetics' of *Doctor Who*[38] and analyse the way that the memory – far from 'cheating' – actually reinscribes meaning for fans. Nostalgia plays a role in memories of past *Doctor Who*, but given the wide availability of DVDs, downloads, and streaming episodes, nostalgia itself becomes tempered with immediacy.[39] This 'immediate nostalgia' reflects a new sense of value within the *Doctor Who* corpus.

This chapter is also accompanied by two case studies. Craig's first study of *The Talons of Weng-Chiang* (1977) explores a story which is frequently cited as one of the finest serials in the show's history. But *The Talons of Weng-Chiang* has nevertheless drawn considerable opprobrium in recent years due to the use of 'yellowface' in casting one of its leading actors. Drawing on reception histories of serials with similarly problematic attitudes towards race and gender (e.g. *The Celestial Toymaker* (1966), *Tomb of the Cybermen* (1967), and *Resurrection of the Daleks* (1985)), and incorporating a survey of representations of race in British television at the time, this case study explores ways in which fan opinion has changed since *Talon*'s broadcast: although still considered a landmark serial, appreciation is tempered with an understanding of the differing racial attitudes then prevalent in British society, as expressed through the serial's production values.

Paul follows this up with a case study of a curious moment in *Doctor Who* history: the juxtaposition of *Caves of Androzani* (1984) and

The Twin Dilemma (1984). In 1984, as the Fifth Doctor (Peter Davison) transitioned into the Sixth (Colin Baker), two serial stories appeared back to back that could not have polarized the audience of *Doctor Who* more. Davison's final story, *The Caves of Androzani*, is widely regarded as one of the best – if not *the* best – story of the Classic era (the Mighty 200 voted it #1). In contrast, Baker's first story, *The Twin Dilemma*, is widely regarded as one of the *worst* stories of the series (Mighty 200 puts it at dead last, number 200). This in and of itself isn't that telling – good and bad markers of quality have always lain side by side – but unusually for *Doctor Who*, which often puts regeneration stories at the end of the series/season, this regeneration story was also broadcast the week before the premiere of the new Doctor.[40] That is, one week saw the 'best' story of *Doctor Who* end while the next saw the 'worst' premiere with no change in script editor or producer behind-the-scenes. This case study will both contextualize these stories and illustrate different ways value can be a defining moment in *Doctor Who* fandom's evaluation of quality. Finally, our last dialogue explores minisodes and extras as the ultimate in ephemeral story-telling. They are paratexts in which ambience trumps substance, and there is more than a hint of the movie trailer about them in their tight focus on striking imagery.

The conclusion to the book, 'Go Forward in All of Your Beliefs, and Prove to Me That I Am Not Mistaken in Mine', offers a meta-view of valuation within academic and fannish works, using this book itself as a case study. Ultimately, the notion of quality undergirds all the explorations of value within this book, including the fact that the authors bring their own biases and expectations to the writing of this book. Only through interrogating our own relationship to the material and topics of the book can we investigate and understand our own unique positioning in terms of fannish value.

Although the above discussion of the contents of the book appears to favour the Classic series over the new, we draw on examples from every era of the show – including the 2018 broadcast series with Jodie Whittaker as the Doctor. How will notions of value and quality affect how fans understand her first series? Or her last? We hope that by uncovering the creation of value and evaluative criteria over the past fifty-five years of *Doctor Who*, we can open up discussion for the next fifty-five years, and beyond.

Chapter 1

The Concept of Evaluation in *Doctor Who* Reception

In June 2012, *The New Yorker* published its first-ever issue devoted to science fiction. That such an avowedly intellectual publication had done so was a source of bemusement to fandom. As Ryan Britt put it in an article for Tor.com, 'the periodical of serious culture is holding up its monocle to our favorite genre. The results? As the Doctor might say, "Highbrow culture likes science fiction now. Science fiction is cool."'[1]

The content of the special issue made for engaging reading. Although eclectic in terms of the types of science fiction discussed (and, indeed, on display – several short stories were included), it is nevertheless provocative to see the types of science fiction (and types of experience of science fiction) that were on offer. The contributions were, at least, pleasingly balanced in terms of gender, with Margaret Atwood, Karen Russell, and Ursula K. Le Guin all writing pieces for the issue. The first two of these, however, were reminiscences of how the writers discovered and 'got into' science fiction in the first place; Le Guin's essay, on the 'golden age' of science fiction, is pungent with affection for an earlier period, even as it castigates earlier, sexist attitudes within the community (Le Guin's editors at *Playboy* were scandalized on making the discovery that they had purchased a science fiction short story from a woman). Furthermore, the picture gracing the front cover – a cartoon, in 1930s pulp fiction style, of a sedate-looking literary gathering being gatecrashed by a tentacled alien, a robot, and a bubble-helmeted spaceman brandishing a ray-gun – speaks straightforwardly of the sort of science fiction that was being valued.

Some of this is pure nostalgia, admittedly; a greater part of it is an insistence on the literary aspect of science fiction in keeping with *The New Yorker*'s origins as a literary magazine, the publisher of landmark works by Hersey, Updike, and Salinger. But this preponderance of writing on 'How Science Fiction Used to Be' signifies in another way: it indicates a value judgment is being made in aesthetic terms. In spite of the issue's more varied content elsewhere, the emphasis in these essays and others like them is on a particular sort of science fiction: pulpy, explicated, innocent. How did 'golden age' science fiction come to be valued this way?

In answering the question, it is useful to consider in tandem another issue – one to do with the difference, often argued over, between intrinsic and extrinsic value. In philosophical terms, a thing may be thought of as having intrinsic value if it is worth possessing or experiencing in itself. In other words, there is something inherent in it that is 'right' or 'good'. In art, we frequently apprehend this quality by the term 'beauty' (though other properties may also fit the bill). In the example of, say, the *New Yorker* cover illustration above, 'golden age' science fiction is clearly thought of as possessing intrinsic value. As a totem for that genre of fiction, it is significant that the cover is not an absolutely faithful reproduction of the art of 1930s pulp science fiction, but rather a reification of it: it is more artfully composed, the lines are more clearly drawn, and the artist was none other than award-winning comic book creator (and long-time *New Yorker* cartoonist) Daniel Clowes.

There remains, however, the issue of extrinsic value. Unlike intrinsic value, extrinsic value is that which is found in something which can lead us to that which is valuable: it is good not because of some inherent property, but because it leads us to something that is good. For example, money has (or is capable of having) extrinsic value, because it can be used to do and create good things. But, as George Eliot knew when writing *Silas Marner* (1861), there is no intrinsic value in money: the miserly Marner is such a fascinating character precisely because he violates this idea, cherishing the gold coins he amasses for their own sake.

One might argue that, between them, these concepts of intrinsic and extrinsic value form the default modes for the average person when it comes to evaluating a piece of art. Whatever it is that is in front of us – a painting, a novel, a graphic novel, a film, a poem, conceivably even a boxing match or a cricket innings – we assess how good it is with one or both of two yardsticks: the qualities inherent to it, typically thought of in terms of beauty, pureness of form, and so on; and the extent to which it can assist us in apprehending such things elsewhere. One of the more influential recent treatments of these concepts in art is Malcolm Budd's 1995 study of intrinsic value and instrumental value, the latter a concept closely associated with (and in the opinions of some, identical to) extrinsic value. Budd's work has informed several recent investigations in fandom studies, including MacDowell and Zborowski's essay on 'badfilms', particularly Tommy Wiseau's *The Room* (US 2003).[2]

Any discussion of fan evaluation must take note of the intrinsic/ extrinsic model. When we hear, say, two fans engaged in earnest discussion of this or that serial's virtues – good production values, clever plotting, suspenseful cliffhangers, or individual performances, even down to the minute details of a line reading or facial expression – we bear witness to a process of assigning intrinsic value. Taken together, these factors will allow fans to arrive at an understanding of how 'good', for want of a better word, a given episode or serial is.

Intrinsic value, however, is more complex than it looks. When we consider fan-acknowledged masterpieces such as *Pyramids of Mars* (1975), 'Blink' (2007), or 'The Day Of The Doctor' (2013), the model operates in easy fashion. Stories of this type are not merely entertaining; they transcend television's ephemeral nature, and excite our aesthetic sensibilities. *Pyramids of Mars* is a prime example. In 1975, *Doctor Who* had weathered a potentially difficult transition in lead actor and a change in production values – away from the James Bond-esque, militaristic feel that pervaded the show during the early 1970s – towards a more sombre, gothic atmosphere. *Pyramids of Mars'* confident fusion of gothic themes with the symbolism of ancient Egypt combined with surprisingly robust production values, stylish directing, and the assured, affable interplay between Sarah Jane Smith (Elisabeth Sladen) and the Fourth Doctor (Tom Baker) to create one of the show's finest serials.

The urge to identify intrinsic value comes under strain, however, as soon as we confront a serial or story that is lesser in stature. How do we go about assessing a merely 'average' story – *The Krotons* (1969), say? Even more confusingly, how do we reconcile the persistent popularity within certain sections of fandom of, say, *Paradise Towers* (1987) – a serial notorious for (among other things) its laughably unconvincing robots, uneven dialogue, ludicrous scenes of peril, and a notoriously hammy piece of acting by guest star Richard Briers – with its seeming shortfall in intrinsic value?

The answer, of course, is that instrumental value is not joined at the hip to beauty, balance, purity, or any of these virtues of art. Assessments in the two areas do not necessarily have to agree, and in *Doctor Who*, they frequently don't: the bad (or the merely mediocre), like the good, benefit from having value assigned to them, merely by dint of being enjoyable. Some of the credit for this can be laid at Susan Sontag's door. Her 1964 canonical 'Notes on "Camp"' was key in identifying the 'so-bad-it's-good' aesthetic so familiar to us today, and the reason why people happily sit through films such as *The Room* or *Battlefield Earth* (Christian, 2000). For Sontag, the artlessness is the artistry:

> The reason a movie like *On the Beach*, books like [Sherwood Anderson's] *Winesburg, Ohio* and [Hemingway's] *For Whom the Bell Tolls* are bad to the point of being laughable, but not bad to the point of being enjoyable, is that they are too dogged and pretentious. They lack fantasy. There is Camp in such bad movies as *The Prodigal* and *Samson and Delilah*, the series of Italian color spectacles featuring the super-hero Maciste, numerous Japanese science fiction films (*Rodan*, *The Mysterians*, *The H-Man*) because, in their relative unpretentiousness and vulgarity, they are more extreme and irresponsible in their fantasy – and therefore touching and quite enjoyable.[3]

The camp aesthetic gains most of its currency from precisely this sort of mismatch. To return to *Paradise Towers*, for many fans the appeal lies in the fact that the serial clearly aspires to a Ballardesque story about urban decay (writer Stephen Wyatt cited *High-Rise* (1975) as an influence), and fails. The 'rezzies' or residents of the eponymous tower block – meant as the apex of luxury living, now derelict – are far too broadly depicted to be believable; Pex, intended as a parody of the type of well-meaning man-child stock character exemplified by the roles of Arnold Schwarzenegger, becomes an obstacle to verisimilitude, being played by the less than muscly Howard Cooke; the slang the Kang gang members use to communicate among themselves, meant to be construed as edgy and dystopic, sounds merely puerile, and the

Kangs themselves, with their dyed hair and baggy jumpsuits, look more suited to late 1980s *Top of the Pops* than to a near-future dystopia. This said, the actors – no less it seems than the makers – are clearly doing their best to transcend the limitations of script and production (Briers excepted), and indeed, their own limited acting experience (for many of the supporting actors, including Howard Cooke, Annabel Yuresha (Bin Liner), and Catherine Cusack (Blue Kang), *Paradise Towers* represented their first major television roles). There is something game about the production; it is biddable and endearing, in the sense that it tries hard to cleave to its tropes. To quote Sontag again: 'What [camp] does is to find the success in certain passionate failures.'[4] In other words, such serials as *Paradise Towers* elicit praise because of what they attempt, rather than what they succeed in doing.

Howsoever fans conceive of intrinsic value, then, the idea of it is clearly present in fandom, and it is invoked regularly and confidently in countless blogposts, reviews, and messageboard debates. Extrinsic value is a more challenging case. Except in the most superficial ways, it is difficult to define ways of assigning extrinsic value in fannish contexts, on the above terms at any rate (Figure 3).

However, there are methods of evaluation used by fans that bear significant resemblances to extrinsic evaluation. They are defined below

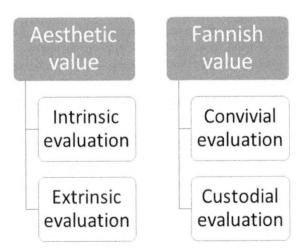

Figure 3 Typologies of evaluation.

as *convivial evaluation* and *custodial evaluation*, and although their functionality may be considered as making them intrinsically valuable, they are far more valuable to *Doctor Who* fandom for truly extrinsic reasons, i.e. because of the role they play in enabling the fandom – and therefore the show – to remain vital and vibrant: a sort of *fannish value*. We shall consider the two ways in which this is bestowed – through convivial and custodial evaluation – in turn.

Convivial evaluation

In our imagining, fannish value embraces multiple perspectives as a natural reflection of the multifaceted nature of today's fandom. It recognizes that, if we at least cannot agree with the next fan on, say, the quality of a guest star's turn on the show, or the impressiveness of this or that studio set, or the punchiness of the script, we can establish consensus in a more general way: namely, by recognizing that the serial or episode under discussion is of value to someone (perhaps many people). In other words, we may ascribe to the story the quality of *worthwhileness*. If we are unwilling to assign intrinsic value to serials we consider 'bad', either for reasons of beauty and form or via camp readings – let us continue to take *Paradise Towers* as our example for the sake of convenience – we may assign fannish value to it instead.

Doing so entails an acknowledgement of the limitations of our own attitude towards the show, and accepting that what is 'worthwhile' for us may not tally with what is 'worthwhile' for others. Changing attitudes towards the way in which stories are told on-screen, borne of generational differences, offer the most instructive example. Post-2005 *Doctor Who* is, after all, 'adventure-oriented, up-tempo flexi-narratives', as Matt Hills puts it, in which exposition is pared back to the barest minimum, plot points are thrown at the viewer at (to some) bewildering speed, and character-based stories are emphasized over concept and situation.[5] The gulf in tone between it and *Doctor Who* of, say, the early 1980s is wide; it is certainly hard to imagine even one of today's two-parters taking almost thirty minutes to reveal the story's antagonists, as happened, for example, in *Earthshock* (1982). For fandom, worthwhileness seems to explain that peculiar and longstanding phenomenon of completism, whereby a fan is impelled to purchase every episode (or even, in extreme cases, every piece of merchandise and so on) connected with the object of their adulation.[6] Today, one might resort to simple brand loyalty for an explanation, but this gambit falls down in the 1990s, when no such concept made sense in *Doctor Who* fandom, when the brand was moribund, and yet VHS releases of even the most boring or risible serials were strong and steady. How else does one explain the otherwise contrary tendency to purchase a serial one will seldom, or never, watch, except to invoke the idea that, no matter how boring, laughable, or lamentable one finds this or that story, it is part of the narrative of *Doctor Who* and therefore worthwhile?

Convivial evaluation finds support in the multiplicity of potential readings available for stories. The fandom is replete with evaluations of serials and episodes of dubious intrinsic value which nevertheless construct plausible ways of assigning value to them. For example, many fans and fan reviewers attempt defences or revisionist assessments of derided serials not according to how they derive pleasure from, say, their campiness, but on entirely serious grounds. Again, *Paradise Towers* provides a good example. Any number of 'serious' treatments exist, but one of the more persuasive ones is Darren Mooney's essay, which, though acknowledging the serial's many faults, makes as compelling a case as could be made for its being 'an underrated gem'. Mooney assesses the story against its exemplars in dystopian science fiction; notes approvingly the impetus to experiment in narrative terms after the nostalgic excesses of the late Davison and Colin Baker eras, which are lambasted as 'four years of [the show] essentially spinning its own wheels'; suggests, by way of a lesbian reading of Tabby and Tilda, the two 'rezzies' who live together, that the Russell T Davies episode 'Gridlock' (2007) owes a debt to the story; and offers convincing explanations for some of the serial's shortcomings, concluding that

> [*Paradise Towers* is] far from perfect, but it's a very clever and very bold piece of science-fiction, and it marks a clear direction for the series. It's the start of great things, marking a path back to consistent quality for the series.

If the defence that the more risible scenes are meant to be read as intentional absurdities is a weak one, the essay as a whole proves surprisingly adept at effacing *Paradise Towers'* failings and re-presenting it as the mostly successful attempt at social commentary it purported to be.[7]

This assessment and others like it posit a sort of redemption from oblivion for stories long thought of as conventionally 'bad' that place little or no reliance on camp readings, replacing that framework with one that treats the text with utter seriousness. Beauty and enjoyableness are obviously still very important, but other, less vaunted factors take their places here alongside these more usual considerations. The disparity ultimately has its roots in who is doing the evaluating. Fans assess within a community, a fact that has important ramifications for how they do so, from the simple need – described by Judith Butler over twenty-five years ago in various books and essays – to perform their identity for others, to maintain, indeed protect, the object of their obsessions. It is suggested here that this second focus for fan evaluation, fannish value, takes its cues not from the text, but from the text's use value for the fan community.

Convivial evaluation is a manifestation of this. Paul Gilroy's recent framing of the concept of 'conviviality' as the commingling within modern societies of people with disparate social and ethnic backgrounds offers a springboard for convivial evaluation's definition.[8] Although *Doctor Who* fandom displays a surprising level of cohesiveness, it is nevertheless a broad church: beyond the bipartite framework that naturally arises from consideration of the show's history, there are other, smaller yet no less significant rifts in opinion, typically centred on the cleaving of fans to particular eras of the show. The vectors for these splits in opinion often involve consideration of the 'eras' of *Doctor Who*, organized according to the actor playing the lead role. More recently, however, there has been an intensification of the discourse surrounding the relative strengths and weaknesses of what we may refer to as the three 'production eras' of the post-2005 series: the 'Russell T Davies era' (2005–10), the 'Steven Moffat era' (2010–17), and the 'Chris Chibnall era' (2017–) named after *Doctor Who's* three showrunners.[9]

Convivial evaluation places emphasis on the points of contact between these various groupings within fandom. Gilroy defines conviviality as a 'social pattern in which different metropolitan groups dwell in close proximity, but where their racial, linguistic and religious particularities do not [result in] discontinuities of experience or insuperable problems of communication'.[10] It is easy to see how such a concept can translate into terms applicable to *Doctor Who* fandom today. Its global popularity has given rise to geographically disparate fan communities. While fan clubs and societies in Canada, Australia, New Zealand, and the United States are of longstanding, the successful *Doctor Who* conventions organized for (and by) groups of fans in Germany and Sweden in recent years demonstrate the show's appeal in places beyond the English-speaking countries that have constituted its fans' province since the 1970s. Such communities will doubtless share certain core values – their fans (presumably) apprehend the Doctor as a force for social change; they may like their science fiction to be eccentric; they are also, perhaps, Anglophilic to varying degrees. Otherwise, it is hard to know what they would agree on when it comes to the show; and yet, when it comes to assigning value to it, the various ways in which *Doctor Who* generates meaning for them may all find expression.

This highlights convivial evaluation's break with the fossilized viewpoints of fandom's past. One of Gilroy's contentions is that multiculturalism is a red herring – that the starting-point for the construction of identities within contemporary societies is the experience of diaspora, and the 'dual consciousness' that comes from being from one culture yet within another. Convivial evaluation posits that value issues not from simple considerations of aesthetic worth or even personal enjoyment, but from the unique perspectives of each participant in the evaluative process. The abiding characteristic of convivial evaluation is its transformative quality: each new discussion frames the text in ways that underline its unfinished nature and emphasize the show's polysemic properties. It is hard to see how such a culture of evaluation could have arisen in, say, 1970s fandom.

However, convivial evaluation presupposes another, related characteristic. Because such discussions admit the viability of multiple viewpoints *within a fandom*, they are inherently convivial in the literal sense: they celebrate the text and shun rancour. Thus in our imagining, the term 'convivial' has a dual meaning: it represents the coming together of fans with hugely differing backgrounds, and also symbolizes the tone of these evaluative discussions. The nature of the discourse is almost always positive, congratulatory, and mutually reinforcing.

At first, this seems counterintuitive. After all, discussions on the value of something by definition involve subjective assessment, and so entail the exchange of conflicting ideas. If one person holds that, say, *Black Orchid* (1982) – a notoriously 'love-it-or-hate-it' serial – is one of the show's masterpieces, while another believes just as strongly that it is the show's nadir, it is difficult to see how positivity can prevail. However, as long as fan consensus can coalesce around a given story's position as part of the canon, good humour is maintained. The quality of worthwhileness is crucial to understanding how convivial evaluation negotiates major schisms in taste and maintains unity within the fandom. Even if there can be no common ground on how good a given story is, in an environment in which everyone is in broad agreement on the worthwhileness of the text or corpus under discussion – in other words, that it means something, to someone – the mood will by default be one where positivity reigns supreme.

One may think that such a mode of evaluation contributes little to the advancement of fan evaluation of a given text beyond the fact of its popularity (i.e. the lengthier the discussion, the more generally the viewpoint it expresses is shared). However, convivial evaluation serves as a site for the generation of value, inasmuch as it fulfils two important roles. First, in the expatiation of the 'nuts and bolts' of the text – including the analysis of scenes, at a level of detail approaching the forensic; the identification of key lines, or even gestures, by the protagonists; references to previous characters, storylines, and tropes, and many other elements – it has a didactic function, educating less well-informed fans and, crucially, assisting in the establishment of a reading of the text that, if not dominant, certainly retains its influence in fandom at least. Secondly, however, convivial evaluation bears an important rhetorical function, amplifying certain elements of the text that the interlocutors deem to be of worth, and identifying key points for future debate. Examples of this mode of evaluation include messageboard threads devoted to a given episode, Twitter hashtags referring to a given episode, and so forth.

Custodial evaluation

We term the second mode of assigning value 'custodial evaluation', and it is a byproduct of the show's extraordinary longevity. Elsewhere, the term 'custodial narration' has been advanced to describe the intense sense of regard for the show's future longevity that the production of episodes such as 'The Night of the Doctor' (2013) seems to exemplify.[11] This minisode – less than seven minutes long – enjoys an exalted position in fandom entirely at odds with its modest length and nominally ephemeral nature. It runs as follows: Cass (Emma Campbell-Jones), the sole remaining crew member of a gunship that is about to crash, is suddenly joined by the Eighth Doctor (Paul McGann), who offers to rescue her. On seeing the TARDIS, Cass realizes that the Doctor is a Time Lord, and mistakenly assumes him to be a participant in the Time War, whose exceptionally violent nature she despises, and she refuses to go with him, preferring death than to be associated with the race that is complicit in the war. The ship crashes on Karn, an alien planet, whose inhabitants – the Sisterhood of Karn – extract the Doctor's body from the wreckage and resuscitate him, giving him the option of regenerating into a warrior. Despairing of an end to the war, and against his moral judgment, the Doctor agrees, and the episode concludes with his regeneration into the character that would become known to fandom as the War Doctor (John Hurt).

Finding an explanation for the high regard in which 'The Night of the Doctor' is held is simple. In addressing three points previously left unexplained – the nature of the Doctor's participation in the Time War (alluded to several times in various episodes since the show's return in 2005 but never explicated); the question of what happened in the Doctor's life between the *TV Movie* of 1996 and the arrival of Christopher Eccleston's Ninth Doctor; and the identity of John Hurt's character, revealed at the end of 'The Name of the Doctor' (2013) – the minisode tied up loose ends, providing crucial backstory. The corollary of this, however, is that there is some value in doing that: *Doctor Who* fandom places value on continuity and in-universe consistency in a way that fans of shows such as (for example) the sitcom *Bottom* (BBC, 1991–95, 1993–2005 (stage)) – whose protagonists die several times during the course of the series, only to reappear in the next instalment without explanation – do not. None of the events depicted in 'The Night of the Doctor' *needed* to be shown, but once they were, they allowed fans to gain a new perspective on other elements in the show's overarching narrative. If custodial narration provides an explanation for why the show's makers – almost all *Doctor Who* fans at this point – so often resort to this sort of gambit, custodial evaluation represents the corresponding process at work among fan communities. Stories are valued for their inclusion of narrative elements that are necessary to maintaining the existence of the show. Backstory and internal continuity have almost always been seen as worthy of consideration to some degree in *Doctor Who*'s history, but custodial narration – and, therefore, custodial evaluation – foreground these elements. Fans assign value to an episode based on the cohesiveness it brings to the show as a whole, and the success with which it enables the creation of nuanced understanding of the protagonists and scenario. 'The Night of the Doctor' was followed by the ninety-minute anniversary special 'The Day of the Doctor' (2013), a story which did not require prior knowledge of 'The Night of the Doctor' in order to comprehend its events. However, the latter served to enhance the viewer's understanding of the former – *and all other episodes of the show*. Evaluation occurs, then, along narratological lines, and with a profound impulse to preserve the show, and by extension, the fan community. What drives custodial evaluation is assessment of what a story contributes to a larger narrative whole, and its profundity. It must resonate – at least, must not clash with – what has gone before, and, in its embracing of Hills' concept of the 'endlessly deferred narrative', it confers intergenerational responsibility on today's viewers, challenging them to play a part in the creation and celebration of key moments in the show, and helping them to orient the generations of fans that follow in their own appreciation of it.[12]

What does it mean to be a custodian of something? Care for the thing under one's aegis is clearly key. So too is preservation, which is why the subset of fandom that obsesses over the continuing search for *Doctor Who*'s missing episodes (ninety-seven at the most recent count, all from the Hartnell and Troughton eras of the show) is held in high regard. However, it is also true that custodians may pass judgment over what it is they are caring for. As with archivists, the choice of what is worth preserving and what is worth caring for resides with them. In this way, they subtly alter the trajectory of fandom: they may exert something like an editorial influence, and help to frame debate over what the show should and shouldn't be. Fan reactions to changes in tone brought on by the arrival of new script editors or producers often assume this form. For example, in 1985 a fan from Burnley found fault with the show's (then recently transmitted) twenty-second series. It is instructive that her criticisms are couched firstly in proscriptive tones (the implication that the show ought to be more adult-oriented), and secondly in terms of 'saving' the show:

> I feel rather sorry for actors Colin Baker and Nicola Bryant, who have to act out pathetic storylines.
>
> Beginning with The Twin Dilemma, it is clear the story was meant for an under-five age group, and failed to make an impact on screen whatsoever.
>
> Attack of the Cybermen was definitely another re-hash of previous Cyberstories. The acting was an improvement on The Twin Dilemma, and the direction was average.
>
> ...
>
> The Two Doctors was a load of rubbish ...
>
> All in all, this season has been the worst ever, and I hope for an improvement when Doctor who [*sic*] returns after its 18 month rest.
>
> ...
>
> I don't want the show to be axed for good, and I am making these comments for Doctor Who to be improved. To save it.[13]

Custodial evaluation is important to fans for another reason. By placing emphasis on the show's continuous narrative, fans elevate it, articulating the sense of profundity and wonder that permeates so many fans' experiences of it. Arguments against this viewpoint are certainly possible, and indeed persuasive in many respects. However, fans who emphasize the viewer's ability to read the show as one enormous story help strengthen the fandom's uniqueness – after all, no other science fiction show is so old, or exhibits such a strident sensibility towards the tropes that formed it. Media outlets can also be complicit in this, by treating the 1963–89 series and the post-2005 series as one. *The Guardian*, for example, maintains the habit of referring to the new series as 'seasons', beginning with Christopher Eccleston's series, which the newspaper calls 'season twenty-seven' (season twenty-six, of course, being Sylvester McCoy's final season (1989)).[14] This is at odds not only with TV listings, but also with the BBC, which refers to new seasons as 'series', the first of which is Eccleston's: an example of the faithfulness that fans exhibit towards a particular set of values, the core identity, so to speak, of *Doctor Who*.

Case Study 1A

The mightiest values: Rankings in *Doctor Who*

Paul Booth

Rankings of particular episodes, or moments, within a television canon are always fraught with value judgments – by their very definition, each ranking has to be debatable and fluid. It is no surprise that many fans have an affinity for ranking elements within the corpus of the text, but *Doctor Who* fans in particular seem particularly keen to rank.[1] When meeting a fellow *Doctor Who* fan – identified, perhaps, by a bow tie, long scarf, or question mark jumper – it's not so hard to imagine that the first question out of anyone's mouth will be, 'who's your favourite Doctor?' I suspect every *Doctor Who* fan has been asked this question and – when appropriate – has a number of different answers depending on their mood. The very question of 'favourite', however, presupposes a ranking of the Doctors: if there is a #1, there must be a #2, #3, #4, etc. In fact, Colin Baker was so upset at being voted last on *Doctor Who Magazine*'s (*DWM*) polls ranking the popularity of the Doctors that he refused to interview with them for a number of years. In *DWM #322* he noted that:

> I think people's attitude to my time in *Doctor Who* is based more on where it sits within the canon, rather than about any actuality. It's perceived in terms of scheduling, or the kind of press it was getting, or how it coincided with a time when those who were disaffected – because John Nathan-Turner wasn't doing exactly what they wanted – started sniping at him regularly.[2]

Today, with a wealth of *Doctor Who* content available to stream, download, or insert into a DVD player, fans have ready access to evaluate multiple aspects of a series; it's harder to imagine how rankings might have occurred before the widespread availability of easy-to-access content (as our next chapter discusses).

Still, the topic of rankings has never quite left *Doctor Who*. Perhaps it has to do with the BBC's policy of releasing audience appreciation numbers throughout the run of the Classic series, or maybe because the constant renewal and regeneration mean there are always different elements to argue about, but from its very beginning *Doctor Who* has seen convivial evaluative judgments – and, importantly, the arguing about these values – as central to the core of fan discussion. As we discussed in the introduction, the quality of even the second episode of the series ('I Suspect That "Dr. Who" Is Now Lost and Gone For Ever') indicates that ranking happens even when only two episodes exist.

In this case study, I interpret and analyse one particular ranking, *DWM*'s Mighty 200, in comparison with two other *DWM* lists – a 1998 poll of Classic *Doctor Who* stories and the fiftieth anniversary poll conducted in 2013 and released in 2014 – to see not how any one episode ranks higher than any other, but rather to see how *changes* in the rankings reflect different sets of value judgments within the fan audience.[3] (While we expand on this in the next chapter, I want to spend some time here introducing some of the concepts before they are fleshed out.) The Mighty 200 list, compiled from votes by *Doctor Who* fans and subscribers to the magazine, attempted to hierarchically rank every episode of *Doctor Who*. As a mirror of what traditional *Doctor Who* fandom values in its episodes, the Mighty 200 list records not just a list of 'must-watch' episodes, but also a systematic method of evaluation. Comparing the Mighty 200 to other lists – including *DWM*'s other polls (which give a solid read on what one particular fan audience values over a period of time) – reveals how evaluation is really cultural co-optation: a 'convivial evaluation' as we argued in the first chapter.

DWM has been a standard presence within the *Doctor Who* fan community since it first arrived as *Doctor Who Weekly* in 1979. Over the past forty years and over 500 issues, the magazine has featured an array of content designed for multiple types of fan audiences: there are critical reviews of episodes, behind-the-scenes facts, photo displays, comic stories, reviews of other media, feature stories about the series, interviews with stars and producers, letters to the editor, columns from the producer/showrunner, and a variety of other features that kept the magazine going even during the hiatus years between the end of the Classic series and the start of the New series. Officially the longest-running TV tie-in magazine, *DWM* was originally published by Marvel

Comics until Panini Comics purchased the magazine, along with the rest of the Marvel UK catalogue in 1995.[4] Today, it publishes monthly, along with twice a year 'special editions' that focus on macro-issues in the world of *Doctor Who*, including issues on non-fiction writing about *Doctor Who*, the fandom of *Doctor Who*, and the toys and games of *Doctor Who* (among many other topics).

The Mighty 200, released in 2009 as part of the thirty-year celebration of *DWM*, was not part of any special issue, but rather was the culmination of a poll *DWM* undertook to create a 'massive and exhaustive survey' of televised *Doctor Who* episodes.[5] Remember, of course, McKee's note that 'personal choices about "favourites" are not the same thing as decisions about which stories are "best", have the most "value"' – these votes were (supposedly) not about what fans' *favourite* episode was, but what the *best* episodes were.[6] The poll also ranked series of *Doctor Who* based on average rankings of episodes within that series, and for fans of a particular demographic, certain eras are remembered more fondly than others. According to Matt Hills, writing about the Hinchcliffe/Holmes partnership on the series, 'Working together on 16 stories featuring Tom Baker as the fourth Doctor, Philip Hinchcliffe and Robert Holmes have frequently been viewed by fans as overseeing one "golden age" in *Doctor Who*'s long history.'[7] Fittingly, Series 13 and 14 (the two Hinchcliffe/Holmes series and Tom Baker's second and third) were ranked first and second in the polls, with just a 0.5 per cent difference of score between them.

According to the article, 6,700 people responded to the survey, with the average age of the voter being thirty-three years old (and reported having read *DWM* since 1990, when they were fourteen years old). As the magazine states, these demographics 'skew older and further back' than most polls, and this 'does have an impact'. Indeed, any poll will be influenced by the types of people who take it, and *Doctor Who* polls are no exception: *DWM* readers tend to skew older and white (and more male) than a lot of newer fans might identify.

As part of the 2009 poll, the compilers also noted how the popularity of a story may have shifted over time, and what it compared to in the previous 1998 poll, concretizing the very idea of *shifting* value judgments within the poll. For example, *Nightmare of Eden* (1979), a story discussed later in this book, is ranked number 167 on the Mighty 200 poll, and rated a score of 5.703 out of 10 by the readers of the magazine. In 1998, *Nightmare* was ranked 138 (out of 159 stories) but received a higher overall ranking of 5.708 out of 10 (admittedly, not that much higher). Some stories changed rankings massively: the very-low ranked *The Twin Dilemma* (1984, and also discussed later in this book) dropped from 4.368/10 to 3.844/10, even though it was ranked bottom of the list both times. It's not just that the episode was disliked the most; it's that *it was disliked even more in retrospect*. Similarly, on the opposite end of the spectrum, the episode that immediately preceded *Twin Dilemma* on air, *The Caves of Androzani* (1984), actually increased in popularity from 1998 to 2009. Voted the #1 story of all time in 2009, it was merely #3 in 1998 (and again in 2014 it dropped to #4). In addition, the actual score increased as well, from 8.851/10 to a whopping 9.164/10. (I discuss the polarization around these two episodes that appeared back to back in Case Study 4B.)

It is very hard to determine why something may change positions on the list, except to say that fans' tastes often change, perhaps as a marker of larger changes in a culture. *The Evil of the Daleks* (1967), an episode almost entirely missing from the *Doctor Who* archives, was ranked #9 in 1998 and #18 in 2009, but dropped to #34 in 2014. Perhaps an influx of new *Doctor Who* fans, who started watching the show with Matt Smith's Eleventh Doctor and recently subscribed to *DWM,* hadn't gotten their hands on the BBC CD of the 1967 episode. Or perhaps a younger demographic no longer concentrates on episodes they can't actually watch.

In fact, age might be a key element of the changing values of the fans. Consider that in 2009, the time of 'The Mighty 200', the average age of the poll-takers was thirty-three; meaning that in 1984, at the time of *The Caves of Androzani*'s airing, many of the poll-takers were between six and ten: arguably the perfect age to discover a strange television show about a time travelling, shape-shifting benevolent alien wearing a cricket uniform. Is it possible the memory really does cheat? If so, it is a selective memory and it's not very good at cheating; as mentioned, *The Twin Dilemma* scored lower in 2009 than in 1998, as did the episode immediately preceding *Caves*, *Planet of Fire* (1984, 6.437/10 compared to 6.808/10). If fans are influenced by their memory, then the episodes they thought the best increased in value, but the episodes they thought the worst decreased – the memory doesn't just cheat, it's also quite polarized. And that polarization increases over time.

Whereas we might remember some things fondly, others we may re-evaluate in hindsight: memory also seemingly cheats in reverse. Take, for example, the episode 'Fear Her' (2006). In 2006, immediately after the episode aired, it received an audience Appreciation Index[8] rating of 83 and a *DWM* rating of 6.096/10 – certainly not the best that *Doctor Who* has ever generated (and the lowest of that particular series), but not the worst either. But in 2009 'Fear Her' dropped even further, to ranking 192/200 and a score of 4.89/10 – a drop of 12 per cent! In 2014, it was ranked 240/241. *Time and the Rani* (1987) – a consistently low-ranked episode – sinks lower and lower in the polls each time it is evaluated. In 1998, it was ranked 154 out of 159 (with a score of 4.68/10). In 2014, it was 198/200 (with a score of 4.247/10). And in 2014, it was 239/241 (rising slightly with a score of 4.574/10). It seems fans' contextual remembrances are affected by much more than just the show itself – they can be influenced by the polls themselves. If something is low ranked in one poll, it tends to be lower ranked in future polls. If something is high ranked in one poll, future polls elevate it to a higher position. While some jostling among the very top or very bottom happens because of fluctuations in particular audience demographics or fleeting feelings, the presence of sentiment itself seems to have a major impact on the way episodes are ranked.

And thus ranking becomes a way not just of evaluating the particular value of an episode at a particular time, but charting how different rankings affect rankings moving forward. A text with a high ranking may continue to rise while lower rankings continue to sink. In the 2014 poll, the most recent episode at the time (the fiftieth anniversary 'The Day of the Doctor' (2013)) topped the poll, a new addition to the canon. If history is any guide, it won't be in the top place in future polls, but it won't be far off. Values reinforce values.

Case Study 1B

Fan reaction videos: Responding to *Doctor Who*

Craig Owen Jones

The relation of fan reaction videos – short productions using the most basic filming equipment, consisting of nothing more elaborate than footage of the creators watching, and reacting to, an episode, film, trailer, or video clip – to fannish evaluation may not at first glance be obvious. Videos of this kind (by *Doctor Who* fans, at any rate) rarely offer conventionally critical perspectives on the text being watched; indeed, most critical evaluation is conspicuous by its absence. However, the very act of watching, of *beholding*, serves to finesse perceptions of the text under scrutiny. By dint of background, dress, comportment, emotional response, and editorial decisions, fan reaction videos constitute a surprisingly coherent set of critical perspectives, emphasizing certain narrative properties of this or that episode while underplaying or omitting others. Most importantly, from the perspective of viewers watching these videos, they offer the opportunity for validation of their own act of viewing, and may even comprise a site of fan pilgrimage, in which fans can share and appreciate each other's responses to an episode without feeling the need to explain or justify their reactions.

The earliest reaction videos appear to have been created in the mid-2000s. They were, at first, uploaded for shock value, or else 'for laughs': videos featuring pornographic or obscene acts, such as *2 Girls 1 Cup* (2007), were the subjects of videos whose emotional focus was the revulsion and horror they evinced in the viewers, while others, such as *Re: Scarlet Takes a Tumble Reaction Video* (2008), featured the often-hysterical reactions to homemade 'outtake' videos.

Fan reaction videos developed on the heels of this earlier phenomenon. Early examples included reactions to the trailer for *Star*

Trek (Paramount, 2009), the BBC television series *Sherlock* (2010–17), and *The Hobbit* film series (New Line, 2012–17). Some of the earliest *Doctor Who* fan reaction videos date to the spring of 2013, when the conclusion of that year's season prompted several YouTubers, including Rosa Magalhães and the Chique Geeks, to upload reaction videos to the season finale, 'The Name of the Doctor' (2013). In November, when the fiftieth anniversary of the show afforded an obvious opportunity for fan production, over a dozen YouTubers uploaded videos of their reactions to the ninety-minute special 'The Day of the Doctor' (2013), *An Adventure in Space and Time* (2013, a dramatization of William Hartnell's tenure on the show in the 1960s), and other texts released and broadcast as part of the anniversary celebrations. These videos have gone relatively uncommented on in the context of *Doctor Who* fandom or scholarship: with the exception of Brigid Cherry's essay, which laid important groundwork for future analysis by outlining the prevailing contours of the phenomenon in the context of *Doctor Who* fangirling and 'squeeing', scholarly attention has been firmly directed towards the more creative texts of fan production.[1]

Fan reaction videos have an allure all their own, a cachet that extends beyond the *schadenfreude* of watching, say, a skateboarder's painful wipeout (a staple of the earliest reaction videos), or the revulsed response to watching the performance of an extreme sexual act, many of which were online pre-YouTube, before 2005. The act of watching is gentler, though emotionally it may be no less intense; the effect for the initiated is one of enablement and, perhaps, validation of one's own reactions, especially if they mirror those of the subject(s) of the video. They provide the Butlerian *sine qua non* of fannish behaviour, inasmuch as they allow the makers to perform their identities, and also allow viewers to perform theirs; yet it may be possible to push the point a little further. Fan reaction videos make it possible to embark on a particular type of fan homage that is distinctly different from fan-produced edits of episodes and scenes. Rather, reaction videos allow for a sort of vicarious pilgrimage – the opening up of a space where fans can participate in the beholding of the show beyond the boundaries of what we might consider to be critical evaluation, reliving the moments when they had their first visceral experiences of this or that revelation free of the need to justify their responses. The application and appreciation of affect become salient.

Anatomy of the fan reaction video

The vast majority of *Doctor Who* fan reaction videos exhibit similar narrative structures. Louisa Ellen Stein has foregrounded how the technological limitations of reaction videos shape the very text they seek to create: reaction videos are (or have the capacity to be) 'moments of interpretive and expansive (or even resistive) authorship [that] are shaped by the digital tools audiences use as well as by the affordances and limitations of the interfaces at play'.[2] The uniformity of structure in the *Doctor Who* YouTube community is certainly reflective of this comment. All videos are shot using either camera phones or laptop cameras, and are therefore, to all intents and purposes, 'locked down'; no panning or zooming takes place. The background invariably constitutes an important performative element. Strategically placed badges of fan identity – or fan devotion, perhaps – such as *Doctor Who* posters, action figures, or toy TARDISes establish and underscore community membership, as does the mode of dress of the subjects, who are frequently seen brandishing sonic screwdrivers, wearing *Doctor Who* T-shirts or pin badges, or even cosplaying as the Doctor.

Most videos begin with a salutation delivered directly to the camera; these may be explanatory or merely phatic, but are never more than half a minute long. There then follows the 'reaction' portion of the video: the YouTuber is seen watching the show on a screen off-camera with the audio in the background. (The more sophisticated videos feature an inset in a corner showing the footage from the show synchronized to the video, so that the viewer is able to see what the YouTuber is reacting to in real time.) Although some YouTubers offer reaction videos covering an entire episode of *Doctor Who*, the vast majority of videos are heavily edited, concentrating on the 'textual "moments"', as Matt Hills has described them, of high drama and emotion in the episode.[3] Afterward, there is a valediction of anywhere from a few seconds to a minute or two in length, containing comments on what has just happened, or further emoting on particular inflection points in the show. Fan reaction videos derive a great deal of their allure from the nature of the narratives they represent. Watching the makers of these videos emote in reaction to inflection points in the episode they are watching allows us to relive those moments of revelation ourselves – *even if our emotional responses differed from theirs.*

What is less intuitive is that these videos offer ways of validating our own experiences. Stein notes that 'response videos', as she calls them, '[become] a site of audience negotiation with the televisual text and with each other regarding what it means to be a fan'.[4] However, Stein's observation does not imply any *uniformity* of emotional response. The sense of community reaction videos engender derives its impetus from elsewhere: namely, the editorial choices made by *Doctor Who*'s YouTubers, which, taken together, serve to underscore the sense of belonging to a community of fans. When multiple YouTubers upload their reactions to the same key sequences or 'moments', a *de facto* consensus is established as to the performative value of those sequences, a consensus rooted in deep knowledge of the show, its tropes, and the overarching narrative added to with the screening of each new episode. The fact that YouTubers upload edited versions of their reactions independently (usually within hours of the episode's screening), and that their understanding of what constitutes a 'moment' so consistently agree with one another as evidenced in the choice of sequences to be included or omitted, speaks to the ubiquity among them of this deep knowledge, and frees the similarly knowledgeable viewer of their videos from received notions of consumption – the unspoken idea that fans should, or perhaps are minded to, comport themselves in a particular way during the act of viewing. By watching the videos, viewers are a party to the reactions of others but not actually present to witness them, and conversely, do not have their reactions witnessed, and are consequently unencumbered by the pressures of performativity within a public context. Rather, the interest for the fan lies in identifying the key 'moments' in the text, because it is this act, with all the accumulated knowledge of the show and its narrative that it entails, that serves as the primary indicator of fan identity.

Affective viewing, self-insertion, and fan reaction videos as pilgrimage

A critical aspect can be located in these videos from time to time. It is not uncommon for a YouTuber to pass comment on this or that development in the story. 'They got him for the 50th!' notes one

YouTuber with satisfaction on seeing Tom Baker's cameo appearance in the anniversary special 'The Day of the Doctor' (2013); 'That was quick!' opines another in bemusement at Matt Smith's abrupt regeneration into Peter Capaldi at the conclusion of 'The Time of the Doctor' (2013).

By and large, however, these are exceptions, and it is suggested here that the prevailing tone of fan reaction videos is not critical but communal. There is no more compelling demonstration of this than the plethora of fan reaction videos to 'The Day of the Doctor' (2013), and in particular, fan reactions to one moment in particular: the cameo appearance of Fourth Doctor Tom Baker in the role of the Curator, an enigmatic and mercurial figure who, the script implies, may or may not be the Doctor's future self. The cameo was spoiled (by Baker himself) the week before the episode aired, but it appears, from compilation videos of fan reactions, that the majority of YouTubers who uploaded their reactions were unaware of his appearance; certainly they would have been entirely unaware of its emotional contours. The scene, a two-hander between Baker and Matt Smith, in which they discuss the success of the Doctor's plan to save Gallifrey in such a way that it disappears from the observable universe, is largely stolen by Baker, who, in a succession of verbal and physical tics, evokes his previous portrayal of the Doctor. His final line, a reference to the immutability of one's future actions – 'Who knows, eh? Who knows?' – is accompanied by a playful tap of his nose. This 'hush-hush' gesture is consciously or unconsciously replicated in the videos of four of the eight YouTubers whose reactions to the moment are archived by reaction video compiler Blake Dale.[5] The aping of the gesture, no less than their modes of dress – three wear bow ties or T-shirts with bow ties designs at the neck, referencing Smith's costume – speaks to nothing so much as vicarious involvement, an instance of affective viewing replicated in bedrooms and living rooms across the fandom.

The narrative style of the videos of Rosa Magalhães approaches the fan reaction from this perspective. Magalhães' videos tend to be 'top and tailed' by very brief addresses to the camera, introducing the viewers to the episode being watched, and thanking them at the end for watching. In between, however, she is almost completely silent: her reactions are overwhelmingly rooted in facial expression and body language. Dramatic revelations are accompanied by a look to camera; another key component in the nexus of emotional responses is the shedding of tears, typically during Doctor/companion farewell scenes or regeneration scenes.[6]

The Chique Geeks similarly privilege affective viewing. One of the most prolific, and certainly one of the most popular, producers of *Doctor Who* reaction videos on YouTube, the pairing of Amy Tandberg and Marita Holm are Norwegian fans who began uploading their videos in 2013, and at the time of writing (2018) have over 23,000 subscribers. The reaction video uploaded in 2013 in response to the transmission of the dramatization of First Doctor William Hartnell's years on the show, *An Adventure in Space and Time* (2013), features a variety of modes of affect. The video is seventeen minutes long, and begins with brief reactions to the early scenes in the drama. These reactions are for the most part muted. They include laughter at comedic moments, indignation as Hartnell's irascibility is portrayed on-screen, and gleeful acknowledgement of actor David Bradley's aping of Hartnell's visual affectations, such as the grasping of his lapels while pontificating (a gesture that had at the time of transmission attracted comment in fan circles due to Peter Capaldi's referencing of it during his televised reveal as the Twelfth Doctor the previous August). The lightness of mood begins to dissipate as the story progresses, and the onset of Hartnell's arteriosclerosis increasingly interferes with his ability to act: a scene showing him repeatedly fluffing his lines draws expressions of sympathy, and the farewell scene with the show's first producer Verity Lambert (see Figure 4) elicits the following comment from Tandberg: 'This is so sad'.

This dynamic abruptly changes during the scene in which Hartnell, having been informed his contract will not be renewed, breaks down in tears in front of his wife (see Figure 5). The key line – 'I don't want to go' – is, of course, a metatextual insertion, the final lines spoken by David Tennant's Doctor in the last episode of his regeneration story, 'The End of Time Part II' (2010). At this, the Chique Geeks hug one another, and Holm begins to weep.

However, the emotional climax of the video occurs a few seconds later. The drama's live action comes to an end on the TARDIS set: Hartnell stands in the console room, ready to film his last scene. As he waits for the call to action, he casts a lachrymose look around the set, and his eye stops on something out of shot. A reverse cut shows us what he is looking at: Matt Smith, who at the time of transmission was the current Doctor. As the music swells, the two men exchange knowing glances, and Smith places his hands on the original TARDIS console in the same manner as he did during his tenure as the Doctor.

The Chique Geeks' reaction at this point (Figure 6) is one of startled disbelief. A 'squee' is followed by exclamations: Amy shouts 'What?' at the screen, while Marita says 'Oh, come on!', apparently chiding the producers for the sentimentalism on show.

In this way do YouTubers come to 'know' a given episode – by touch, feel, and intuition – even though this is a medium of virtual distance. If there is an evaluative hierarchy present, it relates not to the strength of a plot or the clarity of writing, but to the nature of the emotions on display. If popularity is anything to go by, the most noteworthy episodes of *Doctor Who* are, according to fan reaction videos, the ones that elicit the profoundest emotional responses. On the Chique Geeks' *Doctor Who* playlist, for example, the ten most watched videos of full *Doctor Who* episodes are as follows:

1 'The Day of the Doctor' (655,000 views)
2 'The Time of the Doctor' (474,000)[7]
3 'The Name of the Doctor' (256,000)

Figure 4 During Verity Lambert's farewell scene with William Hartnell. Amy: 'This is so sad'.

Figure 5 During William Hartnell's scene after the Newman meeting (14:27). In response to Hartnell's line 'I don't want to go, I don't want to go', Amy looks at Marita; both put their hands to their mouths; they clasp each other's hands, and finally embrace (above).

Figure 6 During Matt Smith's cameo (15:14–15:21). In response to the reveal, both 'squee' in shock. Amy: 'What?!' Marita: 'Oh, come on!' Both put their hands to their chests.

4 'Deep Breath' (226,000)
5 'Listen' (137,000)
6 'Hell Bent' (92,000)
7 'The Magician's Apprentice' (90,000)
8 'The Husbands of River Song' (84,000)
9 'Heaven Sent' (81,000)
10 'Last Christmas' (79,000)

All ten of these episodes are 'moment-heavy', so to speak; they are flush with arrivals and departures; their stars frequently find themselves on the horns of the profoundest dilemmas; they twist, turn, and resolve with more than the usual flair. In these qualities, fans may establish their worth.

Clearly, much of the appeal of fan reaction videos lies in their fundamentally visceral nature. If we put aside the possibility of staged reactions, or at least satisfy ourselves that we can tell staged and authentic reactions apart, then we are left with the conclusion that we watch them because at the moment of truth – the revelation of a companion's death (or miraculous survival), an unexpected appearance by an old adversary, the Doctor's regeneration – they offer the spectacle of a fan emoting. Fan identities may be performed by dint of dress, style of haircut, and merchandise in the background of the video, but the nature of the makers' emotional reaction at these points forms the fulcrum on which the video pivots. The Chique Geeks' videos are so popular – their reaction video for 'The Day of the Doctor' has almost two-thirds of a million hits at the time of writing – because of their affect, their enthusiasm. Or as Daniel Mumby puts it,

What singles out ChiqueGeeks is their unbridled enthusiasm for their given fandoms and the approachable, entertaining way in which it manifests itself. Many fan reaction videos can feel staged as the participants go for the biggest reaction possible, or can just descend into monotonous, unedited screaming (and squeeing), which grates on one's ears and prevents you from understanding someone's passion. In this case, however, the reactions are completely genuine and often hilarious. We grow to like Amy and Marita as people, growing to understanding their obsessions and eventually empathizing with their reactions.[8]

Dialogue 1C

Evolving evaluation of *Doctor Who*
Paul Booth and Craig Owen Jones

Paul: Craig, in your discussion of fan reaction videos, you mentioned that 'the effect for the initiated is one of enablement, and, perhaps, validation of one's own reactions, especially if they mirror those of the subject(s) of the video'…and then go on to call this a 'sort of vicarious pilgrimage' where fans can relive their experiences through watching the visceral experiences of others. I think this is fascinating, especially when we look at the way fan reaction videos tend to highlight the most bodily moments in the text: the ones that we feel within our physical selves. We watch people jump from the jump scares, laugh at comedic moments, cry at the emotions of a death or kiss. Fans want to relive the *physical* experience that they had when they first encountered the text through the emotional reaction of others. This seems to fit with what Linda Williams notes as the 'visceral appeal to the body'.[1] Yet, we also think about reliving the past through the media as a type of nostalgia, what Svetlana Boym calls 'an intermediary between collective and individual memory'.[2] Certainly, my case study of the Mighty 200 list from *Doctor Who Magazine* is all about cerebral discussion rather than physical reaction – maybe a more traditional form of nostalgia for the past ('the memory cheats' indeed). Your discussion seems to indicate that nostalgia can be held in the body as well as the mind. What are your thoughts on reaction videos as a type of immediate nostalgia?

Craig: I hadn't thought of it that way, but it makes a great deal of sense to conceive of fan reaction videos being viewed for nostalgic reasons. There is a disjuncture in the fact that the sense of hankering after a past or an experience long gone is absent – even the oldest *Doctor Who* reaction videos are only five years old, and many rack up thousands of views within days of being uploaded – but it's been almost thirty years since Frederic Jameson wrote of nostalgia for the present.[3] One wonders if the reaction video, and the almost instantaneous taking up of the possibilities for reliving one's experience that it offers, pushes the concept to its furthest extreme, because, as with the 'nostalgia film', the visceral experience that came with the initial viewing of an episode is precisely what you *don't* get when viewing a reaction video; after all, you know exactly what's coming. Comparison with earlier generations of fans probably plays a smaller role. I can't be the only fan who has witnessed older fans speaking of attending the famous Longleat convention of 1983 and felt a twinge of envy. The memorialization of earlier eras is already a phenomenon; both Russell T Davies and Steven Moffat have spoken of inflection points in their experiences as fans revolving around key points in 1980s fandom, such as the return to the show of Cybermen in *Earthshock* (1982), the twentieth anniversary special, or the Fifth Doctor's act of self-sacrifice in *The Caves of Androzani* (1984). Like the GI in the Iraq War film *Jarhead* (US, 2005) who hears a Doors song blaring from an assault helicopter flying overhead and ruefully asks, 'Can't we get our own fucking music?,' today's fans naturally want to make their own memories. Seen from this perspective, fan reaction videos offer a way of identifying and celebrating these inflection points in today's episodes.

The sense of reaction videos as pilgrimage, however, seems to me to derive from the uniquely reverential business of revisiting key episodes in general, and regeneration scenes in particular. It's instructive that the most watched compilations of fan reaction videos are those featuring the Smith/Capaldi and Capaldi/Whittaker regenerations – not the whole episode, but the regeneration only. Older fans did similar things. I grew up with VHS, and can recall forwarding or rewinding tapes to watch key scenes of, for example, *Star Trek: The Next Generation* (CBS, 1987– 94) – the battle scene in 'Yesterday's Enterprise' (1990), or the climax of 'The Best of Both Worlds (Part 1)' (1990) – in greater detail. But as you imply, it was the visceral experience I was attempting to duplicate. The shock of watching the Enterprise losing a battle with the Klingons, or watching Picard turn into a Borg, was always out of reach, though. Try as I might, my foreknowledge meant I couldn't experience it in quite the same way again, and so the act of watching became one of admiration and wonder at how the emotional effect it had on me was achieved in the first place. Watching reaction videos is a form of fan pilgrimage, like a music fan visiting a famous recording studio, say, because, as in that case, it is performative. It doesn't strike me as too fanciful to compare, say, liking the video, or leaving a comment below the line, to lighting a candle at a shrine, or etching a graffito into the church wall. Medieval pilgrims who visited saints' tombs often chipped off a piece of the marble or alabaster,[4] or even bit into the wood of this or that holy relic in the hopes of coming away with a splinter that they could cherish and revere. Isn't bookmarking a video a similar gesture, broadly speaking – a way of leaving one's mark?

Paul: Yes, I think there is a similarity between carving out a piece of a relic and also returning to the scenes of an episode that moved us – both traffic in emotion and (in a sense) religious meaning. But there is a very central difference that I think speaks to the tension that I'm feeling here: actually possessing a piece of marble or a holy relic is to have a *thing*, to note the physical presence of an object. To fast forward to Locutus of Borg threatening the bridge crew is an attempt to recapture a *moment*, a fleeting sense of time. (Although perhaps we can get close to that with something like your beat-up old VHS copy of 'Best of Both Worlds', wherein the more you watched that scene, the more physically destroyed that copy would get. After a while, it would simply disintegrate, something younger *Who* fans today would be shocked at, I'm sure!) In a way, this sense of the importance of the moment marries today's fan's focus on social media. As you mention, Jameson's nostalgia of the present is more relevant now than it was thirty years ago as the constant updatability and *presentness* of social media influences today's fans to live in an eternal sense of now. Personally, I've seen my students be nostalgic for something that happened just a few weeks ago.

Of course, I don't think this is entirely new. There's a great history of fans introducing other fans to episodes at conventions. We like introducing noobs to *Doctor Who* partly because we get to watch their reaction as they see things that we like – and I don't know about you, but I hate it when they don't react the way I would react. But of course, our initial reaction is always tempered by what we've known about the episode before we've seen it. Unless we're really careful, it's almost impossible to see an episode of *Doctor Who* that we've never seen and not already know what to expect – the vast history of the show has been infinitely discussed, and spoilers (even things like knowing the titles of the episode) affect our viewing. I mean, can you just imagine what it would be like to watch *Genesis of the Daleks* (1975) and not know that

that speech was coming up? Perhaps what we are actually nostalgic for is the *absence* of knowledge, of experiencing the show as a blank slate. Forget behind the sofa, we want to be behind our memories.

Craig: Yes, that absence of knowledge is key. A few years ago, a friend of mine and I were having a discussion about 1960s *Doctor Who*, and I mentioned that I hadn't yet seen Patrick Troughton's final serial, *The War Games* (1969). He looked wistful for a moment, and then said, 'I envy you. I would give anything to see that one again for the first time'. I have at times contemplated never watching a film that resonated with me ever again, to preserve the memory in its pristine state, so to speak, but I never had the willpower. Few of us do, I think, and so we try and find ways to offset or slow the process in which the memories change; to stop that first, visceral experience from receding. This may even be a more acute problem for young fans today; after all, if new episodes can be spoiled, so too can the moments within them for which we will soon experience a nostalgic longing. Many years ago, when TV was still analogue, I watched, having not yet seen the film, a trailer for *The Shawshank Redemption* (Columbia, 1994) that contained the central revelatory plot point. (Those who have seen the film will know the one I mean!) And so, when I came to watch it, I had to mentally pivot away from the central question of *if* Andy would overcome his predicament to wondering *how* he was going to do it, an instance of 'operational aesthetics' if ever there was one.[5] That became the focus for my nostalgia later on, but there was always that memory of the spoiler interfering with it.

You mentioned the pleasure we derive from watching someone else experience a show or film for the first time: that is what reaction videos are all about, of course. But the experience of introducing someone to the material...I wonder: could it be that one way of preventing the memory from receding is to make it transmissible? Perhaps that accounts for your annoyance at witnessing a different (errant?) reaction to a given moment. It also makes sense from the perspective of fans wanting to ensure the show continues, harkening back to the custodial narration mentioned earlier. A custodial nostalgia, perhaps!

Chapter 2
Reception History and Fan Perceptions of *Doctor Who*

In an era where the entire history of *Doctor Who* is 'always on' via streaming, download, CD, and/or DVD, how does one go about identifying the essential episodes of the show's television canon? A glut of content can hamper selective viewing. In other words, what aspects of a canon become the central organizational factors for viewers? And how do particular texts become *known* when viewers are spoiled for choice? It seems as though the contemporary media ecosystem is flush with content: so much so that it is virtually impossible to keep up with it all. Certainly, in the historical context of *Doctor Who*, this is a recent phenomenon. In the era of the Classic series (1963–89), episodes were only sporadically re-broadcast in the UK once shown on the BBC, and it was many years before the BBC even considered making episodes available to watch on VHS in the early 1980s, then DVD, Blu-ray, downloads, and streaming services like Netflix, iPlayer, Amazon Prime, or BritBox. The very fact that there are missing episodes of the series – episodes that have been wiped from the vaults and no longer exist[1] – highlights the rather cavalier attitude the BBC held towards the programme (and of course more television than just *Doctor Who* was discarded). It's only relatively recently that the historical and financial incentives (via perceived and actual fan value) to preserve content have made *Doctor Who* available to a 24/7 viewership.

In this chapter, we will develop a holistic approach to understanding how both fans and media professionals shape the 'canon' of a series through an analysis of *Doctor Who*'s professionalized fandom and its influence on the interpretation of the programme itself. There are multitudes of ways that fans can create value – including (and this is important to state) not being influenced by others at all. However, for many fans, value is established through the community of other fans. We explore and analyse the way that fan perceptions of quality and value in *Doctor Who* episodes and the *Doctor Who* canon are influenced in an out-sized manner by the discourses of the production office of *Doctor Who* itself. We contextualize *Doctor Who* professional fandom as a generator of the interpretation of value in the history of the programme as an antecedent to today's official formation of television canon. In order to do this, we first examine the way that the 'value' of various aspects of the series was augmented by one of the official paratexts of the series, *Doctor Who Magazine* (*DWM*), during a period when the series was off-the-air. Indeed, Matt Hills notes that *DWM*'s 'relationship' to *Doctor Who* 'is not simply to an anchoring text' but also as an influencing one as well.[2] We then discuss how the rankings of different *Doctor Who* episodes differ over time, with particular emphasis on the changing valuation of Classic *Doctor Who* episodes. Finally, we apply this analysis to contemporary evaluations of value in the digital age, looking particularly at the commentary of then-showrunner Steven Moffat on an official fiftieth anniversary release documentary, *The Doctors Revisited* (2013).

Value as content; content as value

In the era of the fiftieth anniversary of *Doctor Who*, a host of material – some of it repackaged Classic content – was released by BBC Worldwide in celebration of the show. This 'spike in brand activity', as Matt Hills puts it, 'permits [*Doctor Who*] to be culturally and affectively licensed, positioning it as an issue of (fan) cultural capital rather than as a purely commercial venture'.[3] In other words, the merchandizing of *Doctor Who* for the fiftieth anniversary, a period where *Doctor Who* was seemingly everywhere, became a way not only for the BBC to solidify its branding of the series, but also for fans to concretize their own values of the show. For the fiftieth anniversary, BBC-America aired a series of documentaries about each of the Doctors, one a month in 2013 until the release of 'The Day of the Doctor' (2013). Each of these documentaries accompanied a Classic episode, which was edited into an omnibus format, and included an introduction by showrunner Steven Moffat. Later, BBC-America released a DVD series called *The Doctors Revisited* (2013) that promised 'a curated selection of the best of each of this storied program's eleven Doctors.... *The Doctors Revisited* includes a profile of each Doctor and one Classic story for each'.

These DVDs arguably were released in order to introduce fans who only knew the New *Doctor Who* series to the Classic: and in doing so, they formed an official 'canon' of Classic episodes that narrowed down the glut of content of *Doctor Who* that exists, thus answering the unasked questions, how do fans discern which Classic *Doctor Who* content to approach first? Which is the best? Which should be avoided? Every fan will have their own particular eye towards what is the most important, crucial, meaningful, or essential episodes of *Doctor Who* to watch.[4] Indeed, this has been an ongoing discussion in *Doctor Who* fandom. During the hiatus period between the end of the Classic series in 1989 and the beginning of the New series in 2005, *DWM* featured articles about how to introduce virgin viewers to *Doctor Who*, including one by Tat Wood titled 'How to Make Fans (and Influence People)' that (humorously) argued 'without constant access to *Doctor Who* on terrestrial TV, it's entirely down to us [fans]...'[5] Fans provide the judgment call on which episodes to consider important. But 'every period of *Doctor Who* has its champions and its detractors', every episode has its fans and its haters.[6] When introducing the series to a neophyte, there is a conundrum about the experiences of the viewer: there is almost too much content to begin to approach.[7]

The 'paradox of choice' that Barry Schwartz described in 2004 becomes relevant to *Doctor Who* fandom in the dawning of the digital age and beyond, and a paradox of scarcity becomes relevant to the dearth of *Doctor Who* before its release on home media. It's our argument that *DWM*, as the official spin-off magazine for *Doctor Who*, helped to prescribe fan perceptions of the quality of *Doctor Who* episodes during the hiatus period between the end of the Classic series in 1989 and the start of the New series in 2005. In this chapter, then, we update and revise some of what Alan McKee analysed of *DWM* in 2001. In his article, McKee uses *DWM* as a guide for fans making value judgments on the particular episodes in the series:

For the writers in *Doctor Who Magazine* are involved in making value judgments on stories at many sites – in the Editorials, reviews, letters, annual award votes, feature articles, the 'Time Team' discussions of earlier stories, previews, and so on....The Magazine works as a public site for ongoing discussions about value judgments – and thus represents a valuable archive of empirical textual evidence about the process of making value judgments in popular culture.[8]

McKee noted that 'despite the construction in these [magazine's] discourses of "received wisdom" as being monolithic and unchanging, one of the most interesting and useful aspects of the fan community consensus about the value of *Doctor Who* stories is that it does in fact change over time, in systematic ways'.[9] Change is the operative word: value judgments rarely stay stable.

What we find remarkable is that the same discourses that are happening to shape fandom's perception of quality of *Doctor Who* in an era *before* the wide availability of home media are quite similar to the fannish discourses that shape the perception of *Doctor Who* in an era of multiple points of media access. Schwartz neatly sums up this as:

> When people have no choice, life is almost unbearable. As the number of available choices increases, as it has in our consumer culture, the autonomy, control, and liberation this variety brings are powerful and positive. But as the number of choices keeps growing, negative aspects of having a multitude of options begin to appear. As the number of choices grows further, the negative escalates until we become overloaded. At this point, choice no longer liberates, but debilitates.[10]

Although deciding which episode of *Doctor Who* to watch is perhaps not as debilitating a decision as some others might be, the paradox of choice reflects a similar sentiment from the past. Today, we turn to others – our friends, our family, the fan community – to recommend what we should watch. Which episodes are the best? The most fun? The most interesting? The most connected to the storylines of the New series?

Today's ascription of value mirrors that of the past. In particular, we are interested in the 'hiatus' years between the Classic series and the

New series. As Miles Booy notes, 'the programme's aesthetic history became standardized [in the 1980s] remarkably quickly. This was one effect of *Doctor Who Monthly* [later *Doctor Who Magazine*], but possibly the biggest influence was the twentieth-anniversary volume *Doctor Who: A Celebration.*'[11] As Booy points out, much of the content of this book, attributed to author Peter Haining, actually came from Jeremy Bentham, a writer for *Doctor Who Monthly* and President of the *Doctor Who Appreciation Society*.[12] Bentham's critical commentary on the episodes outlined in *A Celebration* helped 'to solidify an emerging canon of judgments which would last for almost a decade, until videos of old episodes were so common that people could form their own opinions for themselves'.[13] But we question Booy's assumption here: how do fans make their own opinions at all? What influences affect fans' opinions in today's saturation of content? While *Doctor Who* famously does not have an official 'canon' because the BBC has never stated what is or is not canon, fans themselves have established the importance of certain characteristics to a larger state of relevance among a number of elements of the programme, and they have often done this because of external factors and official textual merchandise. Although written by fans of the series, these books and magazines like *DWM* are official guides authorized by BBC Enterprises. The role of critical commentary *then*, which according to Booy ebbed after the VHS revolution in home media, we want to argue is similar to the role of official auteur commentary *now*. At a time when more and more *Doctor Who* is available, fans turn to other sources to help create a canon of value of the series.

Doctor Who Magazine and writing value

We use the term 'hiatus years' to describe the period 1989–2005 (as opposed to the term 'wilderness years', a term used in some fannish circles and even by the production team on the DVD for the 1996 *TV Movie*) because the sixteen-year period between the Classic and New series was not void of content. Although the television series was not on the air, a vast array of additional content – much of it authorized by the BBC – was created, including the Virgin *New Adventures* novels (which continued where the TV series left off), the *Missing Adventures* novels, the *Past Adventures* novels, the Big Finish audio plays, the Paul McGann *TV Movie* in 1996, and of course the comics and articles within *DWM*. Many of these different products spun the series' narrative in multiple often contradictory directions – indeed, because the BBC has never offered an official 'canon' of *Doctor Who* (see Chapter 3), these largely fan-written texts can be seen as alternately part of and apart from the larger, official *Doctor Who* story. Indeed, as Piers Britton notes, this 'unwieldy skein of texts' has 'no clear hierarchy' and

> the maintenance, ordering and enhancement of the *Doctor Who* hyperdiegesis have almost entirely been the work of fans. Nearly all the sustained fictional exploration of the Whoniverse belongs to the phase of the texts' history in which the audience and authors were arguably most homogenous, which is to say the lifespan of the [New Adventures] and [Missing Adventures].[14]

Far from being a wilderness, the period from 1989–2005 saw a huge range of materials for and by *Doctor Who* fans turned media professionals, people like Russell T Davies, Steven Moffat, Mark Gatiss, and Paul Cornell – and by and large kept the concept of *Doctor Who* alive at a period when it wasn't on the air.[15]

From that list above, *DWM* stands out as a steady and key influence on fans. As a 'fanfac' publication – factual information written by fans – *DWM* highlights the importance of the show in the lives of fans, but as an officially authorized venue, it presents ideas sanctioned by the BBC.[16] By presenting themselves as the fans they are, the writers of *DWM* offer a fannish point-of-view through an officially authorized source. The relationship between *DWM/Monthly/Weekly*, its fans, and the producers of *Doctor Who* has usually been friendly, although at times it could be strained. Today, the magazine boasts a monthly column written by the showrunner that answers readers' questions, and in the 1980s then-producer John Nathan-Turner was billed as a 'consultant' to the magazine, which meant that 'he was sent every issue's copy for official approval'.[17] Some fans would write letters to the magazine berating/complaining about Nathan-Turner, and according to former *DWM* writer Richard Marson in his biography of Nathan-Turner,

DWM editor Alan Mackenzie would sometimes butt heads with the producer.[18] Other magazines, like the fan-run *Doctor Who Bulletin,* were extremely critical of Nathan-Turner, and 'in 1987, hardcore fandom's general dissatisfaction grew louder as they reacted to dire stories, declining ratings, the sacking of Colin Baker and the arrival of Langford and McCoy'.[19] *DWM,* however, maintained a relatively close connection to the production team: a special issue devoted to John Nathan-Turner was released after his death in 2002, and when *Doctor Who* reached its fortieth anniversary in 2003, *DWM* readers voted him as the #1 Hall of Famer and the fifth greatest contributor to the history of *Doctor Who* (beating out Verity Lambert and Sydney Newman, the first producer and co-creator of *Doctor Who*). The point is not only how a particular officially sanctioned, fan-produced magazine remembers someone influential in the history of the series, but also how this remembrance becomes influential to fandom at large: in other words, how the values of the magazine shape the values of the fan readership.

DWM creates discourse about which fans of *Doctor Who* speak. In the delineation of any cult television series, multiple elements come together to define how fans understand the nature of the show. The magazine helps 'activate the meanings and associations of "cult" for audiences', highlighting the influence between the magazine and the fandom.[20] The difference between *DWM*, which is officially sanctioned by the BBC, and a fanzine, which is written by fans outside of official circles, can be vast, even if both are written by fans (sometimes the same fans, as in the case of *DWM*, which employed notable fanzine writers like Gary Russell). Fanzines are 'independent and localized, coming out of cities, suburbs and small towns … assembled on kitchen tables'.[21] They are 'a grassroots reaction to … the oft-lamented homogenizing effect of worldwide mass media'.[22] In an early examination of fanzine culture, Fredric Wertham writes:

> In contrast to mass media and the mass circulation publications – which of course have their place in our society – fanzines are intended for small audiences. We have built up an enormous communication machinery which at times confronts us like a superior power and, paradoxically, contributes to our isolation. The individual is apt to be submerged and regarded as a statistic. There is no such tendency in fanzines.[23]

Fanzines offer a space away from official circles, where fans can feel free to criticize or bemoan aspects of a series that may be antithetical in an official venue. Official magazines like *DWM*, alternately, can try to shape fandom in particular ways, encouraging fans to be part of fandoms in an authorized fashion. Official magazines don't have to like everything about a series, but they have a remit to support the show. Writers and editors of official magazines engage with readers as fans specifically, and in doing so, create and delineate a *type* of fan who becomes a synecdoche for *all* fandom – a corporatized and commercialized fan who buys merchandise, researches online, and upholds the value(s) of the text and the fandom.

Measuring value in the hiatus

It is difficult, if not impossible, to make the claim that any one thing written in an official *Doctor Who* publication can have a direct effect on an audience. Indeed, there are so many other factors that go into how individual people claim a particular value on a text that *any* one cause is suspect. We cannot argue that *DWM* has had a direct influence on any fan or fandom. As McKee notes, however, *DWM* 'does not tell us what all *Doctor Who* fans "really" think about *Doctor Who*. But it does give us a useful case study of one institution, with a variety of interesting associated discourses, serving one fan community, and offering a variety of ways to conduct debates around value judgments in popular culture'.[24] There is an imperative to read what *DWM* says as influential in some ways: there are certain value-laden tenets in *Doctor Who* fandom that become repeated time and time again, so much so that they become the stuff of lore. 'The hideously dire *The Krotons*' [1969];[25] '*Genesis of the Daleks* [1975] continues to prove…Baker's best';[26] 'fan ambrosia such as *The Robots of Death* [1977] or *Remembrance of the Daleks* [1988]…';[27] '*Timelash* [1985] was a mistake'.[28] It's true that all fans have their favourite stories. 'But while there are several bones of contention scattered throughout the TV series history…there is a general consensus around particular stories. Nearly everybody adores *The Talons of Weng-Chiang* [1977]; nearly everybody does not adore *Timelash*.'[29] Such value judgments become concretized through repetition.[30] And *DWM*, coming out at least once a month for over thirty years, has repeated a lot of value claims.

DWM, especially during the hiatus period, was the one constant in *Doctor Who* fandom. For fans of *Doctor Who* who grew up in the late 1980s and 1990s (like both of the authors of this book), it is difficult to establish a particular canon of value on past episodes – not only were they hard to find (certainly there was no 'on demand' way to watch every episode), but *Doctor Who* was not a common media property. How would these 'hiatus fans' find their way in *Doctor Who* fandom?[31] We might check out novelizations from the local library or special order titles from a bookstore, but finding an authoritative source of updated *Doctor Who* information would prove invaluable. What *DWM* said would be taken as gospel.

As we described in the previous chapter, *DWM* has run three major polls of the favourite episodes of *Doctor Who*. The first, as described in McKee, was in 1998 during the hiatus years,[32] the second in 2009, 'occasioned by 200 stories having been broadcast … whilst the most recent poll [in 2014] assessed the best of *Who*'s first five decades'.[33] Polls are nothing new to *Doctor Who* fans: 'if there is one activity that most fans engage with', Booth notes, 'it is certain to be the creation of lists.[34] Henry Jenkins illustrates that fan criticism "provide[s] a public forum for evaluating and commenting on individual [TV] episodes and long-term plot developments."[35] Obviously, "audience members … exercise judgment and discrimination in making sense of cultural objects, in a variety of ways,"[36] and "McKee's investigation of *Doctor Who* fans" discussions and debates about the value and quality of episodes of the programme reveals such fannish discriminatory analysis'.[37] Discriminatory is the key word, as 'for *Who* fandom, the "best" story award amounts to a provisional, temporary re-decoding'.[38] What is considered 'best' one year may fall the next, to be replaced by newer episodes, revisitation of Classic episodes, or changes in fan valuations.

But, is it possible that *DWM*'s own descriptions of episodes helped influence fans' polling? There are so many other factors that might also influence fans – for instance, the discovery of a lost episode, or the availability of episodes on home media – which might mean that a particular episode that ranked highly in fans' collective memories may be downgraded after newly viewing it. This happened with *Tomb of the Cybermen* (1967). When *Tomb of the Cybermen* was released on DVD in 2002, it had already been available on VHS for ten years. However, Vanessa Bishop's 2002 review of the DVD release notes that:

> watching *Tomb of the Cybermen* is a bit like being disappointed by an old friend... When *Tomb* was missing, it was everyone's favourite because it sounded like such an exciting idea. The thing is, by the time it came back, we'd got to know it very well... the very things that made it good to dream about make it bland to watch.[39]

Perhaps high definition challenged notions of quality, or perhaps Bishop's review had an effect: *Tomb of the Cybermen* dropped from #8 in 1998 to #16 in 2014 – still a respectable ranking, but still a drop.

Conversely, episode rankings can be based on a number of indeterminate factors: *The Enemy of the World* (1967), ranked #108 and #103 in 1998 and 2009 respectively, jumped to #33 in 2014 – probably because of the recovery of all the missing episodes and subsequent public release of the episodes for home consumption. Actually seeing the episode seemed to give a favourable impression. Thus, while McKee notes that descriptions of the quality of episodes in *DWM* may influence fans, there is a wide variety of other mechanisms by which value might be appraised. Indeed,

> there is a consensus about the relative value of *Doctor Who* stories in the community of *DWM* readers. This consensus has a history in the early days of the magazine, but is not absolute. It is not universally accepted, and is continually being questioned as public debate continues... Through the process of this ongoing public debate, consensus is continually reworked. It is never rendered static; but it is relatively stable.[40]

Fans' perceptions 'of the show [are] incredibly intricate, tangled up in all sorts of emotive issues that often have more to do with nostalgia than with common sense'.[41] We fondly remember episodes that we watched as children that, upon revisiting as adults, may let us down, as Dave Owen writes:

Being a late-comer to the world of *Doctor Who* does have its advantages. Although one lacks that specialized knowledge gained from years of close scrutiny of the show, it also means that one's critical faculties aren't clouded by nostalgia about what terrified you at the age of 12, or which assistant you fell in love with. Nor are they skewed by abstract value judgment about what is or isn't 'canonical'.[42]

At the same time, Stephen James Walker describes loving *The Web Planet* (1965) as a child, and 'years later, when *Doctor Who* fandom became established, I was gratified to find my positive memories of *The Web Planet* reinforced by some highly appreciative reviews. Then, in the early 1980s... It's not overstating things to say that I was shocked when I first heard someone deriding *The Web Planet*'.[43] As Seventh Doctor Sylvester McCoy himself notes in a 1994 interview, 'I remember reading something in some *Doctor Who* fan magazine, some guy who had praised one of my early *Doctor Who*'s at the time; four years later he was doing the opposite.'[44]

Ultimately, then, for fans of *Doctor Who* – especially during the hiatus period – figuring out value judgments about episodes could be based on a number of factors, including how *DWM* discussed the episodes in question, how much of the episodes could be seen, or the availability of the episode for rewatching. It's important to reflect that these value judgments helped to shape the 'canon' of *good Doctor Who* for a generation. If one were to give a list of episodes to watch to a neophyte – as happened in Wood's article about introducing *Doctor Who* to 'not-we' fans – one could do worse than look at the 1998 poll. In the era of the New series, the 2009 and 2014 polls both provided similar shortcuts to understanding which episodes to value more than others. That these lists changed and adjusted over time not only reaffirms McKee's points about the variability of fan valuation, but also indicates the shifting dynamics of influence – more episodes were available to screen, and fans had more opportunities to meet and discuss the value of episodes with other fans, not only in person at the many conventions that were springing up around the world, but also (importantly) online. For as the internet became a more visible and popular route for fandom, it opened up new avenues for exploring value in the *Doctor Who* corpus.

Revisiting *The Doctors Revisited*

Just as *DWM* may lend a particular value to episodes through polling the readership or writing value judgments into articles or reviews, so too can official merchandise offer interpretations of a 'canon' of material for new fans. As Matt Hills asserts, *DWM* 'position[s] readers as part of a "brand community" ... critiquing "bad" *Who* while co-creating value for the BBC by lending "classic" status to a subset of stories'.[45] Similarly, *The Doctors Revisited* (2013) DVD sets also can lend 'Classic' status to particular series, especially through the way showrunner (and 'fanboy auteur'[46]) Steven Moffat describes the Classic episodes on the discs.

   The Doctors Revisited aired once a month on BBC-America, leading up to the fiftieth anniversary episode 'The Day of the Doctor' (2013). The mere inclusion of the episodes themselves within *The Doctors Revisited* collection concretizes these particular episodes as worthy of inclusion in the canon, despite the fact that a number of factors other than fan-value must have gone into the decision to use them. For instance, each DVD needed to include a half-hour documentary, plus the episode and the short Moffat introduction. On the DVD, the episodes have also been altered to streamline them: despite the serialized nature of the programme, the credits before parts 2, 3, and 4 and after parts 1, 2, and 3 of each episode have been removed. However much the production team or Moffat himself might have wanted to include, say, the ten-part *The War Games* (1969) or the seven-part *Inferno* (1970) – both episodes that rated higher on the 2014 *DWM* poll than their corresponding Doctor's included episode *The Tomb of the Cybermen* and *Spearhead from Space* (1970) – they simply wouldn't have been able to fit it all on one disc. In addition, and rather obviously, they had to include episodes that still existed. So while *The Aztecs* (1964) was included as the example of a First Doctor episode, polling from *DWM* might have suggested that *The Daleks' Master Plan* (1965–66) may have been more of a fan favourite – but only three parts of that episode exist.

   Steven Moffat's introduction to each episode also situates the episode within the realm of fan appreciation, with Moffat himself positioned as the fan most clearly. He identifies as a fan, talking about how he went 'racing home just in time to fall through the door and see the beginning of *Remembrance of the Daleks*' (1988).[47] He states his opinions of each episode: 'I think an improved Cyberman' for *Earthshock* (1982);[48] 'This is one of my absolute favourite *Doctor Who* stories' for *Tomb of the Cybermen* (1967);[49] 'For me, a defining moment of *Doctor Who* is the *Pyramids of Mars*' (1975);[50] 'What we got, unexpectedly, and for one glorious night, was a brand new *Doctor Who*. And in Paul McGann, we got one of the very best, I think';[51] '1988, and I remember this one really vividly, because in my opinion, *Doctor Who* had gone off. I thought the first series of Sylvester McCoy, I'll be honest, I didn't think it worked. I didn't think Sylvester worked as the Doctor, and I thought the show was flailing'.[52] Moffat name drops Robert Holmes twice, once in a discussion of *Spearhead from Space* and once in a discussion of *Pyramids of Mars*; Holmes of course is one of the most popular writers from the Classic series of *Doctor Who*, having been voted the #1 writer in 2003 by readers of *DWM*.

But at the same time, he points out his own credentials not just as a fan, but as a professional television executive (and showrunner of *Doctor Who*). He mentions work he's done: in reference to the Doctor getting engaged in *The Aztecs*, 'River Song, eat your heart out';[53] when describing working with Matt Smith, 'I got a phone call from him [Smith] and he was in a state of intense excitement, and he was saying, "I have just seen *The Tomb of the Cybermen*, and it is brilliant"';[54] '8th of March, 1982, *Doctor Who* did something it very very rarely gets to do, and you can take my word on that';[55] 'And at this point, I was delighted to say … I was working on *Press Gang*' (BBC, 1989–93).[56]

Moffat's own discussion of the episodes thus positions him as both a fan of the series and a professional working in the field. He is the 'expert fan' whose opinions other fans should trust. The short documentaries (each one is about a minute long) work to establish the eight *key episodes* of the first eight Doctors through a variety of discursive factors. First, they are positioned as important within the history of the series – fans, they seem to be saying, need to know these episodes in order to understand the New series. For instance, in *The Aztecs*, Moffat first positions the episode as 'a category of *Doctor Who* that no longer exists … the purely historical show'.[57] A bit of *Doctor Who* history encourages fans to see this as a crucial episode in the series' tenure. In addition, the documentary goes on to note that *The Aztecs's* focus on 'what would happen if we changed time' is 'the very first time that we hear the Doctor voice his concerns' on the matter.

The other documentaries each make a claim about the importance of this one episode in the history of *Doctor Who*:

> *Tomb of the Cybermen*: One of the defining archetypal *Doctor Who* stories;
>
> *Spearhead from Space*: I think in the history of *Doctor Who*, I think in the history of all television, no show has transformed as much as this one;
>
> *Pyramids of Mars*: One of the absolutely best *Doctor Who* stories ever made;
>
> *Earthshock*: We're now in the Peter Davison era of *Doctor Who*, and this is the story that absolutely cements him as the Doctor, more than any other;
>
> *Vengeance on Varos* [1985]: I don't suppose the show has ever more reflected its own controversies and its own special nature within the show itself;
>
> *Remembrance of the Daleks*: This is an all-time classic *Doctor Who* story you're about to see;
>
> *TV Movie*: 1996, *Doctor Who* was definitely, emphatically, not coming back.... And then the rumours started ...[58]

By asserting the historical importance of each of these episodes, *The Doctors Revisited* convinces the fans watching that *these* episodes (and by exclusion, not any of the others) are the most relevant and important for understanding the history of the series. Of course, any other episodes could have been chosen for their historical context: *The Daleks* (1964) saw the first appearance of the famous monsters; *Robot* (1975) was Tom Baker's, arguably the most iconic of the Doctors, first outing as the Doctor; *Survival* (1989) was the last Classic episode on the BBC. As we point out in Chapter 3, by citing history, the documentaries are saying more about what they consider important historical events rather than the importance of the episodes themselves. Is *Spearhead from Space* the most important Third Doctor episode because it is the first one in colour or the first made entirely on film? How is value measured? In addition, Moffat makes connections to the New series arguably to appeal to viewers unfamiliar with the Classic series. Along with his mention of River Song in his documentary for *The Aztecs,* he compares the episode to 'The Fires of Pompeii' (2008) as another episode that deals with fixed points in time. For *Tomb of the Cybermen*, he goes on to indicate that Matt Smith based his characterization of the Doctor on Patrick Troughton. And for *The TV Movie* he notes that Paul McGann's Doctor 'of course prefigured the Doctors later, by making him a much more romantic figure, someone who's perfectly at home kissing a lady'.[59]

The Doctors Revisited thus positions particular moments of *Doctor Who* as iconic. Like *DWM* in the hiatus years, it uses its particular branding and positioning as an official part of the series to establish value and canonicity within the series. Of course, fans of the series don't have to take *The Doctors Revisited* as gospel, and they don't have to 'revisit' any of the episodes they don't want to. There are multitudes of ways that fans can create or understand the value of a series. But in establishing a fan-like reading through the guise of showrunner Steven Moffat, *The Doctors Revisited* highlights one particular way this shaping can occur.

Conclusion

In many ways, it has never been a better time to be a *Doctor Who* fan. The show is available to experience in a number of formats – DVD, Blu-ray, streaming, and VHS. While ninety-seven episodes are still missing, every episode is available in audio format. One can log into Amazon Prime or HBOMax, BritBox or iPlayer, and see almost every episode of *Doctor Who*. Big Finish continues to put out hundreds of hours of new content every year. BBC Books has a thriving novel line, and the Titan comic books volumes include Thirteenth, Twelfth, Eleventh, Tenth, Ninth, Eighth, Seventh, Fourth, and Third Doctor titles. Thus, both *DWM* and *The Doctors Revisited* have difficult jobs. They have to appeal to a fan base that is often saturated with *Doctor Who* content and has unprecedented access to the text itself.

Navigating through *Doctor Who* content can be daunting, especially for a new fan. How does one go back to the Classic series and decide what to watch? As we have shown in this chapter, fans often trust the opinion of other fans. And in ascribing fannishness to *DWM* and to *The Doctors Revisited* DVD sets, official BBC-sanctioned values of the past can be transmitted to the fandom. In much the same way as value was ascribed to particular episodes during the hiatus years, when there was very little access to *Doctor Who*, so too can value be ascribed to particular episodes in this period of excess.

Case Study 2A

Tegan: The makers' vision

Craig Owen Jones

For fans unacquainted with 1980s *Doctor Who*, Tegan's reputation is burnished and secure. What little they have to go on – snippets of information inserted into recent episodes of the show and its spinoff, *The Sarah Jane Adventures*, and gasped at by those familiar with Tegan's tenure on the show and hence more appreciative of such 'fan service' – paints a portrait of an attractive, likeable, and above all independent woman. We learn through Sarah Jane's speech in *The Death of the Doctor,* Part 2 (2010) that Tegan is now campaigning for Aboriginal rights in Australia, and even Matt Smith's Doctor's oblique reference to her as 'gobby' in *The Crimson Horror* (2013) has the air of a back-handed compliment – after all, the loud-mouthed do secure for themselves the position of being listened to.

Yet the character of Tegan Jovanka was not meant to be 'independent, empowering nor feminist'. The decision to add Tegan to the cast was strategic and pragmatic – a way of capitalizing on a burgeoning audience for *Doctor Who* in Australia and New Zealand, as well as providing, as John Nathan-Turner would doubtless have put it, an attractive young woman to help retain 'the dads' in the viewing audience. Her dramatic purpose was similarly unprepossessing. The genesis of Tegan – as well as an insight into the intentions of the show's makers with regard to the character – can be found in a slim volume by John Nathan-Turner entitled *Doctor Who: The Companions* – not to be confused with Howe and Stammers' *Doctor Who: Companions* – in which Nathan-Turner reminisced about his time with the various actors to have appeared in that role on the programme. The initial description of Tegan, described as the joint work of him and the show's then-script editor Christopher H. Bidmead, is of interest, not least because of the relative lack of resemblance to the character as she finally appeared on screen:

> Tegan is twenty-one, an attractive and intelligent Australian trainee
> air stewardess, whose brash confidence in her own abilities actually

conceals inner insecurity, a state of affairs that becomes clear in moments of stress.

On her way to her first real flight she accidentally blunders into the Tardis [*sic*] and thus finds herself being inadvertently abducted by the Doctor. Characteristically her inner bewilderment at the new situation in which she finds herself causes her to assume an attitude of overweening self-assertion, and she begins to take charge of the Doctor and Adric.

During the course of the stories, Tegan's superficial self-assurance will build until it becomes a real problem for the other occupants of the Tardis [*sic*], and it will need drastic action on the part of the Doctor to put things to rights and show her the error of her ways.[1]

There is surprisingly little to go on here. The notion of Tegan 'taking charge', which was ultimately never really pursued (how could it have been?), is clearly inserted as an ill-judged attempt to generate some sort of dramatic tension. In addition, the inference that Tegan's 'brash confidence' and self-assertion should be interpreted as recalcitrance that would need to be 'put to rights' by the Doctor hobbles attempts to gloss the character as the makers' intentional continuation of the feminist imperative represented in the mid-1970s by Sarah Jane Smith; instead, one is tempted to read into this brief an attempt to provide a comeuppance for second-wave feminism (but see below).[2]

Nevertheless, this short memorandum, which was written on 1 August 1980 and slightly expanded the following November to include references to the character's Brisbane background, has played a central role in formulating fan perceptions of the character, being repeatedly quoted in books aimed at fans.[3] Emphasis on the character's overbearing qualities was certainly present from an early stage. Nathan-Turner again argues:

When Janet Fielding's photograph arrived, she looked totally wrong. ... There was no mention of her height on her curriculum vitae. ... Nevertheless, the letter accompanying [it] was highly amusing, and said that Janet Fielding was ideal for the part, as she *was* a terribly bossy Australian. ... I agreed to see her.[4]

For the actor who played her, Tegan's success was a blessing and a curse. Fielding did not – in retrospect, at any rate – see her character as extolling feminist virtues, and even went so far as to denigrate her as a mere 'trolley dolly'. This is certainly borne out by the look of the character. *Pace* John Nathan-Turner, who averred in 1986 that Fielding was 'delighted' with Tegan's air stewardess costume,[5] Fielding was ambivalent about the purple ensemble. More generally, Fielding frequently disparaged the role in the years and decades after leaving, as Richard Wallace has been quick to point out:

> It is difficult to believe that many female viewers saw the weak female companions as figures of identification; as Janet Fielding who played Tegan in the 1980s notes, 'Who *wants* to identify with a woman who is stupid enough to climb a cliff in two-inch high-heels and a tight skirt?'[6]

In the same 1994 interview from which the above quote was culled, Fielding pointed out that, early on in her tenure on the show, she was told unambiguously that her function was to be 'something for the dads to watch'. She also called Tegan 'Lucy in space', a reference to the stroppy character from Charles Schultz' *Peanuts* cartoons – hardly a vote of confidence in her character's likeability and empowering credentials.[7]

Such uncharitable descriptions feel like self-deprecation. Viewings of Fielding's appearances do demonstrate a great deal of nuance in the portrayal, more than might have been intended in the scripts, and one suspects that she, as did Elisabeth Sladen and Louise Jameson before her (and Bonnie Langford as Mel after her), did a great deal of the characterization as she worked. Several actors cast in role of the companion later observed how badly planned their characters were. Sladen, for example, later told of the massive gulf she perceived between her time in theatre and *Doctor Who* from this perspective:

> When you work on a play, you open your script and it says: the character is Sarah Jane Smith, she is so many years old, her father died the other day therefore she is seen in black, and so on. When I got my script for *Doctor Who* I opened it up and it just said, 'Enter Sarah Jane Smith', and I thought, 'Oh, hello! Not much here!'[8]

Reactions to Tegan

But if Tegan was seen by the show's writers, its producer, and even the actor who played her as mouthy eye candy with a headstrong streak and a talent for ineptitude, how did she become to enjoy such exalted status among fans? The answer is surprisingly complex, and goes to the heart of the issue of how fans' perceptions of characters have changed over time. In the last forty years, Tegan has been loved, maligned, and then loved again by the show's fans.

We might begin with examining the one constituency at whom Tegan was most obviously aimed – Australians. It is an irony of Tegan's tenure that, in contradistinction to Nathan-Turner's intentions, the character was a relative failure among mainstream audiences in Australia. Reviews were often scathing, as the following extract from a 1982 edition of the *Canberra Times* bears out. The Australian Broadcasting Corporation (ABC) had purchased both *Doctor Who* and the hit period drama *All Creatures Great and Small* (BBC, 1978–90) from the BBC, and, by accident or by design, had scheduled the pair, which both happened to feature Peter Davison in starring roles, within an hour of each other on the same evening:

> Dr. Who steps out of the Tardis [*sic*] before … 6.55pm … and by 7.30pm has entered the Drovers [Arms] as Tristan in 'All Creatures Great And Small'.
> … But the new Dr Who is showing more confidence, and with any luck he'll get the horribly Strine Tegan (Janet Fielding) stranded at Heathrow, and the plague put back to its rightful place in the 14th century before he takes off on another adventure.[9]

The reference to 'Strine' – the slang term for heavily accented Australian English – highlights a recurrent bugbear of Australian commentators, namely, the roughness of Tegan's characterization. It is true that the character exhibited stereotypically Australian traits. In *Black Orchid* (1982), the TARDIS visits interwar England, and she is seen watching a cricket match with evident enjoyment (and knowledge of the game); and in *Four to Doomsday* (1982) she speaks an Aboriginal language, in an episode that prompted widespread derision in Australia, for reasons elucidated elsewhere.[10] However, it is by and large the broad strokes in which the character is painted that jar. In a 1982 edition of the *Sydney Morning Herald*, Fielding again came in for criticism on account of her accent:

> Ms Fielding promises to maintain the high standard of hammy acting the series enjoys. Her BBC Oz accent is something akin to [archetypal Australian film actor] Chips Rafferty yodelling through a didjeridoo…."The doctor's very strynge", says Tegan the Terrible. She is right. He is strynge.[11]

But although attitudes towards the character among Australian social commentators were lukewarm, Tegan was greeted more positively by fans there. In 1982, for example, when a prominent Australian newspaper printed children's *Doctor Who* story ideas based in Australia, no less than five of the thirteen mentioned Tegan; the winning entry of the competition that precipitated the article not only included Tegan, but also placed her in a prominent role, escaping from confinement alongside the Doctor and saving the day.[12] Also, in 1985, only a year after her departure from the show, Fielding attended a science fiction convention in Brisbane as guest of honour, and articles donated by her to the fan auction realized hefty prices.[13]

That Fielding was an immediate success in the role in the opinion of British fans can be gleaned from fan reaction at the time. In a biography of John Nathan-Turner, Richard Marson notes that when she first premiered 'Tegan was destined to be one of the most popular companions'.[14] The letters page of *DWM* regularly featured correspondents praising the character as well as Fielding's performance, even tending towards the hyperbolic on occasion, as a March 1982 comment from a Welsh viewer in Caerphilly demonstrates:

> I have fallen in love with Tegan (Janet Fielding), who I think has great potential and could turn out to be an Australian Sarah Jane Smith, and is, in my opinion, the best partner [for the Doctor] since the aforementioned…[15]

By the 1990s, however, a definite shift in attitude had occurred. Writing in 1992, Katherine Stannard offered comment on Tegan's role as 'critic and complainer'.[16] Howe and Stammers (1995) called her 'over-emotive', adding the following description, albeit tongue-in-cheek, in the character's pen-picture:

> Whining, whingeing, moaning, complaining…. [A] gorgeous brunette with an attitude problem. A request for a drink from this stewardess would probably have been answered with a smack in the mouth. She dressed to kill and then wondered why everyone died.[17]

What is interesting about this is the extent to which assessments of this sort seem to play on – indeed, are informed by – mainstream perceptions of the character. In the British press, as in Australia, Tegan was stereotyped, but the character was glossed less in terms of her Australian identity (though that certainly was seen as important), and more in terms of her 'bossiness'. A *Daily Express* article published to coincide with Fielding's casting announcement quoted Fielding as saying she was 'bossy enough for the part'[18] – one wonders if Fielding, a professed feminist, was attempting to mediate her character's forthrightness, seen as unbecoming of a woman by the standards of the early 1980s, by deploying language that could be easily glossed as gendered, and which would therefore be accepted in mainstream media.[19] But the identification was embraced far more widely, and was frequently invoked throughout Fielding's tenure.

For John Kenneth Muir, Tegan was 'more fiery' and 'abrasive';[20] nevertheless, he ascribes the character's shortcomings to a narrowness of vision on the part of the production team:

> Was Tegan an effective companion? Janet Fielding certainly imbued Tegan with loads of personality and charm, but how many times did writers force this great actress and this interesting character to whine about going home? … Has Tegan no interest in the Doctor, or the universe he shows her? Why is she unhappy all the time? … Fielding had the talent to make Tegan the most interesting and well-loved of all companions, but the writers never gave her a really good story to sink her teeth into. … what else did Fielding really get to do besides whine and cry? She complained her way through "Time Flight" and "The King's Demons," to name just a few episodes. She showed

beautiful charm and joie de vivre in "Black Orchid," but that was the exception, not the rule.[21]

Lastly, and perhaps tellingly, the most recent assessments of the character have increasingly emphasized her credentials not as a feminist, but as an *agent*, while acknowledging that such descriptions can only go so far. Giles and Peloff are quick to note the significant obstacles one encounters in reading Tegan as an instantiation of 1980s feminism, and instead offer an alternative reading, positing that Fielding ultimately invested Tegan with the feelings of irritation she herself was experiencing on being handed a role 'from which', as they put it, 'common sense and basic competence are being withheld'.[22] In comparison with the slew of companions immediately before her, Tegan arrives on the show in a bumbling manner, with a ditsy streak on prominent display – in her debut serial, *Logopolis* (1981), she forgets her passport on her way to work as an air stewardess, her bag, and even to lock her front door. Giles and Peloff explain the character's enduring popularity through her effectiveness as a questioner of the authority of Peter Davison's (unusually biddable) Fifth Doctor, and the 'spunk and wit' she gave to the character.

This said, it may be possible to extend this line of thought slightly, and offer Tegan at least a little of the agency so regularly exhibited by her predecessors. The character displays some considerable competencies, such as to cause one to revisit Giles and Peloff's denial of any agency on her part. *Logopolis*, and the subsequent serial, *Castrovalva* (1982), offer examples of this. For all that Tegan and her aunt come across as, in Giles and Peloff's words, '1980s Lucys and Ethels', it is Tegan who takes the initiative, taking over the task of changing a flat tyre when her aunt is unable to do so. Later, she walks into the TARDIS unobserved by the Doctor, and shortly gets lost in its labyrinthine corridors; while obviously discomfited, she employs sound logic in trying to find her way out, and correctly identifies the TARDIS as a ship, allowing her – in contradistinction to so many companions before her – to comprehend the TARDIS with a certain ease.

It is, perhaps, these qualities that account for the high regard with which Tegan is thought of by fans today. The character frequently draws substantial numbers of votes in fans' polls, including in 2014, when she placed first, above even Sarah Jane Smith, the top spot's usual incumbent;[23] and numbers of fanvids on YouTube amply testify to the qualities that endear her to today's fans: 'Every time Tegan sasses the Doctor, an angel gets its wings', reads the tagline on one, while another, also featuring Tegan's crewmate Nyssa and edited in the style of *Cagney and Lacey*, speaks well to the fondness for the character felt by many.

Case Study 2B

Reception after the fact: Companions in Big Finish

Paul Booth

Big Finish, an audio production company founded in 1996, specializes in a variety of cult media-themed full cast audio recordings. In 1999, it started its longest-running, and most popular, range focusing on *Doctor Who*. (The first series the company made focused on Bernice Summerfield, a companion of the Seventh Doctor first appearing in the *New Adventures* novels.) For most of its existence, Big Finish was licensed to create full cast audio recordings of original *Doctor Who* stories that took place during the Classic series: the licence from the BBC extended to revisiting the Classic Doctors, especially the Fourth, Fifth, Sixth, Seventh, and Eighth incarnations. The original actors continue to portray these Doctors and their companions (in fact, every living actor who portrayed a companion in *Doctor Who* has come back to record with Big Finish, with the exception of Jackie Lane who played the First Doctor's companion Dodo Chaplet[1]). More recent releases have featured actors playing the First, Second, and Third Doctors.[2] In 2015, Big Finish was granted the licence to use characters and themes from the revived series. Actors returning to play their television characters include David Tennant and John Hurt as the Doctor; Billie Piper and Catherine Tate as companions Rose and Donna; and a slew of guest stars like Derek Jacobi, Camille Coduri, Anna Hope, Ian McNeice, Alex Kingston, Michelle Ryan, Simon Fisher-Becker, and Bruno Langley. Currently, Big Finish's licence to produce content based on *Doctor Who* now goes up through the conclusion of Peter Capaldi's final appearance in 'Twice upon a Time'. In this short provocation, I want to demonstrate how the shift in Big Finish's emphasis from the Classic series to the New series has complicated how fans value different elements of *Doctor Who*. In attempting to preserve fans' memories of companions of *Doctor Who*, Big Finish may be shifting what the idea of the Doctor and the companions means in the age of New *Who*.

In 2007, Matt Hills examined the influence of Big Finish as a way of preserving 'fans' memories and discourses of "golden age" *Doctor Who* on the television'.[3] Indeed, much of Big Finish's output is still focused on the Classic series. A monthly series highlights the adventures of the Fifth, Sixth, and Seventh Doctors, while the Fourth Doctor has his own monthly series and the Eighth Doctor has two ongoing bi-annual box sets. While the Eighth Doctor's adventures address unseen moments between the end of the *TV Movie* (1996) and the start of the New series of *Doctor Who*, the other monthly ranges augment the canon, building on bits and pieces of the Classic series in a way that highlights what Hills calls 'discourses of televisuality' – they recall and reflect specific structures and formats of televised *Doctor Who* and 'utilise fan experiences and memories of *Who* on TV'.[4] Big Finish, according to this formulation, specifically hails a particular type of fan audience, one steeped in 'fan nostalgia' within the audio ranges beckoning 'fan-subcultural memories and narratives of consuming *Doctor Who*'.[5] Some examples of this are the fact that Big Finish audio plays follow the format of the Classic series (four half-hour episodes), and the audio plays use the appropriate version of the theme tune with the relevant Doctor's story.

In this, then, Hills' argument rests on the way Big Finish – in 2007 – reflects a fannish valuation of particular characteristics of *Doctor Who*, wherein particular fan expectations are upheld while others are critiqued or subverted. For instance, Hills gives the example of a Big Finish play in which the Sixth Doctor meets the Brigadier – an event 'many fans wished could have happened on TV'.[6] The meeting both highlights a bugbear of the fandom (the Brig had met every Classic Doctor from Troughton's Second to McCoy's Seventh on-screen, barring Baker's Sixth) *and* represents a particular value of the series within the fandom (the consistency of character and universe, the 'fan favourite' Brigadier).

Piers Britton's *TARDISbound* also focuses on this fannishness in Big Finish, addressing the way the company 'has established itself as the chief custodian of format continuity, turning this into a taxonomic as well as an expressive device'.[7] But again, not every part of the continuity is upheld, not every moment from the television series is validated: they are particular moments, particular choices, that reflect a particular sense of what is valued in the series' history (there has never been a mention of the Eighth Doctor being half-human, for instance; and except in the few specially demarcated instances of the alternate history *Unbound* series, Big Finish has stuck to fan-accepted canon[8]). Britton notes that 'fan writers contributing to Big Finish…have avowedly sought to correct perceived transgressions in the handling of [e.g., the Daleks]…during the classic series'.[9] Indeed, Big Finish executive producer (and voice of the TV Daleks) Nicholas Briggs unequivocally stated in *Vortex*, the Big Finish magazine, that Big Finish audio plays 'always were canonical'.[10] In making this determination (one not echoed by the BBC, which has never established a canon), Briggs asserts Big Finish's role in shaping fan values.

One particular emphasis of Big Finish's *Doctor Who* oeuvre is to deepen the characterization and role of the Doctor's companions. In the television series, many of the (mostly female) companions of the Doctor were often given less character development – either by dint of their shorter tenure on the series or the narrative focus on the Doctor – resulting in a decidedly imbalanced depiction of gender. Even in the cases where stronger female characters were brought on board the series, according to Britton, the move 'was compromised by the lack of real change in their relationship with the Doctor'.[11] Partly, perhaps, because of the availability of the actors who played companions, Big Finish has deepened and extended the characterization of companions, turning them into much more fleshed-out beings: a primary example is Sara Kingdom, who appeared in nine episodes of the First Doctor story *The Daleks' Master Plan* (1965–66), but has since developed an entire history through Big Finish's Companion Chronicles line. Other, more prominent companions like Leela have seen huge amounts of character growth in hundreds of hours of Big Finish content.[12] In effect, Big Finish has attempted to rebalance the scales, offering meatier and more fleshed-out roles for all the companions, and focusing especially on the women.

Big Finish has developed and extended the lives of many of the characters from *Doctor Who*, re-evaluating the importance of these characters within the canon(s) of *Who*. However, if Big Finish has traditionally focused on the Classic series, the turn since 2015 to the New series has resulted in a shift in both the output and the focus of the company. Indeed, the New *Who* addition to the Big Finish catalogue – especially the *River Song* box sets (2015–), the *UNIT – The New Series* box sets (2015–), *Jenny – The Doctor's Daughter* (2018), *Lady*

Christina (2018), and the *Chronicles* series (2017, 2018) – complicates the shifting fan values for Big Finish's *Doctor Who* lines. Specifically, the River Song box sets feature the character of River interacting not with New *Who* Doctors, but with Classic Doctors; while the three *Chronicles*, the *UNIT*, the *Jenny*, and the *Lady Christina* box sets – elevate specific characters from the New series as potential leading roles. Each of these sets gives a renewed focus on minor characters from the New series. Thus, while the Classic Big Finish may serve as a type of fan nostalgia, the New Big Finish series re-value particular characters within the *Doctor Who* canon(s) as a whole.

The effect of Big Finish's emphasis on returning characters is to re-value the role of seemingly peripheral characters, turning them from one-time guests (or, in the case of River Song, on/off companions) into fully fledged stars. One consequence of this remaking of minor characters from the New Series into companions or stars is, as Lorna Jowett notes of the *UNIT* series, a refreshing revision of the show's gender divide. Many of these now-major characters, like Kate Stewart and Petronella Osgood, are played by women, and these 'peripheral characters, who are present in the television narrative but not developed to any degree, might also have potential for escaping gendered roles and stereotypes'.[13] Take, for example, the case of *Jenny – The Doctor's Daughter*. In this box set (released in 2018[14]), Jenny, a character from the 2008 episode 'The Doctor's Daughter' who is revealed to be created from the Doctor's DNA, has her own adventures with her own companion. Played by Georgia Moffett, Jenny is a relatively minor character within the *Doctor Who* corpus, but by creating an entire box set around her, Big Finish has re-valued that character through sheer presence. She now has more *Doctor Who* production time (five hours: one TV episode and four audio dramas) than First Doctor companion Katarina.[15] Similarly, *Lady Christina* (2018) is a set of audio plays featuring the character of Lady Christina de Souza, played by Michelle Ryan in the 2009 episode 'Planet of the Dead'. Lady Christina appears in just one episode. The box set – and a special guest appearance in one of the *Tenth Doctor Chronicles* (2018) – augments her time in the series five-fold and promotes her character from one-off to star. In promoting both Jenny and Lady Christina in this way, Big Finish also highlights the importance of female characters (and actors) in lead roles: something *Doctor Who* has rarely done.[16]

In the *River Song* boxed sets (2015–), the titular character – who is already a major character in the television series – is revealed to have a longer and more varied history than what was shown on the screen. On television, River Song is a time travelling archaeologist who meets the Doctor at different times; in fact, they are experiencing the relationship, including their marriage, in a different order from each other. His first meeting with her is her last meeting with him. She was introduced in the 2008 episode 'Silence in the Library' playing opposite David Tennant; she had her last appearance in the show in 2015's 'The Husbands of River Song', which saw her play opposite Peter Capaldi. She married Matt Smith's Doctor in 'The Wedding of River Song' in 2011. During the television series, it is obvious that the Tenth Doctor had never met River before; however, in the ongoing box sets from Big Finish, River has met every previous incarnation of the Doctor (barring the First, Second, and Third, although perhaps these box sets are coming in the future…) as well as four incarnations of the Master/Missy. In effect, the *River Song* box sets reframe the River Song story to make her an important part of the Doctor's entire history, performing the same function as Clara did in 'The Name of the Doctor' (2013) – shaping and sharing the Doctor's entire life (see Chapter 3). Each *River Song* box set takes pains to fit within the established chronology of River's New series adventures: for example, she does not tell the other Doctors who she is, and sometimes only appears over an intercom instead of in person. Regardless, her impact throughout the Doctor's life is felt strongly and has an effect on the way the character is perceived: she is the star of her own series, and the Doctor is merely a bit player. In effect, they have swapped positions in the narrative: listeners to Big Finish follow River's adventures during which the Doctor appears out-of-order. Again, not only does this promote a more egalitarian gender balance, it also highlights the inherent feminism of River Song's role in general.

Similarly, Big Finish's focus on the New series has resulted in a shifting emphasis on the characterization of the Doctor himself in three different box sets: *The Ninth Doctor Chronicles* (2017), *The Tenth Doctor Chronicles* (2018), and *The Eleventh Doctor Chronicles* (2018). In each of these sets, the Doctor is not played by the actor from the television series (despite the fact that they are all still alive), but rather by one of Big Finish's performers playing the role (the Ninth Doctor is handled by Nicholas Briggs, while the Tenth and Eleventh Doctors are played by impressionist Jake Dudman). Dudman in particular is superb at mimicking the Eleventh Doctor's vocal manifestations. However, the effect of having another actor mimic the Doctor is that the stories have to highlight particular vocal traits of the Doctor to make the character more recognizable. For example, when asked by director Helen Goldwyn how Matt Smith's voice differs from David Tennant's in one of the behind-the-scenes discussions of 'The Calendar Man' (2018), Dudman replies:

> They're very different in the way that, if we're talking about purpose and intentions and what the characters are thinking and all that stuff, David's character is all very much about, to me at least, trying to be cool and trying to be the heroic guy to save the day. He's got a bit of arrogance about him, a bit of ego, whereas Matt's doctor is so alien and so just so weird and wacky...he's just very strange. In terms of vocally, the rhythm and pace of them is very different. [in Tennant's voice] David's always on the point like this. And [in Smith's voice] Matt's just all, you never know what word he's going to emphasize, or go soft on, or **loud** on [Dudman]. He's a minefield.

Although speaking in more vague terms (and with the caveat that it's hard to replicate vocal mannerisms in print), these particular vocal manifestations of the characters are simply Dudman's own interpretation of the character. Certainly, Matt Smith does emphasize words in ways we might not expect (as did Tom Baker's Fourth Doctor) but it isn't his entire oeuvre of vocal expressions. However, by concentrating on that aspect of his vocal mannerisms, Big Finish presents a particular version of that Doctor, one steeped in the particular fannish reading that emphasizes that portrayal. In another episode, 'The Top of the Tree' (2018), Dudman muses on the difference between portraying the Tenth Doctor and the Eleventh Doctor: 'I can think of the Tenth Doctor as Tigger and the Eleventh Doctor is like a drunk giraffe.' By 'drunk giraffe', he alludes to Steven Moffat's famous quote (an odd way of using physicality to describe vocal qualities).[17] Yet, in doing so, Dudman also concretizes this particular view of Smith – wacky, dancing, sprawling – rather than any other.

Big Finish's stated mission, then – to augment the larger corpus of *Doctor Who* stories and bring to light new additions to the canon(s) of

Who – finds itself connected to updating the stolid cultural background of the series with fresh, contemporary takes on social issues. Although Big Finish continues to focus on fleshing out Classic companions, the renewed exploration of New series guest stars complicates who even can be considered a companion; fans may question why *these* characters and not *those* characters. In making these determinations, Big Finish helps to establish a canon of value for the series. Certainly, as *Doctor Who* begins a new era under the first female Doctor, it's important to recognize the way some of these issues have been raised, and valued, in the past.

Dialogue 2C

The ends of an era

Paul Booth and Craig Owen Jones

Paul: Craig, one of the things that your discussion of Tegan highlighted for me was the way that the passage of time can have a major effect on the way different fans can interpret the characters of a series. Tegan, as you point out, is a great example of a companion who started off very popular with a lot of fans (although not all), fell out of favour in the 1990s, and has rebounded spectacularly in today's modern *Doctor Who* era. Partly, I think, this is because of the public, playful antagonism that Janet Fielding and Peter Davison have had at conventions, on DVD special features, and over social media. The two of them riff spectacularly and I think that relationship is very appealing to fans who are already primed to see this particular TARDIS crew as a squabbling family anyway. It got me thinking about how the role of the passage of time in fans' valuations of different Doctors has also shifted. Tom Baker continues to top 'best-of' polls for everyone's favourite Doctor (although I suspect this is often the 'safe' answer and many fans have another Doctor they privately like more). I've read that Colin Baker swore off interviews with *Doctor Who Magazine* because they ran a poll where his Doctor came in dead last. And yet, if you look at some of what I wrote about in my case study of Big Finish companion-adjacent characters, new takes on characters through the audio company can rehabilitate fans' interpretations of Doctors as well. Do you have any thoughts about the way time can change fans' views of particular Doctors after they regenerate?

Craig: I speak of custodial narration elsewhere, and that idea also weighs heavily in the balance here. You mention Tom Baker's near-ubiquity at the top of 'best-of' polls. When *Doctor Who Magazine* began running those polls in the 1980s, that was a quite straightforward index of popularity, I think: Baker regularly beat out even the incumbent actors for the title.[1] However, once it became clear the series had ended,

McCoy was voted the greatest Doctor in the 1990 poll.[2] Some of this was doubtless due to his improvement in the role – his performances are noticeably more accomplished in the stories of Series 26 (1989) than those of two years previously. But I think the need to demonstrate to external observers that fandom was behind the most recent version of the show was more important. Then there are the peculiar circumstances of the hiatus. When it became obvious that the show had been effectively cancelled, fandom became more comfortable with the idea of revisiting its own past. Jon Pertwee's appearance in the audio dramas *The Paradise of Death* (1993) and *The Ghosts of N-Space* (1996) led some fans to recognize him as the current Doctor, and not McCoy, as the panel discussion with him during the Liverpool Panopticon convention of 1993 demonstrates.[3] That still strikes me as a strange position to have taken; but then again, as a young fan I was unaware of how warmly appreciated the Pertwee era was, an appreciation that must have grown with the passage of time.

It's clear that the quality of Big Finish's audio dramas has given less well-appreciated Doctors a chance at rehabilitation. The most obvious instances are Colin Baker, whose work with Bonnie Langford in particular has been little short of revelatory, and Paul McGann. One wonders whether the Eighth Doctor would even be seen as canonical at this point were it not for McGann's effortless performances in the audio dramas. In both cases, we are talking about cumulative effects; it is the consistency of performance that drives the change in opinion.

Paul: Oh, yes, definitely: Colin Baker has undoubtedly rehabilitated his Doctor's image via Big Finish, and I think the way he is often given new and exciting aspects within his series is a way Big Finish recognizes that: for instance, he was the first Doctor given a new companion in the Big Finish range, in the guise of Dr Evelyn Smythe. McGann, as well, was given a somewhat new place of honour in the range, when he was taken out of the monthly range of Big Finish episodes and given, first, his own series broadcast on BBC radio in 2006 – becoming something of a companion itself of the New series which premiered in 2005 – and second, a number of special box sets every year which continue his story pre-'Night of the Doctor' (2013).

All of this is a roundabout way of showing that the fans' interpretations of particular Doctors depend on far much more than just what we see on screen. Big Finish appearances can negotiate it (so I wonder if they ever get Eccleston to record episodes, will his year be re-evaluated?), mostly for the better (although I've seen some griping online about Big Finish's tendency to recast certain roles, Tim Trelor has taken over for Pertwee in the *Third Doctor Adventures* (2015–)). But other background elements of knowledge can moderate and mitigate fans' evaluation of different incarnations. For example, knowing that David Tennant and Peter Capaldi were fans before they took over the role may have made fans more appeased to their appearances: they were familiar because they were familial. When Capaldi made his first ballyhooed appearance on the *Doctor Who Live* promotional (2013), he grabbed his lapels like Hartnell, not only echoing the fact he was the same age as the first actor to portray the Doctor, but also signalling to the fandom that he *knew* about the series – he is a fan; he is one of us. But at the same time, when Matt Smith took over the role, largely the fans complained about his age,[4] and his emo look,[5] but rarely about his lack of knowledge of *Doctor Who*. In contrast, fans seemed particularly thrilled to learn that he watched *Tomb of the Cybermen* (1967) to help him understand the role of the Doctor.[6]

This leaves me with a question about regeneration in general – not so much the regeneration of the Doctor, but the regeneration of the audience when a new Doctor is announced. How do you think knowledge about the actor or actress who is cast in the role affects the way fans interpret the performance? Does it make a difference knowing, for instance, that Jodie Whittaker has a long history with Chris Chibnall, or that she grew up not watching the series?

Craig: I doubt it. I daresay many, perhaps most, fans feel in good hands when they know the actor playing the Doctor (or a companion, for that matter) is 'one of them', but it's not a red line. Not much is, frankly; we've already seen the Doctor's gender switch – not without comment, admittedly, but Jodie Whittaker's performance is so assured that it has become a non-issue for most of that part of fandom that had issues with it as far as I can see. Neither does race seem to be problematic, as the sanguine response to rumours of Idris Elba or Chiwetel Ejiofor in recent years indicates. In fact, the only red line I can see when it comes to the Doctor's casting is not what they've been in, nor whether they've seen the show, but their nationality. The Britishness of the Doctor seems to be hard-baked into the show; even the 1996 *TV Movie*, which was tonally misjudged in several ways, cleaved to that.

Paul: Oh wow, can you even imagine the hullabaloo if they cast an American as the Doctor? I'm actually thinking of the horror of casting someone American but making them do a British accent. But the thing is, ultimately, why would that make a difference (I agree it would, I'm just trying to drill down in this)? Tennant changed his Scottish brogue to a generic English accent even though McCoy had let his Scots R's trill magnificently. There is something about the *actor* having to be a certain nationality (or via identification, perceived that way) that makes the Doctor a particularly British character. A similar point is made by Dylan Morris in *Fan Phenomena: Doctor Who*, who writes that:

> America is a country without a (fantastical) medieval European past. There are no castles, no stories of American knights, kings and queens. Young American nerds appropriate Britain as a second heritage that offers stronger mythic and magical possibilities. From prosaic America, they step through the doors of the TARDIS into a fantastical imagined Britain.[7]

And Morris goes on to note that, 'The Doctor himself embodies the show's celebration of British whimsy, wit and intellect'.[8]

Sometimes this applies to the companions as well. In your discussion of Tegan earlier, you noted that having the Australian aboard the TARDIS was largely a positive experience, but the Americanization of Peri (moderate accent given) wasn't particularly notable except insofar as it didn't seem to fulfil the goals of garnering a strong American viewership (fandom aside). Indeed, in a hefty volume that explores the history of US *Doctor Who* fandom, the authors (who are all fans themselves) write that 'a large number of American fans say they like the show because of its "Britishness"' and 'having an American companion was arguably *not* the best approach to take to appeal to those same Americans'.[9]

All this being said, I want to return to the original question I posed here – to what extent does the passage of time make a difference? I think if you'd asked fans in 1966 whether the Doctor could be played by a woman you'd have received a vociferously different reaction than what we had last year. And similarly, as you say, about race. But nationality seems to be a sticking point to the character; will we ever see a non-British Doctor? In an age where Brexit is rending the country apart, I seriously doubt anyone wants to see any more fractures in esteemed British institutions …

Chapter 3
The Error of Eras

This chapter looks at the significance of and consequence for fans categorizing *Doctor Who* into eras – what we are calling 'periodization'. There is indisputably a sense of *'Doctor-Who-ness'* that helps fans characterize how the show has been identified for fifty years, but that sense has been articulated differently over time (indeed, *Doctor Who Magazine* identified this as 'that indefinable magic'[1]). How fans order and define a text reveals underlying values that guide the interpretation of that text. Order begets valuation. But as we will see, contextual factors – history, genre, discourse – become contexts that help fans clarify the text in order to demarcate boundaries in the text. *Doctor Who* is never whole. One might argue, then, that *Doctor Who* is ultimately indefinable as *one type* of text. But in defining *Doctor Who* as indefinable, we have also created a larger paradigm by which to view the show: its very indefinability defines it.

Seeing *Doctor Who* as broken into parts rather than as a coherent whole may not be an incorrect assessment of the show: *Doctor Who* might more accurately be described as a loosely connected series of programmes than one coherent text. Tat Wood goes so far as to call it an 'anthology' series.[2] Indeed, the 'multi-vocality'[3] of *Doctor Who* has prompted scholar-fan Matt Hills to differentiate between Classic and New *Who* 'on the basis that these were produced in radically different industrial and cultural contexts, as well as therefore exhibiting significant textual differences'.[4] As different eras and different aspects of *Doctor Who* become valued differently, however, these textual differences reveal larger concerns about fan hierarchy in interpretations of media texts. Despite fans' propensity to periodize, there are issues with any set of coherent categorizing principles. Periodization teaches one about ruptures in the categorical systems, but illuminates assumptions and conventions within those systems.

In this chapter, we analyse fans' tendency to periodize *Doctor Who* as a discursive act laden with value. We examine three different ways fans have periodized *Doctor Who*: first, through production details; second, through genre characteristics; and third, through articulation of its very indefinability. We then contextualize periodization by augmenting it with an archontic look at *Doctor Who*. In the work of Abigail Derecho, 'archonic' refers to the archive-like properties of a text: the way a text grows with each new addition to the corpus.[5] Rather than do away with periodization, a fannish archontic analysis demonstrates a more nuanced understanding of periodization within *Doctor Who*, where it joins continuity and canon as organizational factors. Fans will never be able to escape periodization, but it can be integrated more fully into fans' understanding of television programming in general. This chapter is an attempt to evaluate what evaluation of *Doctor Who does:* by separating *Doctor Who* into eras, fans need to navigate the binary between continuity and fragmentation; *Doctor Who* is *both* a continuous programme split into fragmented parts *and* a series of fragments cohered to a whole at the same time.

The *Doctor Who* corpus

Periodization highlights the changing evaluative and contextual understandings of *Doctor Who* across multiple cultural/historical moments.[6] There are more than just production personalities at the heart of the periodization, as 'stark contrasts…need to be explained in terms of the forces much more powerful than individual whim or intention'.[7] Fans ascribing particular characteristics to particular eras tells us what these fans value about those eras. Although a useful heuristic in *deepening* segmented forms of knowledge, periodization also disciplines various contextual meanings into particular articulations of significance.

Multiple discourses are necessary for a more coherent picture of *Doctor Who*.[8] This multi-discursive approach was also illustrated in the first major academic analysis of the series, John Tulloch and Manuel Alvarado's *Doctor Who: The Unfolding Text,* when they investigated the programme through a 'wide range of institutional, professional, public, cultural and ideological forces'.[9] Such discursive categorization is also a classic precedent in Foucauldian theories, in which he argues that the *way we articulate determines what we know*. We understand knowledge through different discursive lenses. Each colours what we see and how the various discourses inform us, eliding 'an origin or transcendental subject that would confer any special meaning on existence'.[10] To examine *Doctor Who* in eras is to ascribe meaning to each era; periodizing underscores – but does not create – the mechanisms by which categories are established.

Once again, *Doctor Who Magazine* provides a key example of this. In a feature by Michael Haslett, the magazine reimagined what Classic *Doctor Who* tales might look like transcribed in different eras: 'What glorious chaos might ensue if one were to toss aside the given order of things, and let stories produced in one season of *Doctor Who* – be they fair or foul – be presented, at great variance, in another?'[11] The article is rife with value judgments about different episodes, writing teams, and eras:

> Would, then, tales beloved of few, such as the gruelling *Planet of the Daleks* [1973] or the chronically crass *Time and the Rani* [1987], reveal hidden depths if groomed with loving affection? Conversely, would fan ambrosia such as *The Robots of Death* [1977] or *Remembrance of the Daleks* [1988] become an [sic] low-fat supermarket yoghurt if left to spoil in other, less gifted, hands?[12]
>
> *The Twin Dilemma* [1984] may, at first, seem like a scant compensation for even the weakest of the First Doctor's stories, but if it had been made in the monochrome age, it would undoubtedly have been a superior production.[13]

The effect of the humorous article isn't just to reimagine *Doctor Who*, but to reaffirm the categories into which the fans (especially the professional fans at the helm of the official magazine) have placed *Doctor Who*.

Expanding on this point in his analysis of the New series of *Doctor Who*, Hills shows how 'fan criticisms involve shaping an image of "ideal" *Who*, a kind of Platonic essence of the series (which may never have been realized fully in any one story)'.[14] This 'unattainable' goal is the approximation of the quintessence of *Doctor Who*, something that one could point to and say 'this is what *Doctor Who* is'. Different fans may be able to articulate particular eras as the most ideal (e.g. the Hinchcliffe/

Holmes 'gothic horror' era[15]), but no value judgment can be said to be authoritative. If one particular era of *Doctor Who* may or may not be described by a particular fan as the essence of *Doctor Who*, then *any* era could be said to be ideal *Who*: 'every period of *Doctor Who* has its champions and its detractors'.[16]

Methods of periodization

Doctor Who's 'regeneration' of the lead actor is a particularly visible aspect of periodization; however, it is far from unique. Changes in on-screen personnel help structure readings of many television programmes: *Bewitched* (ABC, 1964–72) infamously featured two Darrins (Dick York, Dick Sargent), creating a rupture in the series; *The Avengers'* (ITV, 1961–69) many partners with John Steed (Patrick Macnee) help structure the DVD releases. In terms of *Doctor Who*, the Doctor's regeneration cycle offers a visible and highly ordered mechanism by which periods of the show can be separated: for each Doctor, a different era. Useful in a superficial sense, the lead actor certainly influences how the show is perceived. Sixth Doctor Colin Baker's rather brash portrayal colours that era of the show. The Third Doctor's heroic, 'James Bond' nature helps to define the five years Jon Pertwee stayed in the role. This organization can be problematic, however: how to define the Eighth Doctor era, when only one televised text and one web-released minisode exists, but hundreds of hours of non-televised material deepens his story?[17] Or the Fourth Doctor era, which saw huge changes in the demeanour of the lead character? Indeed, categorizing *Doctor Who* not only tells us about the show, but also tells us about the categorizer, and what they consider important for the Doctor's character.[18]

In addition, trying to understand the actor of the Doctor as separate from the production staff elides, as Wood suggests, the important behind-the-scenes elements that historicize and periodize the show into even more eras.[19] For example, Chapman defines the era of the first producer/script editor, Verity Lambert (1963–65)/David Whitaker (1963–64), as reflective of the split between historical and science fiction adventures; the 'erratic' Fourth Doctor is characteristic of the three different producers and four different script-editors of his long tenure. Similarly, the production team of producer Barry Letts (1970–75) and script editor Terrance Dicks (1968–74) saw the start of the Doctor's 'Earthbound' adventures, when the Time Lords exiled him to Earth for three years. During this time, the Doctor partnered with UNIT (United Nations Intelligence Taskforce), a military organization, to defend the planet from evil aliens, duplicitous politicians, and the Master. As Chapman points out, 'the Letts-Dicks-Pertwee era is associated with a particular type of story that set the tone for that period'.[20] Defining by production helps see 'marked shifts in the tone of drama'.[21] And the producers of *Doctor Who* themselves have used this production method to periodize. As *Doctor Who* scriptwriter, long-time script editor, and prolific author of the Target novelizations, Terrance Dicks describes:

> *Doctor Who* is like a saga. Every few years there will be a new something. There will be a new companion. There will be new writers. There will be new script editors. There will be new producers. And every chunk of years there will be a new Doctor. So all of these things bring change.[22]

New *Who* regenerator Russell T Davies, in describing the transition between the end of his tenure and Steven Moffat's incoming one, concurs:

> the best thing that a new [production] team can do is move in, trample over the way that we did things, and find new ways for themselves … they'd be better off packing up our stuff and throwing our boxes into the street. New show! New team! New start![23]

In terms of the production strategies, periodization puts an emphasis on dividing *Doctor Who* into eras based entirely around the white, male producer/showrunner (with the notable exception of first producer Verity Lambert). Excepting Lambert, all the producers, stars, and script editors of *Doctor Who* have conformed to the traditional system of cultural privilege. This may be an issue with the BBC production system itself rather than with periodization, but examining the series from a production standpoint emphasizes and reinforces this privilege.[24] That is, highlighting production in *Doctor Who* might be reassuring in its neatness, but brings with it very real cultural consequences that articulate dominant hegemonic meanings.

Furthermore, whatever principles are used to characterize a particular era of *Doctor Who* will inherently be biased towards those very principles. Fans might watch a Pertwee episode and see the 'Earthbound' criteria in the Letts/Dicks story because *they're already expecting that authorial characteristic*. The characteristic has become canon, rather than the unique elements of the series' narrative.[25] These characteristics thus arrive at the expense of other, perhaps just as relevant, characteristics. To deny that the Letts/Dicks period was not primarily Earthbound would be ludicrous. But centralizing the periodization to that characteristic only *typifies* that particular era; it does not define it.[26] Such characteristics become so notable that they can even be mocked by fans; for example, Mike Morris lampoons the key characteristics of the Letts/Dicks/Pertwee era, including constant fight scenes and the Doctor's pomposity – but highlights as his first and most obvious cliché the Earthbound motif.[27]

Lest we forget, however, even during the Third Doctor's supposed exile, he manages to get off-world on multiple occasions, as in *The Mutants* (1972), when he travels to the thirtieth-century planet Solos. Furthermore, the Time Lords released the Third Doctor from his exile just past halfway through his tenure. After *The Three Doctors* (1972), the Doctor takes every opportunity to travel away from London in the late twentieth century: he returns to UNIT only three times in two series. He is not 'Earthbound' for the entirety of the Letts/Dicks era, but using the term 'Earthbound' colours our interpretation of his other adventures as well. Moments when the Third Doctor goes off-Earth are unusual, because they do not fit into the Letts/Dicks/Pertwee paradigm – and, indeed, fans don't normally consider the first Fourth Doctor story, *Robot* (1975), to be similarly 'Earthbound' even though it was produced by Letts and see the Doctor and UNIT fighting on Earth.

As another example, we might assume that the Seventh Doctor manifests the common 'master manipulator' characteristics of a Nathan-Turner/Cartmel production. However, these 'mastermind' elements of the Seventh Doctor are only really present in some of his later episodes. This is also noted in the 2013 *Doctors Revisited* series, released for the fiftieth anniversary, when then-current showrunner Steven Moffat describes how the 'mysterious' characteristic of the

Seventh Doctor only became notable during the latter half of his tenure. We see the beginning of Sylvester McCoy's era as not fulfilling the 'mysterious Doctor' paradigm because the paradigm excludes what does not fit. Fans value the mysterious Doctor more than the clownish Doctor, so that's the characteristic applied to the era. When a particular characteristic becomes shorthand for understanding an entire era, it prescribes, rather than describes, the relevant characteristics. This prescription colours any further reading of the era, not destroying it but subtly shaping its interpretation.

Generic methodology

As the *Doctor Who* corpus grows, genre may be a more convincing way of understanding *Who* than one based in production personnel.[28] On the one hand, *Doctor Who*'s format as a whole 'cannot be pinned down generically'.[29] It has characteristics of science fiction, fantasy, adventure, historical, and romance, among others. The multi-genre format recalls Tulloch and Alvarado, who argue that 'the uniqueness and … durability' of the programme lie in its 'range of different genres'.[30] On the other hand, actual episodes manifest radically different genre characteristics even within that fluidity. Individual episodes may follow more or less in a particular generic template (e.g. *The Robots of Death* (1977) and *Terror of the Vervoids* (1987) are inherently murder mysteries; 'Blink' (2007) and 'Midnight' (2008) are horror), or may reflect multiple genres (e.g., 'The Unicorn and the Wasp' (2008) is a historical-murder-mystery-science-fiction tale). But as Mittell has shown, genre characteristics are themselves problematic in asserting classification strata, as categories can exist only to organize texts, not to delineate what is contained within them: 'The members of any given category do not create, define, or constitute the category … While the members constituting a category might all possess some inherent trait binding them into the category … there is nothing intrinsic about the category itself'.[31] *Doctor Who* is emblematic of this generic issue. 'Blink' might be a horror story, but that does not really tell us about what that 'horror' means, and, with its emphasis on shocks, jumps, and surprises, it is a different type of horror than the body horror of, say, *The Brain of Morbius* (1976). What might be a more telling example of generic periodization of *Doctor Who*, as described by Murray, at least, is the way the script editor functions to impact the development of the show. The script editor oversees the scripts for a particular series, often rewriting (or even writing) individual episodes to keep a consistent generic tone throughout.[32]

Perhaps the most celebrated script editor in terms of *Doctor Who* is Robert Holmes, who script-edited during the mid-1970s, wrote individual episodes for Doctors Two through Six, and 'became a linchpin of the series' writing pool' for the Third Doctor.[33] Indeed, *Doctor Who Magazine* voted him the #1 fan favourite writer.[34] But it is during his tenure as script editor, when he worked with Philip Hinchcliffe and Tom Baker, that he solidified what many fans consider the 'golden age' of *Doctor Who*, with its reputation in the 'gothic' genre.[35] This genre focused on, among other things, an 'uncanny' sense of the body and remaking classic horror stories in a science-fictional context (e.g. *Frankenstein* becomes *The Brain of Morbius*; *The Mummy* becomes *Pyramids of Mars* (1975)).[36] If we can identify the Baker/Hinchcliffe/Holmes period as one filled with monsters and versions of horror, however, it tells us only about that one trait, but not the genre in and of itself. Furthermore, it only describes one generic aspect of these scripts – namely, that many rewrite or refer to classic monsters. Identifying each episode in this generic manner reduces the episode to that genre, eliding characteristics of other genres that may also be present. For example, reading *Pyramids of Mars* as a gothic horror elides the important time travel narrative at the heart of the story, and glosses the narrative discussion of paradoxes.[37]

By asserting a generic distinction at all, fans ultimately participate in what Andrew Tudor calls 'The Empiricist Dilemma', a problematic at the heart of genre studies. Before analysing a genre, critics must isolate texts:

> on the basis of the 'principal characteristics', which can only be discovered from the films themselves after they have been isolated. That is, we are caught in a circle that first requires that the films be isolated, for which purposes a criterion is necessary, but the criterion is, in turn, meant to emerge from the empirically established common characteristics of the films.[38]

In other words, by establishing criteria, genre critics 'merely reproduce the initial assumptions that led to establishing their primary sample'.[39]

To determine the gothic elements of the Hinchcliffe era is to have always seen those elements in the first place; it is a backwards way of establishing periodizing qualities, and hides other facts that go into developing a theory of generic discourse. For example, Rolinson notes how *State of Decay* (1980) was originally written for Series 15, a 'gothic' series, but did not make it into the series until the Series 18, which saw Christopher H. Bidmead, a new script editor, focusing more on science characteristics.[40] By which elements do we periodize *State of Decay*? Identifying the 'gothic' era in this generic way, we also find the very characteristics we are trying to uncover, which colours the interpretation of the story. Establishing generic characteristics for particular eras also elides those characteristics in *other* eras.

Periodizing as discourse

Periodization emphasizes division rather than continuity, encouraging the development of criteria of differentiation rather than unity. Any type of categorization brings with it assumptions that discipline our understanding of the whole. If *Doctor Who* is a 'vast fictional quilt', then, stretching the metaphor a bit, the more fans categorize the quilt via its individual blocks, the less we know about the blanket.[41] A non-generic, anti-hierarchical view of *Who* elides the Platonic ideal of periodization to focus on the show's ability (like its protagonist) to shape-shift as a key factor in its longevity. As David Butler suggests,

> it is this openness to diversity and change that is one of the great strengths of the programme…What makes *Doctor Who* particularly notable, and has perhaps enabled it to last so long, is its blurring of boundaries. *Doctor Who* has defied easy classification.[42]

Hills takes this to its logical conclusion that fans and academics alike could explore 'new *Who* without getting hung up on its "essence" and on whether a given episode is "really" *Doctor Who*'.[43] Because of the nature of *Doctor Who*, it is ultimately antithetical to the essence of the series *to* elide periodization. *Doctor Who* is, and always has been, about change, renewal, and development.[44] *Doctor Who* is never standard, which makes it always in-process.

But if change becomes the lens through which all *Doctor Who* is interpreted, then that too reductively facilitates a specific reading of the corpus – a reading itself based on change as the totalizing principle. Focusing on change in *Doctor Who* makes that change a central, connective tissue across the text, eliding periodization *within* the corpus as well. Thus, whatever mechanism fans use to categorize *Doctor Who* always brings with it a disciplining procedure. As Lindlof, Coyle, and Grodin illustrate, 'a typical media audience is not a cohesive membership that behave according to a shared code'; instead, as we saw in the last chapters, fans have diverse views.

The periodizing consistency of *Doctor Who* fans emerges through the ascription of value to particular eras, stars, producers, or functions of the text. Any assertion of value is thus 'specific to the particular regime that organizes it',[45] the text shaping the 'social hierarchy' of the fan community that follows.[46] To emphasize one particular moment or series of moments fragments meaning within a text. Following a text with a fifty-year history, the 'community' of *Doctor Who* fans must create strata in order to self-actualize. The positioning of individual membership in any fandom depends on the relationship with others' organizational principles, highlighting the impact of periodization on viewers as well. However, by examining alternative conceptions of meaning-making of *Doctor Who*, a more polyvocal understanding of the text can be revealed.

Archives, palimpsests, and periodization

Thus, reconciling periodization within and about *Doctor Who* means seeing ruptures as *both* meaningful and unimportant to the larger serial frame of the text. *Doctor Who* itself has tried to accomplish this revisitation of continuity: 'The Name of the Doctor' (2013), the lead-in to the fiftieth anniversary of *Doctor Who,* featured multiple in-text references to the show's own past via diegetic rewritings. In the episode, in order to save the Doctor (Matt Smith), companion Clara Oswald (Jenna-Louise Coleman) inserts herself into every era of the Doctor's life, rewriting aspects of his history through her very presence. Clara's multiple presences across the Doctor's lives saw her experiencing each Doctor as separate entities, each within his own time and apparel (e.g. she appears in a 1970s-style miniskirt with images of the Third Doctor; in a 1980s leather jacket with the Seventh). But at the same time, the Doctors are seen out of context, digitally animated or colorized, and put in different circumstances (and in one case, so briefly seen it's hard to even make him out). In other words, the episode reveals that Clara permeates (and has permeated) the Doctor's past, reflecting a continuity-laden attempt to both elide and highlight periodization. Such a revelation/revision requires a shift in the conception of all *Doctor Who* knowledge, highlighting both the connectivity and periodization of the show.

Clara's experiences through *Doctor Who* reveal the change and continuity of the show. Continuity and change are consistent elements of the programme: think how canon references make the show coherent but renewal brings new ways of approaching the material. In her discussion of the archive-like qualities of cult media, Abigail Derecho examines what she calls an 'archontic' system of content.[47] Looking at the archive-like qualities of *Doctor Who* as a corpus provides a mechanism for integrating periodizing tendencies within a continually expanding text. Archontic media provides a methodology for conceptualizing *Doctor Who*'s 'unfolding' text.

The term 'archontic' comes from Jacques Derrida, who describes the properties of an archive that allow it to continually open up to allow new and varied inclusions. As Derecho describes in her analysis of the archontic properties of cult texts, 'any and every archive remains forever open to new entries, new artefacts, new contents'.[48] In other words, the existence of an archive *encourages* contributions to enlarge and develop that archive.[49] We would make a correlated argument: that the archontic properties of *Doctor Who* allow it to be continually added to as an archive, not (just) through ancillary texts, but also through canonized and ret-conned information. In this, for example, Clara both *did* and *did not* influence past *Who* at the same time: 'The Name of the Doctor' reveals she *did*, but our collections of DVDs of the original series remind us, of course, that she did *not*. For *Doctor Who*, a continual rewriting is key to the way periodization functions: fans group the 'endless transformations and complex weavings' together, inscribing meaning into each 'entry' as a unique unit of data within a *Doctor Who* 'database'.[50] Clara literally (re)inscribes herself into the corpus, cohering it together. She becomes a connective tissue that both highlights and liberates the show's own history. Far from escaping the issues of periodizing, Clara's inscription onto *Doctor Who* writes the history through imbrication, piling one new reading on top of another.

Of course, 'archive' is both a noun and a verb, and to archive something means to write its place within an already-extant structure.[51] This inherent rewritability applies as *Doctor Who* continually reinvents itself: the notion of particular eras thus flourishes under archontic principles. As Britton notes about *Doctor Who*'s continuity,

> key elements have not always simply been brought into alignment with existing 'truths', or vice versa; some of them have effectively overwritten earlier histories, albeit leaving the original elements partially visible.[52]

Changing the categorization does not alter the text, it alters the category into which the text has been placed. *Doctor Who* thrives on this re-evaluative situation. Each era of the show – however it is defined – undergoes a 'cycle of evaluation', in which its value is 'continually reworked'.[53] Clara's coherence throughout *Doctor Who* reveals the continual rewriting of the show. *Doctor Who* never had a 'production bible' with the history of the Doctor, Gallifrey, and the Universe neatly laid out. Rather, such diegetic canonization has usually occurred after the fact, and unofficially.[54] Clara's trip to visit the Doctors highlights this archontic construction at the heart of *Doctor Who*, as the depiction of her visits can be seen to be rewriting and re-valuing its history on the fly. The inclusion of new material naturally engenders the desire to include more material. But an archive must necessarily exclude some material in order to be separate from the culture that created it. We know *Doctor Who* because there are things that are *not Doctor Who*, and they firmly remain outside the scope of the show.

Lance Parkin describes the desire of *Doctor Who* fans to continually add to or adjust what counts as 'canon' within *Doctor Who*. Although he talks about the books and comics predominantly, his argument can extend to the nominally canonized material of the show itself.[55] With periodization, problems over quality 'always exclude parts of the whole': for fans, some eras of *Doctor Who* are 'less "proper" than other examples, whether it is anything broadcast after the introduction of K-9 in 1977, or seemingly anything after 2005'.[56] As Gillatt notes:

> I'm sure you have your own particular individual tastes in *Doctor Who*.... For every reader of [*Doctor Who Magazine*] who thinks *The Curse of Fenric* [1989] is the acme in sophistication of TV *Doctor Who*, there's another who believes nothing of any worth was produced after the introduction of the Time Lords, UNIT HQ and colour TV.[57]

One relevant example is the 1996 *Doctor Who TV Movie*. As a singular text situated within the heart of the largest rupture in the series' history, it marks a point of estrangement from the programme. Any information within it might fall prey to the categorical tendencies that erase information within a non-canonized text. For example, chillingly, it reveals that the Eighth Doctor is half-human. Within a periodization of *Doctor Who*, such information would taint the entire Eighth Doctor period, underscoring our reading of the era as a whole. Even showrunner Russell T Davies reveals this discourse. In his *The Writer's Tale*, a book chronicling his writing of the series, he describes an original draft of *The End of Time* which included a line that jokingly referred this half-human assertion. However, Davies says he cut the line as a 'silly reference – [it was] kind of confusing, since most of the audience will remember the Doctor being human in *Human Nature* rather than the 1996 *TV Movie*'.[58] Even in its erasure, the Eighth Doctor's half-human nature affects the corpus. Such a reductive move illustrates the way individual elements within a period can overshadow larger concerns.

Through an archontic lens, however, the expansive archive 'always produces more archive, and that is why the archive is never closed'.[59] There is no finality to the archive; it cannot end.[60] The half-human nature of the Eighth Doctor can thus *exist within the same system as the information that he is full Gallifreyan*. Davies could or could not include it equally, as it is always inscribed within the archive. The units of information that are prescribed and described within an archive thus *individually* reflect the category but do not *transfer* that meaning to other entries. Both elements become part of the archive as equally concomitant but contradictory facts.

Although it is constantly expanding, the *Doctor Who* canon must be limited to be recognized. We recognize *Doctor Who* not only for what it is, but for what it is not, and make arguments about canonicity to determine this placement in the archive. There can be no canon without a sense of inside and outside the archive. For example, what do we make of a single 25-minute episode that features no regular cast, introduces new main characters, and is situated chronologically between two unrelated serials? Such an episode exists: *Mission to the Unknown* (1965) is the 'prequel' episode to the mammoth twelve-part *The Daleks' Master Plan* (1965–66). As such, it becomes 'part' of the archive both because it is 'inside' *Doctor Who* and because it reveals an 'outside' to *Doctor Who* as a text. A different example of a similarly liminal *Doctor Who* text is the thirtieth anniversary special, 'Dimensions in Time' (1993), a one-off charity special that, while featuring all the surviving Doctors, the same producer, many of the most popular companions, and some returning enemies, is considered less canonical than *Mission to the Unknown*.[61] Yet it is still part of the archive. Furthermore, *The Scream of the Shalka* (2003), the animated fortieth anniversary episode, features a Ninth Doctor played not by 'canonized' Christopher Eccleston, but rather by Richard E. Grant. Known as the 'Shalka Doctor', Grant's portrayal contradicts the television series, but has received its own DVD release in the official BBC *Doctor Who* line, archiving it within a non-canonized but recognized liminal space.

Alec Charles argues that *Doctor Who* is inherently defined by 'relativity and relativism … not continuity but discontinuity'.[62] There must be elements that are outside the canon that provide a lens to examine within. *Mission to the Unknown* (1965), 'Dimensions in Time' (1993), and *Scream of the Shalka* (2003) are all liminal texts, whose positioning either inside or outside the canon allows a lens through which the archive can be perceived. Drawing from what it is *not*, the television programme tells us more about our contemporary archiving of it than it does about the show itself. This 'inherent paradox at the heart of the archive' engenders the periodizing problematic: 'by archiving, one must necessarily leave something out'; an archive can only record within a culture, within a particular context.[63]

Thus, an archontic examination of *Doctor Who* offers a way of envisioning the television series' ruptures between eras not as periodizing, nor as categorizing, but as part of a continuous archival *process* by which individual discourses and frameworks of meaning become *part of* rather than *constituent to* the development of *Doctor Who*. Ruptures take no more precedence than any other form of archived material. This also avoids the common articulation of *Doctor Who*'s discontinuity as its *most* relevant factor, a feature exemplified in Britton: the 'metaphor of the vast narrative as a "fictional quilt" … can serve to highlight not merely *Doctor Who*'s famous flexibility of narrative premise but rather its inherent and often productive lack of narrative constraint and coherence'.[64] Discontinuity and continuity work together to cohere the *Doctor Who* archive. Ultimately, the archontic methodology allows us a way to see around textual incoherence, a way to see discourse about the ruptures between eras as *equally* productive as that between continuities, and a way to see divisive discourse about different eras as *cohering* an archontic fandom rather than dividing a periodized hierarchy.

Conclusion

The issue of periodizing *Doctor Who* is not just an academic one. In addition to the value that fans place on the text, as described above, the way that television shows become categorized can have a profound effect on their production, distribution, and marketing. For instance, the production machinery at the BBC uses periodization as a key marketing segmentation, as its website illustrates. When Peter Capaldi's Twelfth Doctor regenerated to Jodie Whittaker's Thirteenth (and Steven Moffat handed over the reins of the show to Chris Chibnall), the website regenerated as well, mirroring the aesthetic changes to the TARDIS, the title sequence and even the theme music. The same happened when Moffat took over from Davies in 2010. With the close of one (online) era, another aesthetically begins.

Such a periodized discourse also developed around the premiere of the 2005 reboot of *Doctor Who*, pervading the text of New *Who* so much so that Davies 'establishes a *fully inclusive continuity*' between the two series, bridging the rupture between the Classic and New as well as between 'cult and mainstream status'.[65] This opens up two different avenues of appreciating and understanding the relationship between Classic and New *Who*. By seeing New *Who* within a *continuity* with the Classic, a continuity is preserved but comparison and (implicit) evaluation are thus encouraged. But if New *Who* is discontinuous with Classic, it is not part of 'the text' and thus not subject to the same mode of analysis.[66] Fans who augment their understanding of *Doctor Who* by contrasting New and Classic are following a production-based understanding of where the meaning lies (in the production team, in authorship, in the stars), and ultimately echoing a discourse that implicitly assumes hierarchies.[67]

For *Doctor Who,* each moment, each element, each point in history, is always in a process of revision. Despite what the Doctor intones to Barbara in *The Aztecs* (1964), signalling his reluctance to interfere in history, time *can* be rewritten, both diegetically and non-diegetically. It is arguably impossible to separate text, audience, and context, but that is precisely the point. We make artificial separations with any scholarly or fan analyses, and thus help to create the very meaning that we are attempting to elucidate. Instead of viewing *Doctor Who* as a 'vast, fictional quilt' where the very bricolage nature of the programme becomes its greatest asset, we can instead assert that however we view, analyse, or discuss *Doctor Who* becomes the argument by which we know the show. The discursive lens delimits the view, but using the infinite lenses available via archontic principles develops multiple discourses simultaneously. Periodization creates meaning; fans think around this meaning in order to construct an ontology of television.

Case Study 3A

Nightmare of Eden and the limitations of genre

Paul Booth

In the previous chapter, we described how different periods in *Doctor Who*'s history have become synonymous with particular evaluative properties: the Seventh Doctor era has become known for the 'master manipulator' Doctor in Series 25 and 26 while the Third Doctor era is identified by the Earthbound storylines. The effect of this periodization is to pre-colour the way audiences may interpret particular moments within a series. For example, if one is expecting an Earthbound story in a Third Doctor episode but comes across, say, *The Curse of Peladon* (1972), their expectations may not be met and the way they value that episode (good or bad) can be affected. As indicated in that chapter, however, the many ruptures in these preconceived notions reveal the artifice at the centre of periodization.

In this short case study, I want to investigate one such rupture in depth: *Nightmare of Eden,* a 1979 episode from Tom Baker's time as the Doctor. *Nightmare of Eden* is rarely considered a 'great' episode of *Doctor Who*; in fact, it often sits near the bottom of episode polls. In this case, my argument is that the expected genre context of the episode is contradicted, in different ways, by what the episode actually reveals. My point in this short explication is not to defend a particular episode, or re-value the placement of an episode like *Nightmare of Eden* on a 'best-of' list. Rather, I wish to use the concept of periodization to evaluate how and why particular assumptions and expectations of an episode help frame the analysis of that episode.

Nightmare of Eden

Coming as it does in the middle of the seventeenth series of *Doctor Who*, sandwiched between *The Creature from the Pit* (1979) and *The*

Horns of Nimon (1979–80), neither of which is particularly well-regarded in traditional *Doctor Who* fandom, *Nightmare of Eden*'s 'low budget'[1] and poorly realized monsters have been sticking points for the fandom. According to the *Doctor Who Appreciation Society*, the monsters have been described as 'cute rejects from *The Muppet Show*'.[2] Bob Baker, the writer for the episode, has said 'the special effects didn't come across very well', and 'the monsters looked dippy, looked like soft toys'.[3] However, many other *Doctor Who* stories with similar cheap special effects and dodgy monsters have been much more valued by fan communities: for instance, the mummies in *The Pyramids of Mars* (1975) are quite silly, yet that story continues to rank very highly among fans.[4] Perhaps there is some other reason the story does not rank highly; perhaps, as I suggest, it is because the larger questions and underlying structure of the episode do not fit in with the perceived genre characteristics of the era.

Nightmare of Eden was produced by Graham Williams and script-edited by Douglas Adams; together, the Williams/Adams pair are known for their humorous take on the programme, their tendency to let star Tom Baker have freer rein to improvise, and to focus more generally on the fantastic elements of the series (as opposed to, say, more science-heavy moments).[5] Their tenure together on the show lasted just one year: Adams was script editor for Series 17, and Williams was producer for Series 15–17. But during that time, they created one of the most loved episodes (*City of Death* [1979]) and one of the most loathed (*Horns of Nimon*). *Nightmare of Eden* falls between these two apexes. Perhaps this emphasis on humour is because of Adams himself. As author of *The Hitchhiker's Guide to the Galaxy* (BBC, 1978), Adams is best known for absurdist comedy, and it is not surprising fans watch Tom Baker in a Williams-produced Adams script and expect (and see) such humour. And while there are definitely moments of comedy in the Williams/Adams era, there are monsters, horror, and other non-comedic elements that are elided in discourse about the era, as Smith?[6] points out: 'it's still an era remembered primarily for its over-the-top humour, some dodgy acting and even dodgier special effects',[7] and yet also depicts more diverse villains and shows a greater emphasis on female empowerment.[8] For instance, there are moments that are not humorous at all, but the genre's characteristics overshadow the others.[9] At the end of episode one of *Nightmare of*

Eden, the camera zooms into what appears to be an empty forest only to reveal in close-up a disguised and horrendous face emerging from the foliage. The moment is shocking, but identifying comedy as the 'main' characteristic of the era turns the horrifying moment into a footnote in an 'otherwise' humorous script (see Figure 7). For Smith? and Morris, the humour of the Williams/Adams era has coloured other generic characteristics.

Another element of the episode that seems to counter the predominant view of the series as a whole is the subject matter: *Nightmare of Eden* was deliberately and overtly made, according to Baker, as a treatise on drugs. In the documentary 'Going Solo', found on the episode DVD, he describes how he:

> did quite a bit of research about drug taking and that sort of thing … and read as much as we could about all forms of smuggling and the kinds of drugs, how they took them, that sort of thing. We really took research seriously. The drug theme in *Doctor Who*, well,

Figure 7 The Nightmare of Eden, Part 1. *Doctor Who* © BBC 1979.

I thought why not, really? It seemed to work. Everyone was happy with it, especially Douglas Adams, the script editor....

I think there's about 3 or 4 times that the Doctor mentions the fact how terrible this drug is, and the whole idea of drug taking is opened up, and talked about, is not kept as being clever. And I think the honesty of it is the thing that kept it in, and kept it going.[10]

Far from being a comedic romp, an episode that focuses on drugs lends a more serious air to the discourse, perhaps subverting the generic quality fans may have expected. Indeed, some fans have commented that the episode seems heavy-handed with its lectures on drugs: regardless of the intent behind it, however, the focus on illegal drugs takes the episode outside genre expectations.[11]

Finally, the fact that the episode relied on, and had long sections about, 'real science' may have led fans to devalue it for generic reasons. Baker continues in his discussion on the documentary about the research he did for the various scientific elements in the episode:

The idea of time space crossing, and getting this collision in time space, was a lot of reading in *Scientific American*, and a book called *The Explosion of Science*, which gave me the seeds of the idea. The CET machine, that was the thing I researched quite thoroughly, through *Scientific American,* because it was some idea about someone making a practical version of that at some time in the future, like 50 years in the future. And so I made up the words Continuous Event Transmuter....it transmuted continuous events, so that things could happen right in front of you, like you were there.

Again, those expecting to have a more typical 'Douglas Adams' humour-filled episode may be disappointed by the serious, horrific, and scientific elements of the episode. (Indeed, Series 18, which followed, is known precisely for this generic element, as new script editor Christopher H. Bidmead wanted to bring more science into the series.) The underlying scientific elements within the episode position it within a far more serious-minded 'hard sci-fi' rather than the type of soft, easy-going sci-fi-lite of the rest of the Williams/Adams era, which tended to have created more fantastical or fanciful episodes. This is not to say that one would confuse *Nightmare of Eden* with a science documentary, but the renewed emphasis on the underlying practical science and technology may have seemed in contrast to what might be expected.

The point here is not to 'reclaim' the Williams/Adams era in particular, as Smith? and Morris do, but rather to offer an alternate viewpoint as to the rationale for the generic expectations and subversions of *Nightmare of Eden*. This is not to say that the episode is without fault: as one memorable online review puts it, 'Simplistic moralising, recycled concepts, endless corridors and Romana in the most hideous dress we've ever seen. Nothing the Fourth Doctor's in is ever a complete waste of time, but frankly, there's not much to like.'[12] At the same time, this review also notes the failed comedy elements of the episode, describing it as 'cringeworthy'. However, humour, while fickle at the best of times, is perhaps not the best way of examining this episode, despite the pedigree of the script-editor and the emphasis of the producer. Despite the fact that there are many issues with the episode, perhaps the most salient is simply that it's not quite what one would expect from the genre at the time. And this fact underscores other readings of value within the episode as well.

Conclusion

No one is saying that *Nightmare of Eden* is a good episode of *Doctor Who*.[13] Rather, what I might argue is that it is an *unexpected* episode of *Doctor Who*. It arrives in the middle of a series that contains the incredibly highly regarded episode *City of Death*[14]. The episode that aired immediately preceding it was *The Creature from the Pit*, an episode that featured a green blob with a giant phallus on its front, while it is followed by the poorly regarded *Horns of Nimon*, an episode that Paul Cornell, Martin Day, and Keith Topping call 'wonderfully watchable... [but] brilliant and dull'.[15] As with all things Series 17, *Nightmare of Eden* doesn't quite fit into the mould of *Doctor Who* that has come before: it is neither tragic nor funny, neither scary nor safe. It takes serious themes and treats them silly and takes silly moments with utmost seriousness. It is a contradiction. And it is devalued for thus not fitting into the prescribed notions of what *Doctor Who should* be during this pivotal time in the series.

Case Study 3B

The discovery of *The Time Meddler*

Craig Owen Jones

Nowhere is the changing nature of fannish perceptions more obvious than in the assessment of missing episodes, and for good reason: the absence of the text in its complete form provides all sorts of leeway for this or that interpretation of a story to take hold. In the absence of a corrective, fans can judge a serial not on its merits, but on what they perceive its merits to be in these straitened circumstances of their experience of it, even as they remain aware of the gaps and imperfections in the text.

This process was brought into stark relief in 2013 with the announcement that nine episodes of *Doctor Who* – all five missing episodes of *The Enemy of the World* (1968) and four out of five missing episodes of *The Web of Fear* (1968) – had been discovered in a TV station storeroom in Nigeria. Ken Griffin has noted the opportunity that this discovery afforded to re-evaluate what he refers to as 'the archival surrogates' for these missing episodes: the reconstructions and audio presentations that have done duty for them in fan circles since the absence from the archives was first noted at the turn of the 1980s. As Griffin notes, the reappearance of the episodes has had a profound effect on how these stories are viewed. *The Enemy of the World*, previously considered a humdrum serial on the evidence of its single surviving episode, is revealed to have been uniquely hampered 'in the absence of moving imagery', as so much of the story is reliant on visual cues (even the central conceit, that the Doctor is the spitting image of Salamander, a wealthy aristocrat bent on demagoguery on Earth in the near future, depends on visual imagery for its plausibility). Griffin singles out for scrutiny a ninety-second sequence – derided for years by fans as slow and pointless – in which, as the soundtrack for the episode leads us to believe, nothing much happens. Recovery of the episode in question, however, shows the sequence to have consisted of a lampooning of the ostentatious display of technology in the James Bond and other similar franchises, as Salamander arrives at his destination via a needlessly complicated elevator that pivots from the horizontal to the vertical, much as Virgil Tracy's pilot seat does in *Thunderbirds* (ATV, 1964–66). As Griffin notes,

> The returned serials also highlight the imperfect nature of reconstructions and the potential unreliability of fan evaluations of the series' missing stories. The divergence between previous evaluations and reality is particularly significant regarding *The Enemy of the World*. It is notable that, while some missing serials have been hailed as lost classics, many feature towards the bottom of fan surveys conducted by the likes of *Doctor Who Magazine*. It is entirely possible that these serials have been similarly poorly represented by their surviving fragments, which has subsequently impacted upon their overall position within the *Doctor Who* canon.[1]

Yet while Griffin is correct in noting that continued evaluation of the fidelity of reconstructions to the lost originals will be impossible without further recoveries, fans have frequently evaluated lost serials in ways that turn out to be at odds with those serials' qualities. The compromised nature of surviving elements of the text, no less than the vicissitudes of memory, has conspired to muddy the reputations of several stories from the 1960s onwards.

The Time Meddler provides one such example. A four-part serial, it was broadcast in weekly instalments beginning on 3 July 1965. There being no fanzines or publications devoted to *Doctor Who* at the time, the reaction of contemporary fans is hard to judge, but the audience research reports commissioned by the BBC do exist for the first two episodes, and reveal a great deal about audience sensibilities at the time. The first episode, entitled 'The Watcher', sets the scene: The Doctor, along with Vicki (Maureen O'Brien) and his latest companion, Steven (Peter Purves), lands in Anglo-Saxon England in the year 1066. Before long, they begin to discover evidence of another visitor from the future, who has imprudently dropped a modern-day wristwatch. The culprit is – or appears to be – a monk (Peter Butterworth), who resides in a monastery on a hill above the local village, who uses a modern-day toaster to make his breakfast, and plays a gramophone record of Gregorian chant in order to maintain the illusion that the monastery is occupied. At the climax, and as the Doctor discovers the subterfuge, the monk traps him in a cell.

The audience reaction to this first episode seems to have been sanguine. On a five-point scale (A+, A, B, C, C–), 7 per cent rated it as an A+ episode, and 34 per cent gave it an A; a further 41 per cent rated it as a B; overall, it received a reaction index of 58,[2] just above the then average for the show of 53. However, and as the report notes, a 'substantial minority' were disgruntled at the departure of Barbara and Ian in the previous serial; while still others found the pacing of the episode too slow, even as they acknowledged that expository episodes often had to bear the burden of scene-setting; and 'A minority considered it too fantastic and ridiculous, and some of them became thoroughly confused by the anachronisms which, as far as they were concerned, made nonsense of the episode.'

Reactions to the second episode, 'The Meddling Monk', were far less positive. This time, although 6 per cent persisted in giving the episode an A+ grade, only a further 19 per cent graded it as an A; almost half (46 per cent) thought the episode merited a B, while almost a quarter (22 per cent) gave it a C. The compiler described the majority as having been 'somewhat dissatisfied' on viewing the episode, and was moved to quote one audience member's response at length as being representative of the whole:

> I still can't understand this new Doctor Who story. I was completely baffled after last week's episode and am even more so after this with its mixture of Saxons and Vikings, electric toasters and electric frying pans. The sooner he [the Doctor] gets back to the future the better – these historical adventures are a bit of a bore.[3]

A major obstacle to enjoyment was the continued presence of modern anachronisms in the time of King Harold: 'Certainly there was much speculation as to how various electrical gadgets and other twentieth century items came to be in use in tenth century Britain [sic], but this seemed to irritate rather than intrigue many viewers.'[4] Although various shortcomings in the production were also singled out for criticism, such as the poorly choreographed fight scene, 'stagey' sets, and slapped-on make-up, the obvious conclusion to draw is that the audience *at large* was at this point too inexperienced to envisage the conceit (revealed later) that the monk is in fact one of the Doctor's race, who has journeyed to Anglo-Saxon England in order to rewrite history to his own liking. In the absence of a complete record of audience responses, we can only guess as to how the remainder of *The Time Meddler* was received at the time, though if viewing figures are anything to go by, the serial never recovered from its ponderous opening; over a million viewers switched off between the second and third episodes, and although figures recovered a little for the finale, it was nevertheless seen by only 8.3 million, still noticeably down on the first episode's 8.9 million.

In the interim, *The Time Meddler* was largely forgotten, and fannish opinion seems to have written it off as a quirky but ultimately forgettable serial of the Hartnell years. An in-depth overview of Hartnell's twenty-nine serials featured in *Doctor Who Magazine* in September 1981 omitted the serial entirely; and even a comprehensive article on the 'historical' dramas of the 1960s glossed over it as, according to the author, it was 'predominantly science-fiction oriented'.[5]

At this time, the serial was lost.[6] Following its initial broadcast, *The Time Meddler* was put up for sale by the BBC, and copies were made for broadcast in overseas territories, including Zambia, Mauritius, Sierra Leone, and Nigeria, from the latter of which copies were eventually returned in 1984. Prior to this point, therefore, fan opinion was based solely on recollections of the serial on transmission, as well as reminiscences of cast and crew, and access to the scripts for those with connections.[7] After the serial's rediscovery in 1984, however, there was an upsurge in interest in the serial, and evaluations immediately began to improve. An assessment printed in September 1985 as part of an article on comedy in *Doctor Who* acknowledges that the story has been hard done by in the past, while admiring the introduction of Butterworth's character as a prototype Master, and praising the story's comic chops: '[I]f it wasn't so under-rated [it] might be held as the funniest *Doctor Who* story ever made.'[8] Around the same time, fanzine writer Paul Mount heaped praise on the production, calling it

another of those drastically under-rated and often-forgotten stories that tends to be overshadowed by some of the more spectacular and lavish space serials which surrounded it .... With a perfect blend of subtle humour and a strong, tightly-directed drama, 'The Time Meddler' is certainly in the running as the best serial of its type ...[9]

The serial was novelized in 1987 for Target Books, after which a whole new audience was able to evaluate the story (albeit from a different form of media).

Fan interest continued into the 1990s, and was picked up on by the BBC, which chose the serial as one of the very few Hartnell-era stories to be repeated on BBC2 in 1992, where it achieved respectable viewing figures. By the 1990s, the consensus established was that *The Time Meddler* was a good, and perhaps even great, serial.[10] In 2014, the serial placed 77th in *Doctor Who Magazine*'s 'First 50 Years' poll, an improvement of twenty-one places on its position in a similar poll conducted in 1998, and making it the fifth most popular of the Hartnell era,[11] above such 'classics' as *The Tenth Planet* (1966), *Marco Polo* (1964), and even the debut serial, *An Unearthly Child* (1963).

The disparity in audience responses is key to understanding why *The Time Meddler*'s reputation has undergone such a dramatic change in recent years. Allowing for the fact that the viewers polled for their opinions in 1965 were general or 'casual' viewers, the emphasis in their responses is on the wish to be entertained and not to be confused, a cleaving to straightforward narratives that were inimical to the sustained mystery of a purportedly Anglo-Saxon monk with access to toasters and gramophones. Comments such as 'Rubbish!' and 'It just seems silly' were among those levelled at this plot device, and it is clear that it spoilt the viewing experiences of many, who presumably felt that the eventual explanation (if any) would not be adequate or appropriate to the serial. Still others were dissatisfied with the historical serials that were so common during the 1960s, preferring space-borne stories to anything set in Earth's past.

By the 1980s, however, and with the advantage of hindsight (particularly fannish hindsight), *The Time Meddler*'s significance had become a lot clearer. As the show's mythology began to develop, the elements of the story began to cohere in ways that could hardly have been anticipated by writer Dennis Spooner. Stories began to appear in which the immutability of the past (summarized by Hartnell's Doctor in the phrase, 'You can't change history, not one line!') was increasingly challenged, by both the Doctor's foes and the Doctor himself. As the first time traveller we meet who is bent on changing the past, Butterworth's Monk can be seen as an exemplar for later characters. The Monk's other importance is, of course, that after the transmission of *The War*

Games (1969), in which we are introduced to Gallifrey and the Doctor's race, the Monk was retrospectively glossed as a Time Lord, further enhancing the sense of continuity that so distinguishes the show from other science fiction franchises.

For today's fans, *The Time Meddler*'s other praiseworthy characteristic is the tenor of the serial itself. Although the first episode was derided at the time and since as being slow, the serial is arguably one of the most narratologically mature of *Doctor Who*'s earliest serials. The self-reflexivity it displays sits well with today's fans, for whom the central conceits of the TARDIS and time travel stories are as familiar as sonic screwdrivers and bow ties. There is also a refreshing lightness of touch from the director Douglas Camfield, including several points at which the directorial mores of the era are subverted for narrative purposes. An example is the withholding of a dissolve to another scene in order to focus the viewers' attention on the monk's failure to fully inhabit his role: at the point where the dissolve should occur, the monks' chanting in the background of the scene slows down, implying that it is being provided by a recording.[12] If the plot is somewhat telegraphed by today's standards – few contemporary viewers would be left scratching their heads at the appearance of twentieth-century objects in the monk's possession, as so many of the viewers of 1965 were – the story's setting may be favourably compared with the post-2005 take on historical stories, such as what Burk and Smith? define as the 'celebrity historical',[13] centring on a famous figure from history ('Vincent and the Doctor' (2010) and 'Rosa' (2018) are obvious examples). Finally, it should be added that the deficiencies in production of which 1960s audiences were so unforgiving are now treated in an entirely different fashion: broadcasts of 1960s *Doctor Who* on Twitch, a social media platform allowing for the posting of comments to an online broadcast in 2018, demonstrated the perhaps surprising extent to which today's viewers were happy to indulge the weaknesses of costume, set, lighting, and acting that so annoyed respondents to the BBC's audience reports at the time.[14] As the spinners of camp-fire yarns have long known, the allure of the story is so often in who tells it.

Dialogue 3C

Series 24

Craig Owen Jones and Paul Booth

Craig: I have very conflicted feelings about this series. In terms of quality, Series 26 knocks it into a cocked hat, and yet Series 24 retains its importance. It is McCoy's first series; the hugely popular companion Ace is introduced during it; and it contains the hallmark McCoy moment – the cliffhanger scene from *Dragonfire* (1987).

Fan reception since the series' broadcast has reinforced this view; although *Delta and the Bannermen* (1987) and *Paradise Towers* (1987) have small but vocal sets of admirers who extol their 1950s 'retro' atmosphere and dystopian setting respectively, the series as a whole is almost universally derided; its serials regularly feature towards the bottom of fan polls.

In spite of this – or perhaps because of it – Series 24 has become something of a palimpsest, its meaning having been inscribed and reinscribed by producers and fans alike since its broadcast. Hills has written about the importance of 'moments' to the textual design of the show, averring that fan professionals can be responsible for their creation.[1] The corollary of this is that where such moments are retrospectively identified by a particular subset (or indeed, a particular generation) of fans who are long used to watching shows organized around such principles, it falls to those viewers to reach consensus on which 'moments' are worthy of celebration. The result is a peculiar reification of the show's past, reflecting both the archontic principles on which the show may be said to rely and also fandom as a repository of memory. In this way, such scenes as the famously preposterous cliffhanger to the first episode of *Dragonfire*, which sees McCoy's Seventh Doctor dangling over a precipice for no apparent reason and which was thoroughly excoriated by fans when first broadcast, becomes a defining moment of his era due to Clara's witnessing of it in 'The Name of the Doctor' (2013), and serves to elevate the noticeably hit-and-miss McCoy era into one of the most fondly remembered in the show's history.

My interest, though, is in how those who love it have become its curators. The first serial, *Time and the Rani* (1987), I have yet to see defended by anyone in more than a half-hearted fashion, but apologists have put together all sorts of surprisingly coherent arguments for accepting the others as good, or at least serviceable, stories. Both *Paradise Towers* and *Delta and the Bannermen* obviously benefit from camp readings (see Chapter 1), but I have been astounded to see solemn defences of both stories on multiple occasions on message boards. But this is easy to do, as, so the saying goes, these serials 'don't get much love'; such readings can flourish uncontested, especially as they are so impervious to casual criticism on the grounds of errant production values and hammy acting. Paul, to what extent do you see these types of subsections of fandom acting to dictate particular types of narrative over the quality of this or that story, or series?

Paul: The hallmark McCoy moment? Maybe the most notorious moment! (For my money, the hallmark moment is 'You fight like animals? You'll die like animals!'.) But I will admit from a production standpoint, the cliffhanger has become imbricated into the framework of the show, especially when it became the single McCoy moment in 'Name of the Doctor' and Clara's journey through the Doctor's timeline.

But I see your larger point here. I think it harkens back to the point earlier in the book when we discussed how communities can help focus fan engagement in particular moments, episodes, or series. I've generally seen a revisitation of the McCoy era in the thirty years since it ended. In fact, Lynne M. Thomas has written about this too, arguing:

> Received Fan Wisdom (a vocal portion of the long-term *DW* fandom community who write extensively about such things) collectively agree that Season Twenty-Four mustn't be held up as an example of what makes *Doctor Who* great. We endure it, but we certainly don't celebrate it.
>
> Received Fan Wisdom is *wrong*.[2]

Thomas argues here that Series 24 is a return to the *fun* of the series after multiple dark, depressing series overseen by Eric Saward. I've also seen it re-evaluated in terms of the high quality of the storytelling, the averred socio-cultural critiques, the presence of Ace, and the general moody ambiance that seemed to contrast the key lighting of Baker's and Davison's previous series. For example, the Doctor Who Club that I supervise at DePaul University has watched all the McCoy episodes numerous times; by far they request to watch these the most often. I think they see a tension in them, between the very modern elements (there's a direct line to be drawn between the end of McCoy and the beginning of Eccleston) and the very dated. To your point, I see them try to find the moments that resonate the most; so when we watch *Paradise Towers,* they remember the strong female Kang members, the murderous cannibalism and queer subtext of the Rezzies, and the humorous take on what we now call toxic masculinity with Pex. What they don't fondly reminisce about are things like the Great Architect plot, or the swimming pool monster, both of which seem dated and unnecessary to the enjoyment of the episode – and they do love the episode! Lest we forget, we are now further from the McCoy era than the McCoy era was from the beginnings of *Doctor Who* itself.

So I wonder if the re-narrating of the McCoy era in general is more indicative of the historical presence of the show. For many 'old school' fans, McCoy's era may still seem like the new kid on the block, the part of the series after which they stopped watching. While newer fans are rediscovering Series 24 without the preconceptions of old fandom, they're also making the connection to the New series and watching through that storytelling framework. It's all about the little moments: the camp 'Rezzies' in *Paradise*, the spies in *Delta*, or the way Ace treats the little girl in *Dragonfire*. I have definitely seen *Paradise Towers* re-evaluated as both a thoughtful science fiction story and a feminist discourse,[3] and *Delta* is perennially discussed as a fun romp camping piece.[4] I've seen fewer nice things said about *Dragonfire* but let's change that, shall we? What do you like about that story? Or, for that matter, is there any redemption to *Time and the Rani*? ('Leave the girl, it's the man I want', surely!)

Craig: I'll take a deep breath now, and embark on my own 'solemn defense'! *Dragonfire* is one of my favourites, because it was the first *Doctor Who* serial I ever purchased, and so I rewatched it to pieces, but I can't defend it too staunchly; its faults are too numerous. It disappointed me on my first viewing because what I was looking for at that time was serious science fiction, and I hoped *Doctor*

Who – which I had apprehended through what little I knew of it as a mysterious, even slightly sinister, programme about time travel – would be that for me. *Dragonfire* wasn't, of course; the key lighting, silly costumes, and some awful lines left me deflated. The parts of it that are bad are truly bad. The homage to *Alien* is embarrassingly devoid of tension, the sequences with the child miss their mark, and the scene where the Doctor exchanges philosophical small talk with a guard (who turns out to be unexpectedly well read) is leaden. There is something dismaying about watching two actors play a scene well, with perfect intonation and timing, and yet having to witness the scene nevertheless falling flat on its face, because the underlying premise is not believable. That the scene, and others like it, somehow did not make their way to the cutting room floor indicates at once that the lapses of editorial judgment that characterize, say, *Delta and the Bannermen* are still there.

And yet I kept coming back to *Dragonfire*, because it shares with the rest of the series that crucial characteristic: everyone is pulling in the same direction. It is extraordinarily ambitious, and for the first time in the series, that ambition is somewhat realized. Svartos may not look amazing – it's too tinselly and brightly lit for that – but the sheer scale of the split-level studio sets is impressive. Dominic Glynn's score is a minor masterpiece, haunting and gothic, and a far cry from the orchestra stabs and 808 beats of the preceding serials. We have some fine supporting performances from Tony Osoba and Patricia Quinn, and an excellent performance by Edward Peel as Kane – perhaps the last great villain the show produced before the hiatus. And then there's that wonderful speech by McCoy in the final seconds of the last episode – his audition speech, I believe. For me, that's up there with any of Tom Baker's or William Hartnell's speeches. McCoy is on record as saying that he didn't get a handle on the role of the Doctor until his second series, but I wonder; for me, *Dragonfire* is the first serial where he looks at home in the role.

It is interesting that, in your experience, younger fans find *Dragonfire* and its bedfellows so interesting. There's another aspect to that lack of preconceptions you mentioned earlier: young fans today are also not viewing Series 24 through the prism of televisual science fiction at the time. Part of the reason I was so harsh in my initial assessment of *Dragonfire* was that I was mentally comparing it to *Star Trek: The Next*

Generation, and it naturally came up short. Today's young fans, I would think, can extend their indulgence to it – as they would to a Hartnell serial, perhaps – in a way that I wasn't willing to when I first came to it in the early 1990s as a contemporary (or almost contemporary) production.

Paul: Yes, I think that's it precisely. As academics or as fans we are taught (or, at least, I have always been taught) that we need to read texts in the contexts in which they were written: try to put yourself in the mindset of a viewer from 1987 watching *Dragonfire* for the first time. But that sort of historical telepathy ignores the actual reality of a great many viewers of *Doctor Who* today and can become a dangerous sort of mind game, one that is tempted to forgive things like the yellowface in *Talons* because it is 'historical' even if it's still not accurate for the time. (Plus, even as an academic AND a fan, I can't imagine what it would have been like to listen to the 'semiotic thickness' speech with or without the knowledge of Tulloch and Alvarado.[5]) Yet, when we do view things out of context, in the present, we may find more things to enjoy than just the preconceived fan-authorized moments of value.

Chapter 4

Re-Evaluating Value in the Canon of *Doctor Who*

Doctor Who's interest in its own past has been analysed to weariness by academics. The modern-day viewer of HBOMax or Amazon Prime can easily comprehend the early onset of the show's self-reflexivity as an outlier, the product of three things: its unusually obsessive fandom, even for science fiction; the central conceit of the show, that is, the Doctor's ability to regenerate, which as time went on increasingly lent itself to intertextual referencing; and lastly, the indignance – it is not too strong a word to call it grief – among fans over the junking or discarding of old episodes, knowledge of which became general in 1981. Almost a decade before *Star Trek: The Next Generation* (CBS, 1987–94) premiered, fandom obsessed over the tiniest details of the Doctor's life, the working of the TARDIS, and other elements of the show. This interest was acknowledged by the show's makers, particularly producer John Nathan-Turner, who went out of his way to cater to fan opinion and actively courted it.

These factors complicate the job of assessing value in the *Doctor Who* canon in unexpected ways. For one thing, the fact that the debate over the show's past has been around for so long – it is over forty years since the first *Doctor Who* fanzine was produced, and *Doctor Who Magazine* (*DWM*) will celebrate its fortieth anniversary in 2019 – means that fan assessment today must take into consideration something that, say, assessments of *Firefly* (Fox, 2002–03) or *Andromeda* (sci-fi, 2000–05) do not: a *fan historiography*. Newcomers to the critical territory, full of enthusiasm and eager to explore its contours, find (perhaps, are disappointed to find) that the map already exists: its fidelity to the landscape may be argued over, but it is there, and to ignore it is to wilfully lop off an important part of fandom's prevailing narrative. Fans who, say, first encountered the show in the guise of its post-2005 series, even if hailing from places outside Britain where the show does not form a part of the popular consciousness, do not remain ignorant of the show's past for very long. If the clips of previous Doctors inserted into episodes such as 'The Eleventh Hour' (2010), 'The Day of the Doctor' (2013), or 'Twice upon a Time' (2017) (not to say seemingly incomprehensible references to 'gobby Australians' ('The Crimson Horror', 2013)) do not pique their interest in the show's past, actual appearances by pre-2005 Doctors – as in 'Time Crash' (2005) or 'The Night of the Doctor' (2013) – surely will.

Secondly, however, it becomes possible to discern particular camps within fandom that value the show in divergent, or at least different, ways. Given the enormous gap in tone and format, it is unsurprising that there is a subset of (generally older) fans who view the post-2005 show as somehow inferior to the show they remember, while younger fans may take the opposite view.[1] It ought to be said that the larger number of fans by far seems to hold that each of these overarching periods in the show's history has its own merits, and accordingly value each equally, in principle at least; and it is this majority that has resulted in the dichotomy between the 1963–89 series and the post-2005 series in fandom being far more subtle than it might perhaps have been under different circumstances.[2] Nevertheless, it exists, and to return to the earlier metaphor, it emplaces on the critical landscape reverence for the past as a sort of waymarker for those wishing to traverse the territory, and there it has remained.

The perspective of fans prior to 2005 is not without its own biases and agendas. Many came of age in the late 1970s and early 1980s, by which time the show already had the best part of twenty years of production behind it, and as Miles Booy has pointed out, for this part of fandom, 'the present was more-or-less accessible in that it could be remembered (and later videoed), but the past was always in desperate need of recovery and it always seemed to be better than the present'.[3] While the focus of official publications such as *DWM* today is often and inevitably on the post-2005 series, a significant minority of each issue is given over to discussion of the 1963–89 series in some shape or form, or articles that deal with the show in its entirety. This reflects the perspectives of the show's makers, who, as fans reared on the show in the 1970s and 1980s in particular, have made great efforts to maintain continuity since its return. However, for most of today's young fans, earlier eras of the show have no day-to-day bearing on their consumption of it, for obvious reasons. For such fans, viewing what is invariably referred to as 'Classic' *Doctor Who* becomes something akin to an excursion, with all the connotations of extraneousness that implies.

A recent instance of this garnered media attention in early 2018, when a minor controversy arose among members of *DWM* regarding the reintroduction of a feature called 'Time Team', in which a panel of fan writers rewatch episodes from the show's history and pass critical comment on them (see our next section on *Talons of Weng-Chiang* as well). For older readers, the problem was not the premise, but the makeup of the team, which had an average age of twenty-two, and none of whom were over twenty-six. 'It [the magazine] has become a party that I don't feel invited to' was the opinion of one reader, while another remarked: 'Looks like *DWM* have replaced the Time Team with the cast of [BBC children's drama] *Grange Hill* [BBC, 1978–2008]. Not sure why but it makes me feel depressed. Diverse in everything but age.'[4] Blogger Maria Kalotichou has conceived of the controversy in similar terms, noting that it is not about preserving a favoured interpretation of the 1963–89 show, but about representation:

> I would say to bring older fans along with the changes.... the issue is only having young people....I suppose what I'm saying is I agree let's have more diversity, men, women, different ethnicities sure yes, in the Time Team [*sic*] but let's not exclude the age demographic. Would it REALLY hurt that much to do it? Surely by excluding the older fan, [the editorial team] are doing the opposite of promoting diversity?[5]

While diversity of opinion is clearly a factor, there seems to be an underlying rationale in these opinions that articulates a fear of a particular view of the show coming to prevail, one that sees older episodes as inadequate or unworthy of serious scrutiny due to production shortcomings, slow pacing, or sexist or racist gambits in terms of plotting, casting, and dialogue.[6] Singled out for criticism here was Time Team member Christel Dee, who opined in one early feature that she always watched 'old' *Doctor Who* at 1.5x speed because of the slow pacing.[7]

But if to a goodly portion of today's digital natives, 1963–89 *Doctor Who* simply isn't very good – a curio experienced for laughs on Twitch at best, and a poorly made, racist, misogynist embarrassment at worst – how can the show's longevity be explained? Nostalgia for childhood memories of being 'behind the sofa' does not on its own suffice. As Booy notes, while many British viewers began watching the show at the age of four or five, *Doctor Who* fandom tends to cater to older viewers, and has signified as such since the 1970s via 'a wealth of implicit minimum age barriers': advertising in horror magazines, the adult register in which many fanzines were written, and so forth.[8]

The answer can instead be sought in the interplay of fan memory and quality. As we mentioned in the Introduction, long-time producer John Nathan-Turner was fond of saying to fans who decried the show's uneven quality in the 1980s, 'the memory cheats'; fans often remember serials and episodes as better and more resonant than they might have been on their initial viewing. Fan memory is replete with situations in which, as Wood and Miles put it, the focus of the process of remembering is on 'moments when something happened' – that is, something particularly dramatic or pertinent to the development of the Doctor's or a companion's backstory – even if it occurs within the context of an episode we otherwise apprehend as being 'bad'. The following indignant speech, delivered in the courtroom in defiance of his grilling before the Time Lords' Inquisitor (Lynda Bellingham), perhaps embodies Colin Baker's finest moment as the Sixth Doctor:

> In all my travellings throughout the universe I have battled against evil, against power-mad conspirators... I should have stayed here. The oldest civilization, decadent, degenerate and rotten to the core. Ha! Power-mad conspirators, Daleks, Sontarans, Cybermen – they're still in the nursery compared to us! Ten million years of absolute power – that's what it takes to be really corrupt!

This barnstorming speech, delivered with intensity by Baker, occurs partway through *The Ultimate Foe* (1986), the notoriously underwhelming finale to Series 23; nevertheless, it is regularly quoted as emblematic of the Sixth Doctor's personality,[9] and the clip from the episode is often shown in clip shows and documentaries, including *Thirty Years in the TARDIS* (1993). In other words, the moment acquires a meaning quite independent from that attached to it within the story containing it. The memory has hardly 'cheated' on this occasion: *The Ultimate Foe*'s decidedly middling reputation is hardly open to debate. Rather, the passage of time has allowed for evaluation to proceed along other lines. We value the speech for what it is, punchy wordsmithery delivered with conviction and in a suitably fiery fashion; its failure as a dramatic device is forgotten.

This may be thought of as a type of nostalgic recollection. As Boym and others have pointed out, nostalgia is necessarily selective; we remember what we want to remember, or what is most redolent of the experience of place we wish to evoke, while disregarding the rest. Christina Goulding has written of 'vicarious nostalgia', the way in which individuals can develop a preference for the unlived or imagined 'past' that dismisses the lack of lived experience as irrelevant, and embraces sources other than personal experience as wellsprings of nostalgic feeling.[10] However, where this process is to some extent a conscious one, at other times fan memory does indeed 'cheat', suppressing some incidents in the show while creating others out of whole cloth. There are many instances in the history of the show where a purported memory or memories are taken up by fandom and reified, to the extent that they even come to constitute integral components of the show's mythology.

One such example relates to the First Doctor. Interest in William Hartnell's First Doctor was particularly acute by the 1970s, by which time his era had sufficiently receded into the past to lend it a sense of mystery and unknowability. The transmission of Hartnell's regeneration scene from *The Tenth Planet* (1966) on a November 1973 episode of children's magazine programme *Blue Peter* (BBC, 1958–) combined with Hartnell's appearance in the tenth anniversary special *The Three Doctors* the previous January probably worked to reignite interest in the show's heritage in general and Hartnell's era in particular.[11] As the initial incarnation of the show's titular character, the assemblage of the show's mythology by fans often impels fans to seek defining quotations from that period that not only embody the First Doctor's personality and demeanour, but also speak to the prevailing moral attitudes that the show espouses. This imperative is discernible as early as the mid-

1970s, but the triumvirate of defining quotations that crop up most often today – the 'exiles' speech (from *An Unearthly Child* (1963)), the 'one day, I will come back' speech (from *The Dalek Invasion of Earth* (1964)), and the 'have you no emotions, sir?' line (from *The Tenth Planet* (1966)) – were all superseded by a speech of the First Doctor of striking imagery and pregnant with the spirit of adventure:

> Can you imagine silver leaves waving above a pool of liquid gold containing singing fishes? Twin suns that circle and fall in a rainbow heaven, another world in another sky? If you like to come with me, I'll show you all this – and it will be, I promise you, the dullest part of it all. Come with me and you will see wonders that no Human has ever dreamt possible. Or stay behind and regret your staying until the day you die.

Table 1 Published versions of David Whitaker's 'another world in another sky' quote

Source	Date	Quote
Hulke and Dicks, *The Making of Doctor Who*, 8–9	1972	Can you imagine silver leaves waving above a pool of liquid gold containing singing fishes? Twin suns that circle and fall in a rainbow heaven, another world in another sky? If you like to come with me, I'll show you all this – and it will be, I promise you, the dullest part of it all. Come with me and you will see wonders that no Human has ever dreamt possible. Or stay behind and regret your staying until the day you die.
Jack Waterman, 'Who's Who in the Time Warp?', *The Listener* (United States/ Canada), 438 (edited version of Hulke and Dicks)	2 October 1975	
Doctor Who Digest, Vol. 1 No. 1 (1976), p. 1 (attributed 'Dr. Who, 1965')	July 1976	
Ottawa Journal, p. 15 (edited version of Hulke and Dicks)	9 October 1976	
Doctor Who Yearbook, inside cover (edited version of Hulke and Dicks, with 'another world in the sky' for 'another world in another sky')	1992	

Source	Date	Quote
DWM #51	5 April 1981	Can you imagine silver leaves waving above a pond of liquid gold, twin suns that rise and fall in a rainbow heaven. Another world in another sky.
http://bluishtigers.tumblr. com/post/34865019134/ imagine-if-you-can-silver- leaves-waving-above-a	2 November 2012	Imagine, if you can, silver leaves waving above a pool of gold filled with singing fishes. Twin moons in an alien sky. If you like, I'll show them to you and they will be, I promise you, the dullest part of the journey. Come with me and I will show you sights that you have never dreamed of. Or stay behind, and regret it until your dying day …
'heymickey', http://cultbox. co.uk/features/trivia/10- classic-doctor-who-quotes- the-doctor-on-his-enemies, 'think it was William Hartnell and it's from memory'	*c.* 2014	Imagine, if you can: silver leaves waving above a pool of liquid gold containing singing fishes, twin suns that circle and fall in a rainbow heaven, another world in another sky, if you care to come with me, I'll show you all this, and it will be, I promise you, the dullest part of it all. Come with me and you'll see wonders no human has ever dreamed possible, or stay behind, and regret your staying until the day you die. Will you come?

As Table 1 illustrates, fans have long held the importance of this quote; however, it was never uttered on screen. Its earliest appearance in print appears to be in the pages of *The Making of Doctor Who*, a slim volume written by the show's writers, Malcolm Hulke and Terrance Dicks, and was attributed therein to David Whitaker, who wrote for the show during Hartnell's era.[12] The misconception that it was an actual speech delivered by Hartnell had extraordinary staying power, and continues to be believed, and repeated, by fans even today.

The vectors for the dissemination of this supposed speech are worth considering. For fans, the most important fora from the 1970s until the popularization of the internet were the dozens of fanzines produced by fan clubs, local groups, and individuals, and *DWM*. These publications allowed fans to critique and debate individual episodes and serials, as well as the show's history more generally. An important component of early numbers of *DWM*, for example, is a feature devoted to the synopsis of a serial from the past. These features, often illustrated by photographs taken during filming, were surprisingly detailed – some ran to four pages or more in length – and not only offered particular fannish interpretations of serials, but also provided glosses for this or that element that tied it in to the show's continuity as established later in its run. They were also didactic. In the early 1980s, many of the featured serials were about missing (or partially so) episodes, and therefore these synopses became important carriers of identity for fandom, allowing these serials to be experienced in some form: a particularly important role in cases where not even a Target novelization existed to mediate between the original text and the fan audience of the time. Decisions on one story or another's quality and importance within the canon often proceeded on evidence no more substantial than these articles, supplemented by memories of the original transmission shared by fans in print and orally at fan meetings and conventions.

In such a media environment – print-based, reflexive only on timescales of weeks or months (depending on frequency of publication), and permeable to hearsay and distortion – fan memory could also work in the opposite direction, confabulating this or that scene, reimagining the dynamic between, say, the Doctor and a long-forgotten companion in errant ways, or focusing on one interpretation of a serial to the detriment of others. For many years, a key forum for this type of recollection was the regular *DWM* feature, the 'Matrix Data Bank'. More often than not, the feature, which tackled points of detail concerning the Doctor's backstory, the functioning of the TARDIS, and the workings of the Whoniverse in general, engaged with these points through the mechanism of fans' memories of the show. The above 'liquid gold' speech, for example, appeared in an April 1981 edition of *DWM*:

'Can you imagine silver leaves waving above a pond of liquid gold, twin suns that rise and fall in a rainbow heaven. Another world in another sky'. Many publications [have] listed this quotation as an example of 'magic' in the Doctor Who series but Philip Davies of Southampton has asked when it was actually said in the programme.

The answer, I'm afraid[,] is never. It was not said in the programme and neither have I been able to find mention in any rehearsal or camera script to indicate that it might have been written but later edited out from recording [*sic*].[13]

The feature goes on to suggest this 'quote' is in fact a mangled conflation of two separate speeches from the very beginning of the show: William Hartnell's speech to a disbelieving Ian in the second episode of *An Unearthly Child* (1963), and a line uttered by Susan (Carole Ann Ford) in *The Sensorites* (1964). The source for the 'quote' has been speculated to be an uncredited short story written by Whitaker, but the present authors have been unable to locate any such story. Published versions of the quote are summarized in Table 1.

Hulke and Dick's book clearly provides the source material for all the subsequent versions of the quote shown here, but the most noteworthy aspect of the table by far is how the quote was shortly embraced by fandom. The fact that it appeared on the front cover of the first *Doctor Who* fanzine, the news instrument of what would become the *Doctor Who Appreciation Society*, as early as 1976 speaks to its appeal, and the passage appended to it in *DWM* in 1981 quoted above implies that it was well known in fandom as emblematic of the First Doctor. It still enjoyed currency in 1992, and more recently it has come to be represented as a quote from the show itself: writing *c*. 2014, 'heymickey' even frames the quote as an actual line uttered by actor William Hartnell. There can be no more persuasive demonstration of the mutability of fan memory. How, then, do fans reconcile these discrepancies with the way things actually happened, and what effect does the unreliability of fan memory have on assessments of quality?

Speeches such as the above endured in fan consciousness for so long because they do a duty for fandom. They help to create, as Van Wyck Brooks' ground-breaking 1918 essay put it, a 'usable past', a sense of history that shunned what Brooks saw as the incipient 'hectic individualism' of his time, and would enable those beholding it to seek progress in the present.[14] It may also be the case, however, that fans impose modern ways of viewing on older episodes. Fans may not be academics, but they possess critical mechanisms for assessing the quality of a given story. The model embraced by Steven Moffat in particular of 'moment' television – in which elements such as pacing and even exposition are rendered subservient to the need to provide regular inflection points in a given episode, a series of revelations, instances of dramatic tension, and the like, and described by Hills – may be mapped, either advertently or inadvertently, onto earlier stories during rewatches. Other peculiarities of viewing today, such as 'binge' watching all the episodes of a serial at once instead of in weekly instalments, fast forwarding or skipping metatextual elements such as the title sequences and credits, and watching with on-screen production notes or a commentary soundtrack (both of which are more or less ubiquitous features in the *Doctor Who* DVD range) fundamentally alter the meaning of the original. They may even transfigure it; moments such as Hartnell's 'one day, I will come back' speech from *The Dalek Invasion of Earth* acquire added beauty and poignancy not only because of our knowledge of the show's (and Hartnell's) extraordinary history, but also because they have been referred to so many times in the show subsequently.[15]

Finally, generational difference alters meaning. Modes of viewing that complement what Mittell referred to as the sorts of 'complex narratives' represented by shows such as *Buffy the Vampire Slayer* (WB/UPN 1996–2003), *The X-Files* (Fox, 1993–2018), *24* (Fox, 2001–14), and *Lost* (ABC, 2004–10) – that is, endlessly deferred, capable of telling stories using disparate genres (musical, mystery, psychological drama), ready to flaunt devices that encourage idiosyncratic readings such as unreliable narratives, and so on – compel today's viewers to seek ambiguities and wonder at the complexity of the storytelling on display. The resultant atmosphere of 'operational aesthetics', whereby the viewer marvels at how the story works,[16] correlates well to, for example, time travel stories, but has rather less to say when it comes to the sorts of relatively straightforward narratives of, say, the 'base under siege' and 'monster of the week' stories that characterize the Troughton era, or the 'historicals' of the first three seasons. Applied to narratives from the 1960s that were intended for viewing by less experienced audiences, and were therefore told in less complex ways by default, this viewing position can result in some interesting interpretational developments. Old texts become akin to palimpsests; their original received meanings are effaced, and peculiar new meanings are inscribed on them in their stead. Thus, it was a source of surprise and even bemusement in some circles when, in mid-2018, the appearance of 1963–89 *Doctor Who* serials on the live broadcast social media platform Twitch prompted young fans hitherto unaware of the show's origins to begin shipping Barbara (Jacqueline Hill) and Ian (William Russell).[17]

This avowedly modern approach to a show over fifty years old should not be thought of in terms of aberrant decoding. It is true that more recent television shows habitually feature will-they-won't-they relations between pairs of characters. Even when such impulses as read into the demeanours of the characters are not acted upon, the possibility of their coupling remains; and yet this is fairly transparently not the case in an early 1960s serial of *Doctor Who*'s type, in which relationship dynamics do not change except at the departure of actors, and familial relationships are subsequently ossified. Today's sophisticated young viewers know, or at least intuit, this. It seems clear that they are entirely aware of the gloss they place on Barbara and Ian's relationship by, say, reading romantic intent into their (occasional) holding hands and Ian's frequent embracing of Barbara in moments of alarm and peril (see Figure 8). In the same way, the recent proliferation of reaction videos taking 1963–89 serials as their subject matter supports the idea that younger viewers take contemporary modes of viewing and apply them to older work.

It remains to be seen how the relationship of memory and quality will play out in the coming years. Certainly those who grew up with post-2005 *Doctor Who* are in a hitherto unimagined position: the show as they have known it is as safe for posterity as any television series or film can be, and the sorts of debates that embodied fandom in the 1970s and 1980s in particular over the show's past are now

Figure 8 'i mean look me in the eye and tell me you don't think they're adorable'. Barbara and Ian as OTP (One True Pair), Unwilling Adventurer Tumblr account; last accessed 9 November 2018. *Doctor Who: The Chase*, © BBC 1965

easily resolved by a few clicks of a mouse; differences over the show's past are now differences of taste and interpretation, not of opinion over the facts of the show's production, which are as well understood as they will ever be. However, it is inevitable that, once enough time has passed – perhaps as the cultural power and influence of British society wane further (a process that will surely accelerate due to Brexit), the show is cancelled, or the moving image is replaced by emergent forms of transmedia storytelling – the episodes of, say, the Eccleston, Tennant, Smith, Capaldi, and Whittaker eras will come to be viewed as anachronistic after their own fashion, in their subject matter, production, and telling. As more and more new fans come to the show with no memories of the Eccleston era, such a realignment is already happening. One suspects it will continue to happen, and then happen again. *Doctor Who*, as the Seventh Doctor once said, is difficult to get rid of, and it is too deeply embedded in the minds of viewers across the world for it simply to be effaced. It will continue to be evaluated and re-evaluated for as long as we continue to appreciate the moving image.

Case Study 4A

Evaluative changes of *The Talons of Weng-Chiang*

Craig Owen Jones

More than any genre, science fiction is a prisoner of the time in which it was written. Perceptions of the future are more apt to bear the anachronisms of the age that gave rise to them than perceptions of the past. By the same token, however, they reflect the cultural sensibilities of their own time, a fact put to use for comic effect in *Twice upon a Time* (2017), in which writer Steven Moffat made light of the casual misogyny displayed so frequently by the First Doctor during serials of the 1960s, when gender roles within *Doctor Who* conformed to a different set of ideals. What could have been a source of embarrassment is neither accepted with a shrug nor airbrushed out of history; instead, it becomes a source of levity, with Peter Capaldi's Twelfth Doctor rushing to apologize for his previous self's unthinking characterizations of women as being fragile or neglectful of their natural duty in keeping the TARDIS clean and tidy.

Such conservative social mores are, however, not always so easily dealt with. Representations of race in older serials have frequently made for uncomfortable viewing for fans eager to establish the beginning of the show's current multicultural credentials; Danny Nicol's recent declaration that, in the 1960s, 'The show's racism was indeed thunderous', if hyperbolic, is certainly an entirely defensible position.[1] In *The Celestial Toymaker* (1966), a racist slur in a nursery rhyme then current passes without comment;[2] in *Tomb of the Cybermen* (1968), the character of Toberman is the archetypal black savage – surly, strapping, and unquestionably obedient to his (white) masters.

However, the problems extend further than merely the sorts of portrayals of black, Asian, or other non-white characters on display in previous instalments; race in *Doctor Who* may also be problematized in terms of the sorts of stories the show is *not* interested in telling. Lindy Orthia has written illuminatingly on the show's marked lack of postcolonial narratives. Orthia positions the show in terms of its Eurocentrism, noting that the 'stagist ideology' it exhibits is problematic because it does not admit other modes of political or cultural existence.[3] Furthermore, she suggests that the show's essentialist attitude towards humanity effectively debars the show from presenting coherent narratives of humankind's future where race is concerned: the 'unself-consciously monocultural and white' depictions of future times that pepper the show's 1963–89 run have their corollary in post-2005 episodes, which, though offering a far more balanced representation of a multicultural society, persist in depicting a global culture in which cultural differences deriving from race and ethnicity have been effaced: 'There are no battles for cultural dominance; it seems the West has already won that fight, because the future most closely resembles the West.'[4]

Given such problematic attitudes, it is instructive to discover how fans negotiate the problem of race – or, more precisely, racism – within *Doctor Who*. *The Talons of Weng-Chiang* (1977) is selected for analysis here because it probably offers the most glaring example of apologetic assessment in the show's history, a stance some fans of the serial are all the more disposed to adopt because, by common consensus, it is one of the finest serials the show ever produced.[5] The episode became the focus of a late-2018 generational controversy in *DWM*, when the 'Time Team', a group of young, multi-cultural *Doctor Who* fans who watch and comment on Classic *Doctor Who* stories, saw *Talons*. In their write-up, they identify the many points of racism within the serial, decrying the stereotyping of the Chinese characters and the exceptionally poor choice to cast British Caucasian actor John Bennett as Chang, one of the serial's principal villains, complete with a fake Chinese accent and appearing in 'yellowface'. In response, the editor of *DWM*, Marcus Hearn, posted a rebuttal to their assessment in his Editor's column, effectively superseding their own views with what he perceives as the specific positive qualities of the episode. Today, many fans like Hearn are compelled to excuse the racism the episode displays, even as many younger fans are horrified by the overt caricatures and stereotyping.

Kate Orman writes in her thoughtful exploration of how fans reconcile *Talons* that 'when a story we cherish contains racially charged elements, we must show that it's not *really* racist – and neither are we for loving it'.[6] Fans usually employ one or more of three distinct strategies in this regard. Firstly, the serial is defended on the grounds of historical exceptionalism. *Talons*, so the theory goes, is a product of 1970s television, and what would today be regarded as unforgivable treatments of Asian actors was considered acceptable. A second strategy is to claim that the producers (or more specifically, the serial's author, Robert Holmes) sought to lampoon or send up contemporary attitudes towards race. Finally, the serial may be interpreted as straightforwardly reflecting prevailing attitudes towards race of the Victorian era.

None of these strategies do very much to enable unproblematic readings of the story. The first is, on the face of it, the most attractive. As commenter 'Lynda Day'[7] put it, in response to a blog decrying the serial's racist elements:

> I think you're falling into the trap that more and more people are falling into these days, i.e.: looking at something from decades ago and judging it by today's standards. TV of that era was marked by a ton of stuff which, by today's standards, is stuff that wouldn't fly on TV today. But does that make it wrong? On balance, I'd say no. It might well put a guy in yellowface but in no way, shape or form is it done as parody, or to laugh at the character.[8]

This standpoint, however, fails to address the fact that such practices as 'blacking up' and stereotyping non-white characters and communities were already coming under criticism in British society at the time of transmission. Although Gavin Schaffer has convincingly demonstrated that programmes such as the massively popular BBC1 comedy *Till Death Do Us Part* (1966–68, 1972–75), which derived its comedy from the debates between the racist and ultra-conservative Cockney patriarch Alf Garnett (Warren Mitchell) and his socialist son-in-law (Tony Booth), were not understood at the time via the modern gloss of a dialogue on race but as a series of left-wing attacks on the British Establishment,[9] other shows were and still are understood in racialist terms. In September 1975, Harold Wilson's Labour Government's White Paper on *Racial Discrimination* was published, which called for the establishment of a Race Relations Commission and for the recognition of discrimination by effect (i.e. without intention to discriminate) within the framework of law. The formal broaching of the subject of racism at the highest levels of British society, particularly after the relatively recent passing of the Race Relations Act (1968), helped to legitimate re-examinations of depictions of race and race relations in television. Actor (and *Doctor Who* guest star) Louis Mahoney was not slow to seize the opportunity, attacking on-screen depictions of racist behaviour and rhetoric in a well-argued broadside in an October 1975 edition of *The Stage*. Mahoney pinioned the 'racially biased nature of those responsible for comedy, drama and news in the various media, who rather than trying to eradicate racial prejudice in multi-racial Britain, tend to condone or uphold or it':

> [The mass media's supposed] concern for racial equality in multi-racial Britain would have prevented comedy programmes such as 'Till Death Do Us Part', 'Love Thy Neighbour', [and] 'Curry and Chips'[10] from being transmitted (forget the blacks and race relations, think of large viewing figures). Contrary to popular belief in the benign influence of national tolerance and in the power of laughter to defuse tension, these programmes tend to enhance prejudice and exacerbate racial discrimination.[11]

Doubtless the white author of *Till Death Do Us Part* and *Curry and Chips* (1969), Johnny Speight would have vehemently disagreed, being a committed socialist and having frequently gone on the record regarding his intent to lampoon and discredit characters such as Alf Garnett, whose racist tirades are invariably exposed for their logical inadequacies and moral shortcomings by other characters. One suspects, however, that Mahoney was in a far better position to judge, for obvious reasons; and indeed, Schaffer has shown that research conducted by the BBC during *Till Death Do Us Part*'s second run in the early 1970s indicated that, far from acting as a source of condemnation, the sitcom tended to reinforce existing racial prejudices for an older, working-class subset of the white viewing audience.[12]

Similarly, the 'yellowface' makeup of the type worn by John Bennett had been decried in the years leading up to *Talons'* transmission. Beyond the world of comedy, *The Black and White Minstrel Show* (BBC, 1958–78), in which singers and dancers performed in blackface, had been a staple of the BBC's schedules until it was cancelled in the face of mounting criticism in 1978; indeed, a stage revival in Liverpool in 1982 was the subject of determined protests by the local community.[13] The issue had even been commented on earlier in the Jon Pertwee era of *Doctor Who*, when a white actor had played the part of a Tibetan monk in *Planet of the Spiders* (1974). This instance of 'yellowface' was the subject of press criticism in an Equity survey of 1975, the results of which made it into the press.[14]

It is therefore disingenuous to excuse *Talons*' racial attitudes on the grounds of their supposed normality in 1977; as Orman states, 'the yellowface is only the most conspicuous component of a collection of contemptuous clichés in which *Talons* is involved'.[15] Nor can the suggestion that *Talons* comprised a critique of racial attitudes be made to stand up: if it were so – if, as Tulloch and Alvarado aver, the Doctor always espouses '"liberal" values of antiviolence and racial tolerance'[16] – then what is he doing in *Talons* mocking the Chinese as 'little men'?

The final strategy, to claim fidelity to Victorian sensibilities, retains some viability, revisionist histories of Victorian culture notwithstanding. Nevertheless, it is invoked on a less frequent basis than ever in fan circles, due in part perhaps to the growing incidences in the post-2005 series of what Nicol has called 'creative nostalgia' – the 'optimistic' grafting of contemporary values onto earlier time periods in the service of 'representing not [Britain] in earlier times but the country today'.[17] Nicol's example is 'Empress of Mars' (2017), in which a unit of British soldiers from Victorian times features a black private among their number. Rona Munro's 'The Eaters of Light' (2017), in its depiction of homosexual and bisexual Britons in Roman times, similarly repudiates received notions of life in Roman Britain, though with the important caveat that sexuality in Roman Empire was indeed far more fluid than in Britain until very recently.

Given the willingness of *Doctor Who*'s makers to indulge in this type of trope, it is hardly surprising to find that *Talons* is less and less defensible along essentialist lines; and yet it seems that *Doctor Who* fandom is unwilling to cut ties with it, in the way that, say, *Star Trek: The Next Generation* (CBS, 1987–94) fans find common cause in castigating 'Code of Honor' (1987), whose racial politics are similarly objectionable.[18] Perhaps the difference lies in the fact that the former is in the end a good story, and the latter is not. *Talons* and other, similarly well-received serials like it from the Hartnell, Troughton, and Pertwee eras are the Wagner operas of *Doctor Who*: wonderful to watch, if only one can perform the mental sleight-of-hand necessary to reconcile the impulses that shaped them to the values of decency and egalitarianism with which the show's central character is so associated.

Case Study 4B

The Caves of Dilemma: Or, The Twin Androzani? Evaluating value at the poles

Paul Booth

There is a curious moment in *Doctor Who* history that allows us to re-examine how particular episodes are valorized while others are discarded. It's a moment that's been discussed before, in different venues. It's a moment of change, a moment of renewal, a moment of reboot. It's the moment when Peter Davison transferred ownership of the role of the Doctor to Colin Baker, and the unusual values of two back-to-back serials in the series history.

In *DWM* issue #295, for example, Alan Barnes notes that:

> not long ago, a friend (a fan, not a Norm) proposed the theory that a member of the general public wouldn't be able to see any substantial difference between, say, *The Caves of Androzani* and *The Twin Dilemma*; yer average punter, he supposed, would either like or dislike both, but would be unlikely to vastly prefer one over the other.[1]

Later, in issue #413, Gary Gillatt echoes Barnes:

> It's such an unfortunate coincidence, you have to laugh. The same month *DWM* publishes the results of its Mighty 200 survey, *Doctor Who*'s 200th most popular adventure [*The Twin Dilemma*] is released on DVD.... And of course, we find *The Caves of Androzani* at the top of the list. So we have two serials, produced on the same watch – with the astounding final episode of *Caves* broadcast just six days before the astonishing first episode of *The Twin Dilemma* – but when we judge their relative worth, we find the whole history of *Doctor Who* slotted between them. It's a remarkable thing.[2]

Tat Wood and Lawrence Miles are a bit more meta about the dissonance:

> Even now, it's hard to understand exactly what happened...the whacking great gulf between 'The Caves of Androzani' and 'The Twin Dilemma' seems startling. It felt wrong at the time, and it still feels wrong now.[3]

The oddity of the moment is, how can one of the most negatively regarded episodes in the history of *Doctor Who* appear immediately after one of the most praised? In fact, it's not *just* that it's immediately after: it's also that, unusually, they are part of the same series. Unlike most regeneration stories, the first full-episode appearance of the new Sixth Doctor does not appear in the first episode of a new series, but rather in the first episode of the *final* serial of a series. Typically, a new series might engender some new faces (new writers/directors, new producer, etc.); however, in the case where one week saw the 'best' episode of *Doctor Who* end while the next saw the 'worst' premiere, there was no perceivable changeover of most of the main crew behind-the-scenes (barring the regeneration itself and, as I touch on below, the all-important writer and director). The last episode of *Caves of Androzani* was broadcast on 16 March 1984 while the first episode of *The Twin Dilemma* aired just six days later on 22 March 1984. Critics and fans argue it's 'baffling that the highest and lowest rated *Doctor Who* stories of all time could be shown one after the other....It just doesn't seem to make any sense. How can quality and audience appreciation differ so wildly in the space of one week?'[4] Elizabeth Sandifer argues, 'While on television, we go from the supposed best *Doctor Who* story ever to the supposed worst', although she goes on to note that 'On basic quality, this might not be quite fair. It's very bad, but as a matter of competent production and provision of a modicum of entertainment it's not demonstrably worse than many others.'[5] Damning with faint praise indeed.

This case study will contextualize and historicize *Doctor Who* fandom's evaluation of quality through a discussion of discourse around these two episodes. In 1984, as the Fifth Doctor (Peter Davison) transitioned into the Sixth (Colin Baker), these two serial stories appeared back to back but could not have polarized the audience of *Doctor Who* more. Davison's final story, *The Caves of Androzani*, is widely regarded as one of the best – if not *the* best – episodes of the Classic era (the Mighty 200 voted it #1). In contrast, Baker's first episode, *The Twin Dilemma*, is widely regarded as one of the *worst* episodes of the series (Mighty 200 puts it at dead last, number 200, as does the poll following in 2014). Television critic Christopher Bahn notes that this scheduling may have affected value: 'Part of its bad rep was just bad timing: It had the ill luck to follow directly after "The Caves of Androzani," Peter Davison's final and most well-received story.'[6] But of course, this in and of itself isn't that telling – good and bad markers of quality have always lain side by side.

Behind-the-scenes production also helps shape the discourse of the value of the episodes. While some people are consistent in their production roles (Eric Saward was the script editor for both episodes, John Nathan-Turner the producer), there are some significant differences that mean a lot to fans. One point of difference is that *Caves of Androzani* was written by Robert Holmes, one of the most established and notable *Doctor Who* authors (as we alluded to in Chapters 2 and 3), while *Twin Dilemma* was written by Anthony Steven, also an established television writing but with very few *Doctor Who* credits to his name. Holmes is widely considered by fans to be one of the greatest writers of the series, while Steven is largely forgotten (even I had to look his name up while writing this). According to the *Doctor Who* wiki, Steven's difficulty 'in trying to conceive and write a story for a new Doctor under short notice following the decision to push it forward to the end of Series 21 led to a languished production, eventually forcing Eric Saward to make a large number of hasty edits to his script'. Saward, it should be noted, is a divisive figure in *Doctor Who* fandom, with some fans in favour of his violent and adult stories (for instance, Booy indicates he was ahead of his time, writing stories that would later be akin to the adult-themed *New Adventures* novels[7]), while others finding them too graphic and confusing.[8] Saward himself left the programme in 1986 and immediately attacked John Nathan-Turner in the press, alienating some parts of the fandom as well, and perhaps shaping the way fans valued his previous work.[9]

Another production role that shifted between the two episodes was that of director. Graeme Harper directed *Caves of Androzani* while Peter Moffatt directed *The Twin Dilemma*. Although he worked on previous *Doctor Who* serials, *Caves* was Harper's first on-screen credit for directing *Doctor Who*.[10] Moffatt had previously directed four *Doctor Who* stories, and was an old hand at the BBC. Unlike as with the writers, in this case, Harper's inexperience may have been an asset. Fans have called him 'more than the sum of his parts' and his original camera work was unlike anything seen on *Doctor Who* before; he created 'pacy scenes of action' and 'slow, lingering dissolves' that allowed deeper understanding of the material.[11] In contrast to the stalwart writing of Holmes – fans know what they're going to get – Harper provided new and exciting visuals. Moffatt, whose experience on stories like *The Five Doctors* (1983) and *Mawdryn Undead* (1983) was conventional (and solid), may have made *The Twin Dilemma* look pedestrian.

Of course, the on-screen change between Davison and Baker also helps cement fan sentiment. Fans may love one actor over another, but the appearance of Baker playing a wild, angry character who tries to murder his companion may have taken it too far. In fact, in his assessment of the episode, Muir (who actually likes the episode quite a bit) blames this one bloodthirsty part as 'one isolated incident' that makes 'this story…not at all popular with *Doctor Who* fans'.[12] But for other fans, like Lawrence Miles and Tat Wood, 'Colin Baker's performance isn't great, and it'll certainly get better, but you can tell he's getting a kick out of this and he's not taking anything for granted. His maniac laughter in the costume room is genuinely unsettling'.[13] Sandifer, alternately, sees this as the worst possible representation of the Doctor, as a domestic abuser:

> Because Baker's Doctor isn't just unlikable here. He's intolerable. He's an overtly bad person who any reasonable audience should actively dislike and want to see get his comeuppance. Whereas the series still visibly thinks he's the hero. It's not just that Baker's Doctor is prickly and hard to like, it's that he's a bad guy…He physically and violently assaults her in a manner that is chillingly familiar as a real-world phenomenon that happens to women at the hands of their male partners…Peri is violently assaulted by a man who overtly sees her only purpose as being to serve him, and chooses happily to stay with him. The show treats this man as its hero and expects the audience to tune in nine months later to watch his continuing adventures…That's how you kill Doctor Who in under a hundred minutes. You make it about a battered woman idolizing her abuser.

In contrast, Davison, in *Caves of Androzani*, is at the top of his game, with Miles and Wood calling it 'probably the best of his entire career, a savage poke in the eye to all those who seriously believed he was a "bland" Doctor'.[14] It can always be hard to switch from one Doctor to another (as we discussed in the Introduction), but the transition from the 'nice' Doctor to a violent one, a change of pace indeed, could rattle viewers' sense of value.

From a story standpoint, *Caves of Androzani* seemed gritty, realistic, and situated within its own reality. *The Twin Dilemma* is more fantastical, colourful, and ethereal (despite the violent beginning). It's not that either one of these is necessarily better or worse than the other, but that it seems that, for fans, the realism is itself a point of value. *DWM* seemed to sum this up when Gary Gillat reviewed the two by writing, 'But what does *The Twin Dilemma*'s placing, and that survey as a whole, tell us about how we judge success and failure within the world of *Doctor Who*? To my mind, what the top stories have in common is a *robust commitment* to the fictional world they offer.'[15] Value, for these *Doctor Who* fans, is seemingly associated with the authenticity with which the series can create a believable alternate reality. It's these same fans who believe that the stories under Graham Williams's production were less authentic than those under Philip Hinchcliffe, because they were more campy. Humour, emotion, colour, fantasy: these are the sign (for these fans) of a less mature, more capricious tale. The value for these fans comes through an appearance of grittiness. Yet, realism like this is just one more icon, one more simulation of a type of appearance that doesn't actually exist: realism is just a series of codes that reflect back on what previous media texts have told us is realistic. Value again falls back on tradition.

Regardless of how you or I or any individual might feel about these two episodes, the general regarded 'truth' of them is that the apex and the nadir of *Doctor Who* appeared within a week of one another. It is an oddity, to be sure, but it is one that, whether through production personnel, actor changes, or story tone, can be explained by how fans have always viewed the relationship between authenticity and value. A hypothetical mind-game that imagines how *Caves of Androzani* would look directed by Peter Moffatt, or what *Twin Dilemma* might be like if written by Robert Holmes, helps to indicate how capricious these value judgments actually are. It's not that there's one thing that shapes how fans view a text: it is a combination of many, a prism of viewpoints, that creates our notion of value.

Dialogue 4C

Minisodes and changing appreciation

Craig Owen Jones and Paul Booth

Craig: As a self-described 'hiatus fan', it's hard for me to overstate how important 'The Night of the Doctor' (2013) was to me.[1] I have a vivid memory of where I was when I first watched it (on lunch break at work), my reaction (a sort of giddy disbelief – was I actually watching this?), and the first thing I did when it was over (phone a friend, and tell him to drop whatever he was doing, and watch it!). Elsewhere I have written of the story as an example of custodial narration, but I'd like to approach it here as an episode that is frequently treated from a standpoint of custodial evaluation. I do get the impression that for younger fans, for whom it lacked the emotional resonance that it had for older fans (Paul McGann's Big Finish appearances notwithstanding), this so-called 'minisode'[2] is viewed merely as another 'piece of the puzzle' – they're happy it exists because it fills in the Doctor's backstory, but their appreciation ends there. In other words, they don't actively engage in assigning it what we have called in Chapter 1 'intrinsic value' – and this in spite of the fact that it is beautifully produced and directed, with pitch-perfect performances from Paul McGann and Clare Higgins (Ohika). Paul, do you think that concentrating on the custodial aspects of this or that episode can lead fans to ignore the more conventional ways of evaluating stories? In other words, does assigning fannish value generally, and custodial evaluation in particular, privilege the importance of a story to fandom, leading us to ignore (or underplay) how good it is as a story?

Paul: Craig, my reaction to 'The Night of the Doctor' is quite a bit like yours, transplanted six hours earlier (I believe at this time you were still living in the UK and I was in the United States). As was my habit in 2013, I woke up at 6 am and went to check my email/social media on the computer – and immediately saw this minisode had come out. My exclamations when 'not the Doctor [I] was expecting' showed up were so loud, the dogs woke up and came running in to see if I was in peril! Then I rewound it and we all watched it together.

I replay this story every year when I teach my *Doctor Who* class and we get up to Paul McGann's era: the hiatus period during which you (and I, really) became fans of *Doctor Who*. And the reaction I get from the students is never quite what I would expect, largely because of what you're suggesting. I think the students see this as simply filling in one more gap in the series. McGann's Eighth Doctor has always been part of the series for them, while I remember the debates about whether or not it 'fit' into the larger 'canon' of *Doctor Who* from the 1990s and 2000s. My students binged Series 3 over a day, while I watched it week by week and nearly broke my remote trying to freeze frame on the face of the Eighth Doctor in John Smith's diary in 'Human Nature' (2007). The confirmation was electric.

My roundabout answer to your question, however, is a qualified yes. Stories that are perceived as 'important' for one reason or another may be evaluated on that sense of importance rather than any intrinsic value they may have. Your point (which I agree with) that 'The Night of the Doctor' is extremely well-made but is known more for its stitching together of two eras is spot on. I think we could easily see the same for 'important' stories like regeneration episodes. But I wonder if this only works in the positives; or, in other words, perhaps the cart has come before the horse. Stories that are already perceived positively because of their value may also be seen as important for different reasons. In my case study about *Caves of Androzani* (1984) and *The Twin Dilemma* (1984), it is inarguable that both are 'important' stories (being the last and first story of a particular Doctor), but does that importance overshadow the 'intrinsic value' (or not) that the episode might have? I'm not sure that it does. Beyond which – and maybe this is getting a bit too controversial – but I wonder if 'intrinsic value' is even a worthwhile term to be using here? As you've pointed out in previous dialogues, even the detritus of *Who* is worth a second look, and sometimes the things of value that we've assumed through 'fannish wisdom' do not always hold up to the stringent light of contemporary times. Can something even have an intrinsic value when we continually re-evaluate what it means to have value (and what value itself means) depending on any number of factors? I hesitate to even go here, but maybe it's time to re-evaluate 'Dimensions in Time' (1993)?

Craig: Well, some philosophers hold that extrinsic value is just a species of intrinsic value. Not being a philosopher, I didn't touch that line of reasoning with a bargepole, for fear of falling in the canal![3] But in a way, I think the same argument could conceivably be true of fannish value – you could make a case for, say, preserving continuity or maintaining the Whoniverse as a coherent place as having intrinsic value. In which case, even the most dreadful episode could be thought of as having intrinsic value, if it makes a contribution to that effort.

'Dimensions in Time' is such a strange case. I was only on the fringes of *Doctor Who* fandom at the time, but from what little I remember, it was thoroughly vilified on transmission because of the ridiculous plot, the shoddy and rushed production, and the campiness of the crossover between it and the soap opera *Eastenders* (BBC, 1985–). However – and I never thought I'd see this – in 2018 a thread was started on the Missing Episodes messageboard enquiring in all earnestness after the master tapes,[4] and subsequently, a poll begun (rather waggishly) by a member on the subject of whether the master tapes should be erased resulted in an overwhelming show of support for the episodes.[5] The reasoning in these two threads was fascinating. Some people thought that it should be kept because of its 'cultural value', even if 'Dimensions in Time' weighed very lightly in the balance on that score. Others thought it could be released at some point in the future, the special arrangements regarding it notwithstanding, possibly alongside the 1996 *TV Movie*.[6] And still others wanted to see some sort of re-edited version using footage cut from the transmitted episodes. Now, why would that be, if not to make it adhere more closely to what they thought *Doctor Who* should be? That's the essence of custodial evaluation, I think. It is proscriptive, but only about the things that enable the show's continued existence. Everything else – the gender and ethnicity of the Doctor, the look of the TARDIS, even the pacing and tenor of the stories – is fair game, as the experience of fans since 2005 as told us.

Paul: Our discussion about intrinsic and extrinsic value (which extends back to our first chapter as well) makes me think about the discussions I've had with fans about the relative weight we (in the fandom) put on 'canon', despite the fact that there is no established canon of *Doctor Who*. But it does seem like some fans need to have something external, some presence, something to point to in order to give validation for their belief about the intrinsic value of something. For example, we can point to 'The Night of the Doctor' as something with *intrinsic* value because it adds on to the larger narrative arc of *Doctor Who*, it coheres the Classic and the New series together, and it provides a sense of closure for a number of threads left dangling in the *Doctor Who* Universe. There are canonical reasons for liking it. But we could make the same arguments about 'Dimensions in Time', especially concerning things like the Brigadier meeting the Sixth Doctor, following the stories of Ace and of the Rani, and even (dare I say it) linking to scenes like in 'The Pandorica Opens' (2010) where all the monsters come together to defeat the Doctor. Looked at through the lens of canon, 'Dimensions' gives us closure while also opening up new avenues to explore. (On a side note, a friend of mine who had never seen it recently watched it, and loved it for its camp nature, harkening back to our earlier discussion of convivial evaluation.) Canon seems to work both ways.

Ultimately, though, I'm going to contradict myself here: maybe acknowledging the intrinsic value of an aspect of *Doctor Who*'s vast lineage (absent *any* relation to something outside of itself) is a worthwhile experience in empathy. In all my fandom and research, I've never met a part of *Doctor Who* that's unimportant. And when we recognize that something might be important simply because of what it is, we are reminded of the best parts of *Doctor Who*. Every creature in the universe, no matter how small and seemingly insignificant, is meaningful in and of itself, and is deserving of respect and care. That's the Doctor's ethos, and maybe it is the best of what we, as *Doctor Who* fans, can offer as well.

Conclusion

'Go Forward in All of Your Beliefs, and Prove to Me That I Am Not Mistaken in Mine': Thoughts on Value

First, a story: one of the authors of this book teaches a class on fandom every year. During the discussion of fannish evaluation, he runs an activity. Rummaging in his office, he produces two action figures to bring to class, both of Captain Jean-Luc Picard from *Star Trek: The Next Generation* (CBS, 1987–94). One is individually numbered and packaged in its original plastic/cardboard framework. The bottom of the plastic shell contains a certification of the action figure's unique status in the world. The other action figure is out of the box. It's a 'sword-fighting' Picard, complete with epee and fencing stance. There's a switch on the back – when flicked up and down, Picard's hand gesticulates and, with the sword clutched in it, he appears to battle any number of unseen enemies. (He also has a phaser.) In class, he gives one to one side of the room, the other to the other side of the room. He asks the class to look at the figures, and then pass them on. He tells the class to be gentle when handling the in-the-box figure. He mentions that it's individually numbered. He then tells the class that the out-of-the-box figure is one he's had since he was a kid. He tells them that it's seen battles against other *Star Trek* action figures, *Doctor Who* figures, even *My Little Pony* figures. He then passes this action figure around the class as well, and encourages the class to play with it. The class gingerly handles the in-the-box Picard, dutifully passing it from one hand to the other, silently agreeing that their Professor has some strange hobbies. But when the fencing Picard stumbles by, often separate from the fencing foil that is hastily reinserted into his hand, the students laugh. They flick the switch and make him sword fight. They bonk each other on the head. They enjoy the heck out of it.

Then comes the professor's inevitable question: 'Which of these has the most value?'

Savvy classmates (or those who had simply done the reading) will know the answer that he is going for, but many in the class will simply look up and say 'Picard in the box'. Because it's 'unique' through its individual numbering, and because it's still in the box, they imagine it is worth more money. And maybe it is, the professor says, but does that mean it's more valuable *to me*? Or is the playful figure, the one that *every student who's ever been in the class* has handled and laughed with, the one with value?[1] The memories associated with the fencing Picard are worth more to me, he says, than any amount of money he might get for that in-the-box Picard.[2] It is valuable in a way the other simply cannot be.

The activity breaks students out of the commercial mindset that so many fans and viewers have today. In a capitalist culture, of course, value takes on monetary significance – the more 'valuable' something is, the more it has financial wealth associated with it. When we collect the one-of-a-kind items, we do seek them out because they are worth money, but there is more to the relationship between the item and its value than we can see through money. Capital is just one measure of value. In fan communities, it may not even be the most practised way of ascribing value. As Karen Hellekson has noted, fandom doesn't just exist in a capitalist engagement: the gift economy also guides fannish relationships with each other.[3] One of the authors, Paul, goes so far as to say that while the media industry might see fandom as a monetary value, fans interpret the products of the media industry in a gift-like way, a process called the 'digi-gratis', where the media texts themselves are valued as gifts.[4]

Throughout this book, we've been asking the question 'what is value, and how does it fit into a procedure of evaluation?' In the realm of fan and media studies scholarship, the terms 'value' and 'evaluation' are often used as placeholders to indicate emotional reaction or affective meaning within a community about a particular text. Or 'value' takes on the added heft of individual assessment – the value of a media text within the context of an individual's life.[5] Value can be personal, or it can be universal. Value can be friendly, or it can be antagonistic. Value is mutable; evaluation is fluid. If nothing else, the preceding pages have demonstrated that value is mutable across any number of axes: fannish interpretation, production information, contextual and cultural milieu, temporal placement, and generic sensibilities, among many others.

We've specifically focused on *Doctor Who* for a number of reasons. First and foremost, we are fans of *Doctor Who*. We know it and its history very well. Episodes come to mind readily. We have found ourselves within and around different *Doctor Who* fan communities for years. We have had many of these conversations contained within these pages. At the same time, both of the authors are also academics who have written scholarly articles and book chapters about *Doctor Who*. The two of us first met at *Doctor Who: Walking in Eternity*, a conference organized at the University of Hertfordshire in 2013 to celebrate the fiftieth anniversary of the show. At the conference, academics gathered to hear insightful scholarly work about all aspects of *Doctor Who*, and then in the evening got together in the pub to talk about what their favourite episodes were and why. Attendees were as excited about the academic keynote speakers as they were about meeting the original K-9, the Doctor's trusted robot dog companion.

We believe that being both fans and academics about *Doctor Who* gives us a unique insight into the relationship between the two, and reveals the underlying tension between the different notions of value that underscore fannish appreciation. This dual identity has been discussed in academic literature before: it is the 'aca-fan', according to Henry Jenkins, or the 'scholar-fan' as Matt Hills puts it.[6] Yet, in discussions about these hybridized identities, there is a genuine fear of losing credibility in both. For Hills, the scholar-fan 'must still conform to the regulative ideal of the rational academic subject, being careful not to present too much of their enthusiasm while tailoring their accounts of fan interest and investment to the norms of "confessional" (but not overly confessional) academic writing'.[7] In other words, to be credible to an academic audience, an author's fannishness must not show … too much. Similarly, Katherine Larsen and Lynn Zubernis note in their book *Fangasm* (a fan-side companion to their academic-side book *Fandom at the Crossroads*), their fannishness and scholarship about *Supernatural* (WB/CW, 2005–20) collided when a colleague discovered their 'racy fanfiction ... Here we were extolling the virtues of fanfic and the liberating value of fandom, only to be struck (painfully) with the reality that we were far from immune to shame ourselves.'[8]

From the fannish side, the opposite is true as well. As Kelli Marshall, an academic who also runs a fan site for Gene Kelly, notes,

> In certain fandoms, nonacademic fans seem to resent academics who identify themselves as such. One scholar/fan told me there was a significant backlash against Ph.D.s (aka "elitists") in some fandoms, and that having a doctoral degree is "grounds enough for some fans to assume we think we're better than everyone else."[9]

Certainly, within some fan circles, even the whiff of academia can raise hackles; there are still enough negative or pathologizing articles written about particular types of fandom that some fans are hesitant to trust academics.[10]

Value is perceived differently in both cases.

And yet, the 'liminal' position of the aca-fan does have some advantages.[11] With one foot in each world, so to speak, researchers who are fans (and fans who are researchers) have the ability to reach two different audiences in new ways. We can codeshift, flit in between roles. We see value in both. As Matt Hills notes, fans and academics analyse texts in different ways. Fans tend to view the text as 'thick', full of multiple meanings and larger contexts; academics tend to view texts 'as a finished, fixed and bounded object'. As aca-fans, we simply try to unite these disparate views.[12] The unique spheres of knowledge that fandom and academia both bring can be reconciled – or, at least, imbricated – through writing that brings these knowledge bases together. Speaking two languages, the aca-fan can be a bridge that highlights the similarities between the two groups and celebrates the unique positionality each can bring to the conversation.

As aca-fans, we are aware that both fans and academics are passionate. We believe that emotion is an important characteristic of academic work; and the subjective positioning of the academics themselves is a relevant and crucial factor in understanding their work. It is impossible to separate the academic from their writing; nothing will ever be truly objective (there are always shades of subjectivities), as even the choice of topic to study is itself a value judgment. We have chosen to lean into this, rather than avoid it all together. We have chosen to embrace our *selves* as important factors in this book.

This, of course, comes with additional complications. Both the authors are white, middle-class, cis-gendered masculine, heterosexual men. Both are in their mid- to late thirties. Both of us have US and UK roots that have shaped our childhood and adulthood. We both live in or near major metropolitan areas. In many ways, we are the ür-stereotype of *Doctor Who* fans, the ones that people think of when the term '*Doctor Who* fan' (or anorak) is thrown into a conversation. Yet, the reality of *Doctor Who* fandom is far more vast, wildly convoluted, wonderfully diverse, and wholly different from what your humble authors can provide. We both celebrate and honour this diversity and encourage the plurality of viewpoints that something as complex and simple as *Doctor Who* can provide. Our perspective is just that: one perspective. It is not the whole of fandom, it is not the whole of academia.[13] It is simply us, for better or for worse; not speaking for others, but speaking through our own experiences.

All this being said, the authors of this book have attempted to bring their fannish knowledge of *Doctor Who* into their academic knowledge of evaluation and notions of quality; at the same time, they've attempted to bring their academic knowledge of *Doctor Who* into conversation with their fannish opinions of particular episodes and tropes within the series. There are times when, we're sure, we landed too far on one side or the other, but the goals of this book have been largely to unite these two worlds, so similar and yet interpreted so differently.

The result has been a book built from two traditions. On the one hand, academic publishing rewards the thoughtful presentation of research in advancing human knowledge, and engagement with relevant aspects of the world. Academic writing – especially that of the humanities or cultural studies genres – is often stereotyped as jargon-filled or obtuse. Why use one word when fifteen will do? Why use a short word when a complicated, hyphenate will do? On the other hand, fan writing – especially that dealing with issues within the media – is often stereotyped as too emotional or esoteric. Why are personal opinions relevant? Why become lost in the minutiae and details of the text?

Of course, any reader of the above paragraph will realize that both academic and fan writing lead to similar outcomes. Each is simply writing for their own audience, and using language, styles, and connections that may be unintelligible to the other. That both become the focus of ire from conservative cultural critics perhaps speaks to the insularity of all the communities; a lack of translatable moments that can reach across boundaries.

In this book, we have attempted to bring together these academic and fannish writing styles to discuss how fans' interpretation and evaluation of *Doctor Who* have changed given any number of factors. Some chapters – longer, more engaged in previous scholarship, and often more theoretical – hewed closer to the academic tradition. Other chapters – made up of shorter case studies, heaped with value judgments, and often more specific – emerged out of fannish writing and traditions. Yet, throughout all our chapters, we have tried to write in a style that appeals to academics, fans, and other readers. In this attempt, we also hope that we have not alienated every group, a very real fear.

Doctor Who?

So why *Doctor Who*? Beyond our fan and academic interest in the topic, there is much to be learned from a television series that has lasted over half a century. Since it first premiered in 1963, *Doctor Who* has, deliberately or not, represented aspects of the culture in which it was made. The show has changed over time – indeed, the only constant in the show is change. We could point to the ecological stories of the 1970s that matched the growing green movement, or the political jibes of the 1980s as relevant at that time. We could focus on the 2005 series that dealt with post-traumatic stress disorder just as troops were returning home from the Middle East and both the United States and UK were dealing with the aftermath (and continuations) of a number of wars. As we write this, the 2019 series of *Doctor Who* is complete: Jodie Whittaker has completely inhabited the role, and for hundreds of thousands of fans, *she is the Doctor.* At a moment when more women are running for political office, when #MeToo radiates and validates survivors of sexual harassment and assault, when women are asserting their rights, it makes sense for a show like *Doctor Who* to embrace change and diversity.[14]

But beyond cultural changes, *Doctor Who* has always been about *value changes*. When a new series comes out, a new Doctor regenerates, or a new showrunner replaces an old one, there comes with it an inherent comparison that other shows or stories may not have. Part of the reason for this value change with *Doctor Who* specifically is because the show itself is one long narrative: a palimpsest of one, where the narrative continually gets rewritten over, but a single narrative nonetheless.[15] Identifying changes within a single narrative invites valued comparisons. The same can be seen in a series like *Star Trek* (CBS, 1966–69), where multiple iterations have taken place over fifty years' time as well (the Original Series, the *Next Generation*, *Deep Space Nine* (CBS, 1993–99), *Voyager* (UPN, 1995–2001), *Enterprise* (UPN, 2001–05) the Abramsverse movies (Paramount, 2009, 2013, 2016), *Discovery* (CBS, 2017–), etc.), and intra-universe comparisons are rife (who is the best captain? Which ship is the best in battle?). Shows without that history or that do not have that extensive of a narrative tend not to generate the same sort of intra-comparative evaluations.[16]

As a marker of cultural change, and as a vehicle for understanding value change, *Doctor Who* is relevant to examine different ways that evaluation occurs within a fandom. At the same time, the fluctuating popularity of the series also serves as a barometer for fannish evaluation. An abbreviated overview shows that the show's popularity waxed and waned over time. When the show premiered, it was very popular, especially when the Daleks appeared and children were enamoured of the metal pepperpots. In the 1970s, *Doctor Who* was reliably one of the most popular shows on British television, although it only retained a cult following in the United States.[17] At times, it was *the* most popular show on in the UK. In the 1980s, declining ratings of the series coincided with increasing numbers of fan conventions and collectables. Fewer people appeared to be watching, but the strength of the passion of the fans seemed stronger. When the show came back in 2005, it again premiered to a popular audience, and with the 2010 switch to Steven Moffat/Matt Smith, there was again great international appeal.[18] Peter Capaldi's three series as the Doctor were less popular, at least in the United States, but Jodie Whittaker's appearance galvanized the show once again in 2018.

This very brief summary articulates our point: the value of a particular component of a text can change depending on the larger cultural valuation of the text as a whole. As our first chapter demonstrated, evaluation is often a communal activity, one that examines not just the relative merits of a particular aspect of canon, but rests this evaluation on the reception of the community at large. At the same time, the ability to pass judgment – to have knowledge about the canon, expertise on the history or production, or informed opinions about the text – itself becomes a marker of membership within a community. In the second full chapter, we demonstrated some of the methods that particular communities use to evaluate, using *Doctor Who Magazine*, *Doctor Who* fanzines, and promotional documentaries about *Doctor Who*. Value becomes ascribed from the community, rather than generated by the individual. At the same time, it's important to see the effects of this evaluation, so in the third full chapter in the book, we critiqued the very common fan practice of splitting *Doctor Who* into eras. This 'periodization' disciplines readings of particular assumptions about eras of any show. When fans are already primed to be looking for one particular moment within a text, because of the contextual information they know about it (this Doctor acts in *this* way, this writer produces *this* type of script), they automatically pre-value and pre-judge the texts under review. To get around this periodization, we argued in the fourth full chapter that the tension between quality and memory, especially as particular episodes in *Doctor Who*'s history, can become re-examined in fan critical memory. Examining the role that time and specifically *the past* play in an interpretation of value, we indicate that this 'immediate nostalgia' reflects a new sense of value within the *Doctor Who* corpus.

In order to demonstrate the theoretical explorations of valuation that we endeavoured to explore in the longer chapters, we also presented eight shorter 'fan takes', or case studies seen through a fannish lens, which focused on specific moments within the history of *Doctor Who* that problematized or exemplified concepts of value. We looked at rankings in professional/fan publications, fan reaction videos, the roles of the companions both in and out of the television series, moments of rupture within the expectations of the canon, and fan interpretations of particular moments over time. Finally, at our most fannish selves, we conducted four debates about issues of value where both authors discussed their own points of view as fans and as academics.

Conclusion

So what did we learn? And what, if anything, can readers take away from this book?

Although *Doctor Who* is unique in the history of television for a variety of reasons – many of which we've enumerated above – it is also not particularly alone in the way that fans will create judgments about what they see on screen. As we might expect with most things fandom, these judgments are based on emotion and belief – the affect of a strongly passionate audience. But surprisingly, these value judgments are also based on a number of self-reflexive, almost academic, interpretations. Fans use empirical data presented on screen, historical reflections about larger issues in the text. Valuations are not tossed off like opinions about what colour shirt to wear today or likes/dislikes about the weather. Rather, they are strongly held, often well-reasoned, and stringent.

Yet, fan value judgments are also mutable. They are changeable over time. Fans may modify and adjust their valuations based on any number of elements seen or unforeseen. Matt Hills notes that

> for fans, each episode of *Doctor Who* is something anticipated, speculated-over, looked-forward to, and then picked apart: it exists in a special kind of fan chronology that stretches from long before broadcast (usually from an initial press/publicity announcement) through to immediate post-episode debate, and then onwards into years of evaluation and re-evaluation.[19]

We've explored what that 'evaluation and re-evaluation' looks like, where it comes from, how it's shaped, and what effects it has on the larger *Doctor Who* fan community.

The same sorts of evaluative components could be used to analyse the fan communities of other television programmes or media. But fan evaluation isn't limited to just media texts. The way that evolution is created, developed, spread, and promoted can apply outside the media sphere. For instance, it is certainly the case that fan methodologies have been used by politicians on both sides of the Atlantic to develop strong followings. Whether Donald Trump or Jeremy Corbyn, Theresa May or Hillary Clinton, the same typologies of evaluation that fans use to analyse their favourite programmes apply. Fans of May could see their knowledge of British politics tested as a way of joining a community. Fans of Trump might be swayed by what other political actors (or fans) are saying in different contexts. Fans of Corbyn may find themselves arguing with others about the role that typification/periodization plays in understanding his position on issues. Fans of Clinton might remember particular moments in her history differently, given the distance of time and space.

We argue that these same efforts of fan evaluation and re-evaluation take place across any text, over any time period. They may arrive in different ways, or be experienced within different contexts, but interpretation is always going to be evaluative. This book will be evaluated differently on the day you're reading it than it was on the day it was published – and will be evaluated quite differently twenty years from now, we're sure.[20] The typologies, principles, and ideas that we've promulgated here will themselves be evaluated, judged, and interpreted. Those that continue to explore the topic of evaluation will find things to argue with in this book, and (hopefully) things to agree with. But it's only through valuation that difference is articulated, that change is noted. Advancement only happens at the level of valuation.

That is the inherent element of all creation; it is the value of value.

Notes

Introduction

1 Paul Booth, *Playing Fans: Negotiating Fandom and Media in the Digital Age* (Iowa City: University of Iowa Press, 2015).

2 Matt Hills, '*Doctor Who*'s Textual Commemorators: Fandom, Collective Memory and the Self-Commodification of Fanfac', *The Journal of Fandom Studies* 2, no. 1 (2014): 31–51; Matt Hills, *Fan Cultures* (London: Routledge, 2002); Henry Jenkins, *Textual Poachers: Television Fans and Participatory Culture*, 2nd ed. (New York: Routledge, 2012).

3 Alan McKee, 'Which Is the Best *Doctor Who* Story? A Case Study in Value Judgments Outside the Academy', *Intensities: The Journal of Cult Media* 1, no. 1 (2001). https://intensitiescultmedia.files.wordpress.com/2012/12/mckee.pdf

4 Miles Booy, *Love and Monsters: The Doctor Who Experience, 1979– Present* (London: I.B. Tauris, 2012); Matt Hills, *Triumph of a Time Lord: Regenerating Doctor Who in the Twenty-First Century* (London: I.B. Tauris, 2010).

5 See Hills, *Triumph*, 147–77.

6 Alan McKee, 'Why Is "City of Death" the Best *Doctor Who* Story?' in *Time and Relative Dissertations in Space: Critical Perspectives on Doctor Who*, ed. David Butler (Manchester: Manchester University Press, 2007), 233–45.

7 McKee, 'Which Is the Best?' (*emphasis ours*).

8 Although to date, after Verity Lambert's (1963–65) tenure as producer, it would always be 'his'.

9 Tom Steward, 'Author Who? Masterplanners, Scribermen, and the Script Doctors: The Producers, Writers and Script Editors of *Doctor Who*', in *Ruminations, Peregrination, and Regenerations: A Critical Approach to Doctor Who*, ed. Chris Hansen (Newcastle: Cambridge Scholars, 2010), 313.

10 James Chapman, *Inside the TARDIS: The Worlds of Doctor Who* (London: I.B. Tauris, 2006), 10.

11 See Lawrence Miles and Tat Wood, *About Time 5: The Unauthorized Guide to Doctor Who 1980–1984, Seasons 18 to 21* (Des Moines: Mad Norwegian Press, 2004), 9–11.

12 See Jonathan Bignell, 'The Child as Addressee, Viewer and Consumer in Mid-1960s *Doctor Who*', in *Time and Relative Dissertations in Space: Critical Perspectives on Doctor Who*, ed. David Butler (Manchester: Manchester University Press, 2007), 43–55; Andrew O'Day, 'Event TV: Fan Consumption of Televised *Doctor Who* in Britain (1963–Present)', in *Doctor Who in Time and Space*, ed. Gillian Leitch (Jefferson: McFarland, 2013), 7–24.

13 Matt Hills, 'Foreword', in *Fan Phenomena: Doctor Who*, ed. Paul Booth (Bristol: Intellect, 2013), 5–9.

14 See Booy, *Love and Monsters*; Piers Britton, *TARDISbound: Navigating the Universes of Doctor Who* (London: I.B. Tauris, 2011).

15 See Dave Rolinson, '"*Who* Done It": Discourses of Authorship during the John Nathan- Turner Era', in *Time and Relative Dissertations in Space: Critical Perspectives on Doctor Who*, ed. David Butler (Manchester: Manchester University Press, 2007), 187.

16 See Miles and Wood, *About Time 5*, 9–13.

17 Ian Levine, Twitter, 16 July 2017, Tweet archived at https://www.bleedingcool.com/2017/07/16/ian-levine-jodie-whittaker-doctor-who-hi-nrg-song.

18 Ian Levine, Twitter, 16 July 2017, Tweet archived at https://www.bleedingcool.com/2017/07/16/ian-levine-jodie-whittaker-doctor-who-hi-nrg-song.

19 Anonymous letter to *Huddersfield Daily Examiner,* 7 December 1963, retrieved from Graham Kibble-White Twitter at https://twitter.com/grahamkw/status/935527337898233856.

20 Anonymous letter (*emphasis ours*).

21 Jenkins, *Textual Poachers*; Camile Bacon-Smith, *Enterprising Women* (Philadelphia, PA: University of Pennsylvania Press, 1992).

22 Hills, *Triumph*; Booy, *Love and Monsters*; Henry Jenkins and John Tulloch, *Science Fiction Audiences* (New York: Routledge, 1995).

23 Rukmini Pande, *Squee from the Margins* (Iowa City, IA: University of Iowa Press, 2018); Suzanne Scott, *Fake Geek Girls* (New York: New York University Press, 2019); Mel Stanfill, *Exploiting Fandom* (Iowa City, IA: University of Iowa Press, 2019); Booth, *Playing Fans*; Ashley Hinck, *Politics for the Love of Fandom* (Baton Rouge, LA: University of Louisiana Press, 2019).

24 Mark Campbell, *Doctor Who: The Complete Guide* (Harpenden: Pocketguide, 2007); Chapman, *Inside the TARDIS*.

25 Elizabeth Sandifer, *TARDIS Eruditorum* blog (2014–16). http://www.eruditorumpress.com/blog/author/phil/tardis-eruditorum/, accessed 15 January 2019.

26 Graeme Burk and Robert Smith?, *Who's 50: The 50 Doctor Who Stories to Watch Before You Die – An Unofficial Companion* (Toronto: ECW Press, 2013).

27 Janet McCabe and Kim Akass, 'Introduction: Debating Quality', in *Quality TV: Contemporary American Television and Beyond* (London: I.B. Tauris, 2007), 2.

28 Bart Beaty and Benjamin Woo, *The Greatest Commit Book of All Time* (London: Palgrave, 2016), 2–3.

29 McKee, 'Which Is the Best?'

30 Lincoln Geraghty, *Cult Collectors: Nostalgia, Fandom and Collecting Popular Culture* (London: Routledge, 2014); Booth, *Playing Fans*.

31 Hills, *Triumph*, 9.

32 Burk and Smith?, *Who's 50*.

33 Katharina Freund, '"We're Making Our Own Happy Ending!": The *Doctor Who* Fan Vidding Community', in *Fan Phenomena: Doctor Who*, ed. Paul Booth (Bristol: Intellect, 2013), 96–105.

34 Chapman, *Inside the TARDIS;* Sandifer, *TARDIS Eruditorum;* Lawrence Miles and Tat Wood, *About Time*, series (Des Moines: Mad Norwegian, 2008–).

35 Matt Hills, 'Televisuality without Television? The Big Finish Audios and Discourses of "Tele-Centric" *Doctor Who*', in *Time and Relative Dissertations in Space*, ed. David Butler (Manchester: Manchester University Press, 2007), 280.

36 Britton, *TARDISBound*.

37 Tat Wood and Lawrence Miles, *About Time 2: The Unauthorized Guide to Doctor Who 1966–1969, Seasons 4 to 6* (Des Moines: Mad Norwegian, 2006), 237.

38 Jason Mittell, *Complex TV: The Poetics of Contemporary Television Storytelling* (New York: New York University Press, 2006).

39 Svetlana Boym, *The Future of Nostalgia* (New York: Basic Books, 2001).

40 The same thing occurred with the regeneration of the First Doctor (episode 4 of *The Tenth Planet,* 29 October 1966) into the Second Doctor (episode 1 of *The Power of the Daleks*, 5 November 1966).

Chapter 1

1 Ryan Britt, 'Genre in the Mainstream: *The New Yorker*'s Science Fiction Issue', *Tor.com*, 31 May 2012, https://www.tor.com/2012/05/31/genre-in-the-mainstream-the-science-fiction-issue-of-the-new-yorker/, accessed 24 November 2018.

2 James MacDowell and James Zborowski, 'The Aesthetics of "So Bad It's Good": Value, Intention, and *The Room*', *Intensities: The Journal of Cult Media* 6 (2013): 1–30.

3 Available at: Susan Sontag, 'Notes on "Camp"', 1964, https://faculty.georgetown.edu/irvinem/theory/Sontag-NotesOnCamp-1964.html, accessed 24 November 2018. Originally published as 'Notes on "Camp"', *Partisan Review* 31, no. 4 (1964): 515–30.

4 Sontag, 'Notes on "Camp"'.

5 Matt Hills, 'The Dispersible Television Text: Theorising Moments of the New Doctor Who', *Science Fiction Film and Television* 1, no. 1 (2008): 28.

6 The word was in common use in science fiction fans in the early 1990s, if not earlier; see Benjamin Woo, 'Understanding Understandings of Comics: Reading and Collecting as Media-Oriented Practices', *Participations: Journal of Audience and Reception Studies* 9, no. 2 (2012): 186–7, http://www.participations.org/volume%209/issue%202/12%20Woo.pdf, regarding comic collecting, accessed 15 January 2019.

7 Darren Mooney, 'Doctor Who: Paradise Towers (Review)', *The M0vie Blog*, 2 July 2013, https://them0vieblog.com/2013/07/02/doctor-who-paradise-towers-review/, accessed 25 November 2018.

8 Paul Gilroy, *After Empire: Melancholia or Convivial Culture?* (London: Routledge, 2004), 40 and elsewhere.

9 Although see our Chapter 3 for a refutation of this tendency.

10 Gilroy, *After Empire*, 40.

11 Craig Owen Jones, 'Custodial Narration in *Doctor Who* – Or Why "The Night of the Doctor" Is the Most Important Episode You'll Ever See', in *New Worlds, Terrifying Monsters, Impossible Things: Exploring the Contents and Contexts of Doctor Who*, ed. Erin Giannini (Chicago, IL: PopMatters, 2016).

12 Hills, *Fan Cultures*, 157.

13 *Doctor Who Magazine #100* (May 1985): 5.

14 See for example Dan Martin, 'Doctor Who Recap: Series 37, Episode 7 – Kerblam!', *The Guardian*, 18 November 2018, https://www.theguardian.com/tv-and-radio/2018/nov/18/doctor-who-recap-series-37-episode-7-kerblam, accessed 29 November 2018. The decision seems not to have been an editorial one, as earlier reviews from the 2000s abide by the BBC's numbering system (albeit frequently using 'season' instead of 'series'. Rather, it seems to have been introduced on the initiative of reviewer Dan Martin – a *Doctor Who* fan).

Case Study 1A

1 Paul Booth, 'Fans' List-Making: Memory, Influence, and Argument in the "Event" of Fandom', *MATRIZes* 9, no. 2 (2015): 85–107. I don't mean to deny the very apt ranking procedures of other fandoms, of course.

2 Colin Baker, interview with Benjamin Cook, *Doctor Who Magazine #322* (16 October 2002): 24.

3 *Doctor Who Magazine #265* (7 May 1998); *Doctor Who Magazine #413* (14 October 2009); *Doctor Who Magazine #474* (July 2014).

4 'Doctor Who Magazine', Wikipedia (2018). https://en.wikipedia.org/wiki/Doctor_Who_Magazine

5 Peter Griffiths, 'The Mighty 200', *Doctor Who Magazine #413* (14 October 2009): 18.

6 McKee, 'Which Is the Best?'

7 Matt Hills, '"Gothic" Body Parts in a "Postmodern" Body of Work? The Hinchcliffe/Holmes Era of Doctor Who (1975–77)', *Intensities: The Journal of Cult Media*, 4 (2007). https://intensitiescultmedia.files.wordpress.com/2012/12/hills-gothic-body-parts-in-postmodern-body-of-work.pdf

8 The Appreciation Index is 'a score out of 100 which is used as an indicator of the public's appreciation for a television or radio programme, or broadcast service, in the United Kingdom'. 'Appreciation Index', Wikipedia (2018). https://en.wikipedia.org/wiki/Appreciation_Index

Case Study 1B

1 Brigid Cherry, 'Squee, Retcon, Fanwank, and the Not-We: Computer-Mediated Discourse and the Online Audience for NuWho', in *Ruminations, Peregrinations, and Regenerations: A Critical Approach to* Doctor Who, ed. Christopher J. Hansen (Newcastle: Cambridge Scholars Press, 2010), 228.

2 Louisa Ellen Stein, *Millennial Fandom: Television Audiences in the Transmedia Age* (Iowa City, IA: University of Iowa Press, 2015).

3 Hills, 'Dispersible Television Text'.

4 Stein, *Millennial Fandom*, 75.

5 'Doctor Who 50th – The Curator/Future Doctor (Reaction Mashup), part 4 of 5', https://www.youtube.com/watch?v=B2oSM4cU-_s, accessed 22 October 2018.

6 Among the plurality of physical reactions which are on display in *Doctor Who* fan reaction videos, the only one that even approaches the ubiquitous is the shedding of tears.

7 At the time of writing, this video was subject to a copyright strike by the BBC, doubtless decreasing its viewing figures.

8 Daniel Mumby, 'BLOG SPOT #24: ChiqueGeeks', *Mumby at the Movies*, 14 May 2014. http://mumbyatthemovies.blogspot.com/2014/05/blog-spot-24-chiquegeeks.html, accessed 22 October 2018.

Dialogue 1C

1 Linda Williams, *Hard Core: Power, Pleasure, and the Frenzy of the Visible* (Berkeley, CA: University of California Press, 1999), 5.

2 Boym, *The Future of Nostalgia*.

3 Fredric Jameson, *Postmodernism, or, the Cultural Logic of Late Capitalism* (Durham, NC: Duke University Press, 1992).

4 Diana Webb, *Pilgrims and Pilgrimage in the Medieval West* (London: Bloomsbury, 2001), 25.

5 Mittell, *Complex TV*.

Chapter 2

1 Barring their recovery in other countries.

2 Matt Hills, *Doctor Who: The Unfolding Event – Marketing, Merchandising and Mediatizing a Brand Anniversary* (Houndmills: Palgrave, 2015), 11.

3 Hills, *Unfolding*, 4.

4 We keep lists to hand out to people, of course.

5 Tat Wood, 'How to Make Fans (and Influence People!)', *Doctor Who Magazine #320* (21 August 2002): 13.

6 Philip MacDonald, 'Sign "O" the Times', *Doctor Who Magazine Special Edition #10: The Complete Seventh Doctor* (2005): 4.

7 The authors have seen this first-hand, teaching courses about *Doctor Who* to students in University and running *Doctor Who* fan clubs. These young *Doctor Who* fans and scholars are usually quite familiar with Matt Smith's Eleventh Doctor episodes, as this is the Doctor most of them have grown up with. Some of these young fans may have gone back on Netflix or Amazon Prime to watch the Christopher Eccleston series and the David Tennant series. In one rather excruciating conversation with a student, Paul was discussing the differences between the Classic series of *Doctor Who* and the New series of *Doctor Who*, and the student thought he was referring to the Russell T Davies-produced episodes compared to the Steven Moffat-produced episodes. Much consternation was had. In a discussion with students, we discovered that many haven't seen the Peter Capaldi Twelfth Doctor, not because of lack of interest, but because these particular episodes hadn't been available on streaming yet. The almost-ubiquitous Netflix housed New *Doctor Who* in the United States until 2016, but included very little of Capaldi's episodes or the Classic series. It was removed to make way for the BBC's own BritBox service, which now has almost all the Classic episodes, and Amazon Prime, which has almost all the New episodes – but for those without access to the sites, the episodes were unavailable. Those adventurous New *Who* fan-students who were interested in *Doctor Who* and wanted to keep watching didn't know where to begin with Classic *Who*, and many went straight to the beginning with *An Unearthly Child* (1963). In almost all cases, they didn't watch past 'The Firemaker' (1963, the fourth episode of *An Unearthly Child*.) The conversation then turns back to us: 'well, you're the expert! What Classic episodes should we watch?'

8 McKee, 'Which Is the Best?'

9 McKee, 'Which Is the Best?'

10 Barry Schwartz, *The Paradox of Choice* (New York: HarperCollins, 2004), 2.

11 Booy, *Love and Monsters*, 84.

12 Peter Haining, *Doctor Who: A Celebration* (London: WH Allen, 1983); see also McKee, 'Which Is the Best?'

13 Booy, *Love and Monsters*, 86.

14 Britton, *TARDISbound,* 11, 21.

15 For a discussion of 'The *Doctor Who* Mafia', see Hills, *Triumph.*

16 Hills, 'Textual Commemorators'.

17 Richard Marson, *JN-T: The Life and Scandalous Times of John Nathan-Turner* (London: Miwk Publishing, 2013), 275.

18 Marson, *JN-T,* 276.

19 Marson, *JN-T,* 308.

20 Matt Hills, 'Defining Cult TV; Texts, Inter-Texts and Fan Audiences', in *The Television Studies Reader*, ed. Robert Allen and Annette Hills (London: Routledge, 2004), 509–10.

21 Stephen Duncombe, *Notes from the Underground: Zines and the Politics of Alternative Culture* (London: Verso, 1997), 2.

22 Vicky Vale, ed. *Vol 1. Zines!* (San Francisco, CA: V/Search, 1996), 4.

23 Fredric Wertham, *The World of Fanzines* (Carbondale, IL: SIU Press, 1973), 35.

24 McKee, 'Which Is the Best?'

25 Garye Russell, 'Off the Shelf: *The Krotons*', *Doctor Who Magazine #171* (13 March 1991): 12.

26 Gary Russell, 'Off the Shelf: *Genesis of the Daleks*', *Doctor Who Magazine #179* (30 October 1991): 25.

27 Michael Haslett, 'Swap Shop', *Doctor Who Magazine #310* (14 November 2001): 8.

28 Baker, interview with Cook: 24.

29 Gareth Roberts, 'Same Old Story?' *Doctor Who Magazine #332* (23 July 2003): 14.

30 Even if we may disagree.

31 Craig Owen Jones, 'Life in the Hiatus: New *Doctor Who* Fans, 1989–2005', in *Fan Phenomena: Doctor Who*, ed. Paul Booth (Bristol: Intellect, 2013), 39.

32 McKee, 'Which Is the Best?'

33 Hills, *Unfolding,* 53.

34 Booth, 'Fans' List-Making', 86.

35 Jenkins, *Textual Poachers,* 95.

36 McKee, 'Which Is the Best?'

37 Booth, 'Fans' List-Making', 88.

38 Hills, *Unfolding*, 54.

39 Vanessa Bishop, 'Review: *Tomb of the Cybermen*', *Doctor Who Magazine #313* (February 2002): 46.

40 McKee, 'Which Is the Best?'

41 Vic Camford, 'If You Tolerate This Your Children Will Be Next', *Doctor Who Magazine* #284 (17 November 1999): 9.

42 Dave Owen, '*Talons of Weng-Chiang*', *Doctor Who Magazine Special Edition #6: We Doctor Who* (2003): 15.

43 Stephen James Walker, 'The Web Planet', *Doctor Who Magazine Special Edition #7 – The Complete First Doctor* (2004): 49.

44 Nick Briggs, 'The Real McCoy: Part Two'. *Doctor Who Magazine* #217 (26 September 1994): 43.

45 Hills, *Unfolding*, 54, citing Martin Kornberger, *Brand Society: How Brands Transform Management and Lifestyle* (Cambridge: Cambridge University Press, 2010), 131; Simone Murray, 'Brand Loyalties: Rethinking Content within Global Corporate Media', *Media, Culture & Society* 27, no. 3 (2005): 426.

46 Suzanne Scott, 'Who's Steering the Mothership? The Role of the Fanboy Auteur in Transmedia Storytelling', in *The Participatory Cultures Handbook*, ed. Aaron Delwiche and Jennifer Jacobs Henderson (New York: Routledge, 2013): 61–70.

47 Steven Moffat, Introduction to *Remembrance of the Daleks, The Doctors Revisited vol. 2* (New York: BBC America DVD, 2013).

48 Steven Moffat, Introduction to *Earthshock. The Doctors Revisited vol. 2* (New York: BBC America DVD, 2013).

49 Steven Moffat, Introduction to *Tomb of the Cybermen. The Doctors Revisited vol. 1* (New York: BBC America DVD, 2013).

50 Steven Moffat, Introduction to *The Pyramids of Mars. The Doctors Revisited vol. 2* (New York: BBC America DVD, 2013).

51 Steven Moffat, Introduction to *The TV Movie. The Doctors Revisited vol. 2* (New York: BBC America DVD, 2013).

52 Moffat, *Remembrance.* We discuss Series 24 later in this book.

53 Steven Moffat, Introduction to *The Aztecs. The Doctors Revisited vol. 1.* (New York: BBC America DVD, 2013).

54 Moffat, *Tomb.*

55 Moffat, *Earthshock.*

56 Moffat, *Remembrance.*

57 Moffat, *Aztecs.*

58 All Moffat quotes from *The Doctors Revisited* introductions.

59 Moffat, *TV Movie.*

Case Study 2A

1 John Nathan-Turner, *Doctor Who: The Companions* (Piccadilly Press: London, 1986), 39.

2 Valerie Estelle Frankel, *Women in Doctor Who: Damsels, Feminists and Monsters* (Jefferson, NC: McFarland, 2018), 188 notes the difficulties many female members of the cast encountered on working with Nathan-Turner.

3 See, for example, David J. Howe and Mark Stammers, *Doctor Who: Companions* (London: Virgin, 1995), 96. Howe, Stammers, and Stephen James Walker also drew extensively on Nathan-Turner's recollections of his dealings with Fielding (including the memo) in *Doctor Who: The Eighties* (London: London Bridge, 1996), 17–18.

4 Howe, Stammers, and Walker, *The Eighties*, 40.

5 Howe and Stammers, *Companions*, 41.

6   Richard Wallace, '"But Doctor?" – A Feminist Perspective of *Doctor Who*', in *Ruminations, Peregrinations, and Regenerations: A Critical Approach to Doctor Who*, ed. Chris Hansen (Newcastle: Cambridge Scholars Press, 2010), 106.

7   Quoted in Howe and Stammers, *Companions*, 97.

8   Quoted in Howe and Stammers, *Companions*, 69–70.

9   *Canberra Times*, 20 May 1982, 22.

10 For a full discussion of the various incongruities, colonialist subtexts, and racist implications of this incident, see Lindy Orthia, 'A Very Good Googly – Race in Four to Doomsday', 23 May 2013, https://doctorwhoandrace. com/2013/05/23/a-very-good-googly-race-in-four-to-doomsday/, accessed 19 March 2018). Orthia notes that Fielding was herself aware of the enormous incongruity of a white Australian possessing the linguistic ability to converse with an Aboriginal in their native language (and tens of thousands of years removed from the 1980s at that!), and raised them in production, but the response of the production team was inadequate (ibid.).

11 *Sydney Morning Herald*, 26 April 1982, http://cuttingsarchive.org/index. php/A_new_face_for_%27Dr_Who%27, accessed 19 March 2018.

12 *The Age* (Melbourne), 23 September 1982: 4; *The Age*, 9 September 1982: 4. Interestingly given the backstory given to Tegan later in the show, the winning entry was a synopsis of a story where Tegan and the Doctor come into contact with a group of Aboriginals in ancient Australia.

13 *Semper* 10 (November 1985), 11–12.

14 Marson, *JN-T*, 114.

15 *Doctor Who Magazine #62* (March 1982): 6.

16 Quoted in Lee Barron, 'Intergalactic Girlpower: The Gender Politics of Companionship in 21st Century Doctor Who', in *Ruminations, Peregrinations, and Regenerations: A Critical Approach to* Doctor Who, ed. Chris Hansen (Newcastle: Cambridge Scholars Press, 2010), 136–7.

17 Howe and Stammers, *Companions,* 94–5.

18 'I'm Bossy Enough to Take on Two Doctors!', *Daily Express*, 28 February 1981, http://cuttingsarchive.org/index.php/I%27m_bossy_enough_to_take_on_two_doctors! accessed 20 March 2018.

19 For an early expression of Fielding's belief in the importance of strong female role models in science fiction, see 'Dr Who Companion Wants to Be Role Model', *Sarasota Herald Tribute*, 26 May 1987, http://cuttingsarchive.org/index.php/Names_in_the_News,_May_25,_1987, accessed 19 March 2018.

20 John Kenneth Muir, *A Critical History of Doctor Who in Television* (Jefferson, NC: McFarland, 1999), 302.

21 Muir, *Critical History*, 339–40.

22 David Boarder Giles and Amy Peloff, '"There's Nothing Only about Being a Girl": Learning to "Play" the Doctor's Companion', in *Who Travels with the Doctor? Essays on the Companions of Doctor Who*, ed. Gilliam I. Leitch, and Sherry Ginn (Jefferson, NC: McFarland, 2016), 52–68.

23 Other recent showings include fourteenth (*Radio Times*, 2010, http://
news.thedoctorwhosite.co.uk/radio-times-online-companion-poll/,
accessed 23 March 2018), and fifteenth in a poll conducted by *Doctor Who
Magazine* in 2014, https://theparadoxcycle.wordpress.com/2014/05/31/
doctor-who-magazine-474-2014-poll-results/, accessed 23 March 2018.
Both place Tegan in the top 25 per cent of companions.

Case Study 2B

1 Some actors have come back but cannot, due to licensing issues, play
their original character; e.g. Daphne Ashbrook and Yee Jee Tso, who
played Grace Holloway and Chang Lee in the *TV Movie*, have returned to
play UNIT agents because Big Finish does not have the licence for their
original roles. One companion, the android Kamelion, is scheduled to come
back in 2019 but voiced by a different actor.

2 Peter Purves and William Russell often portray the First Doctor in their
releases, although David Bradley has reprised the role from the 2017
Christmas special *Twice upon a Time*; Frasier Hines is noted for his
portrayal of the Second Doctor, and new-to-*Who* actor Tim Treloar plays
Pertwee's Third Doctor.

3 Hills, 'Televisuality', 280.

4 Hills, 'Televisuality', 281.

5 Hills, 'Televisuality', 283.

6 Hills, 'Televisuality', 282. Of note, this meeting did also happen in the 1993
'Dimensions in Time' special, as we discuss in our fourth Dialogue.

7 Britton, *TARDISbound*, 15.

8 Karen Hellekson, '"Doctor Who Unbound", the Alternate History and the
Fannish Text', in *Fan Phenomena: Doctor Who*, ed. Paul Booth (Bristol:
Intellect, 2013), 128–34.

9 Britton, *TARDISbound,* 59.

10 Nicholas Briggs, 'Letters', *Vortex – The Magazine of Big Finish*, 2014, 21,
https://www.bigfinish.com/vortex/v/60.

11 Britton, *TARDISbound,* 111.

12 There have also been new Classic companions created for Big Finish –
Charley Pollard with the Eighth and Sixth Doctors and Dr Evelyn Smythe
with the Sixth Doctor being two of the most prominent – who demonstrate
a renewed focus on female characterizations.

13 Lorna Jowett, *Dancing with the Doctor: Dimensions of Gender in the
Doctor Who Universe* (London: I.B. Tauris, 2017), 108.

14 Although no further titles in the *Jenny* series have been announced as of
the time of this writing, Big Finish has rarely released a box set without
adding in additional titles later.

15 A low bar, admittedly: Katarina was in five half-hour episodes in the 1960s
before producers changed their mind about keeping her in the show and
killed her off in episode four of *The Daleks' Master Plan* (1965–66).

16 Jowett, *Dancing with the Doctor.*
17 Steven Moffat, 'The Time Is Now! The DWM Interview: Steven Moffat',
Doctor Who Magazine #418 (3 March 2010): 18; cited in Richard Hewett,
'Who Is Matt Smith? Performing the Doctor', in *Doctor Who: The Eleventh
Hour*, ed. Andrew O'Day (London: I.B. Tauris, 2014), 22.

Dialogue 2C

1 Cf. *Doctor Who Magazine #150* (July 1989), 8; Baker received 28.8 per cent
of the vote, against Sylvester McCoy's 24.1 per cent.
2 *Doctor Who Magazine #160* (May 1990).
3 A recording is included as an extra on *The Three Doctors'* (1972–73) DVD
release.
4 See WhySoSerious123, https://forums.digitalspy.com/discussion/1318449/
series-5-completely-ruined-doctor-who-for-me, accessed 8 November 2018.
5 See https://www.reddit.com/r/gallifrey/comments/2dud3k/how_did_
people_react_when_matt_smith_was/, accessed 8 November 2018.
6 Moffat, Introduction to *Tomb of the Cybermen.*
7 Dylan Morris, 'Britain as Fantasy: New Series Doctor Who in Young
American Nerd Culture', in *Fan Phenomena: Doctor Who*, ed. Paul Booth
(Bristol: Intellect, 2013), 51.
8 Morris, 'Britain as Fantasy', 57.
9 Steven Warren Hill, Jennifer Adams Kelley, Nicholas Seidler, and Robert
Warnock, with Janine Fennick and John Lavalie, *Red White and Who: The
Story of Doctor Who in America* (Illinois: ATB Publishing, 2017), 475.

Chapter 3

1 Gary Gillatt, 'The Fan Gene: Part One: Defining the Indefinable', *Doctor
Who Magazine #326* (5 February 2003): 14.
2 Tat Wood, *About Time 6: The Unauthorized Guide to Doctor Who 1985–1989,
Seasons 22 to 26, The TV Movie* (Des Moines: Mad Norwegian, 2007), 15.
3 Britton, *TARDISbound,* 12.
4 Hills, *Triumph*, 4.
5 Abigail Derecho, 'Archontic Literature: A Definition, a History, and Several
Theories of Fan Fiction', in *Fan Fiction and Fan Communities in the
Age of the Internet*, ed. Karen Hellekson and Kristina Busse (Jefferson:
McFarland, 2006), 61–78.
6 Lee Barron, 'Proto-Electronica vs. Martial Marches: *Doctor Who, Stingray,
Thunderbirds* and the Music of 1960s British SF Television', *Science Fiction
Film and Television* 3, no. 2 (2010): 239–52; Alec Charles, 'The Crack of
Doom: The Uncanny Echoes of Steven Moffat's *Doctor Who*', *Science
Fiction Film and Television* 4, no. 1 (2011): 1–23; Anne Cranny-Francis

and John Tulloch, 'Vaster than Empire(s), and More Slow: The Politics and Economics of Embodiment in *Doctor Who*', in *Third Person: Authoring and Exploring Vast Narratives*, ed. Pat Harrigan and Noah Wardrip-Fruin (Cambridge: The MIT Press, 2009), 343–56.

7 John Tulloch and Manual Alvarado, *Doctor Who: The Unfolding Text* (New York: Simon and Schuster, 1984), 4.

8 Hills, *Triumph*, 14–15.

9 Tulloch and Alvarado, *The Unfolding Text*, 2.

10 Hayden White, *The Content of the Form: Narrative Discourse and Historical Representation* (Baltimore: The Johns Hopkins University Press, 1987), 105.

11 Haslett, 'Swap Shop', 8.

12 Haslett, 'Swap Shop'.

13 Haslett, 'Swap Shop', 11.

14 Hills, *Triumph*, 5.

15 Chapman, *Inside the TARDIS*, 98; Hills, 'Gothics'; Andy Murray, 'The Talons of Robert Holmes', in *Time and Relative Dissertations in Space: Critical Perspectives on Doctor Who*, ed. David Butler (Manchester: Manchester University Press, 2007), 223.

16 MacDonald, 'Sign "O" the Times', 4.

17 Jones, 'Life in the Hiatus'.

18 Matthew Kilburn, 'Was There a Hinchcliffe Era?', in *Time Unincorporated 2: Writings about the Classic Series*, ed. Graeme Burk and Robert Smith? (Des Moines: Mad Norwegian, 2010), 167; Paul Booth and Jef Burnham, 'Who Are We? Re-Envisioning the Doctor in the 21st Century', in *Remake Television: Reboot, Re-Use, Recycle*, ed. Carlen Lavigne (Lanham, MD: Lexington Books, 2014), 203–20.

19 Wood, *About Time*, 11.

20 Chapman, *Inside the TARDIS*, 83.

21 Steward, 'Author Who?', 314; see also Rolinson, "*Who* Done It"', 179.

22 Quoted in Tulloch and Alvarado, *The Unfolding Text*, 3.

23 Russell T Davies with Benjamin Cook, *The Writer's Tale: The Final Chapter* (London: BBC, 2010), 133, 469.

24 However, it is notable that some of the producers of *Doctor Who* have been gay, breaking this paradigm.

25 Hills, 'Gothic'.

26 Jonathan Bignell, 'Exemplarity, Pedagogy and Television History', *New Review of Film and Television Studies* 3, no. 1 (2005): 15–32.

27 Mike Morris, '10 Official Writers' Guidelines for the Pertwee Era', in *Time Unincorporated: The Doctor Who Fanzine Archives, Vol. 2: Writings on the Classic Series*, ed. Graeme Burk and Robert Smith? (Des Moines: Mad Norwegian, 2010), 112–14.

28 Daniel O'Mahoney, '"Now How Is That Wolf Able to Impersonate a Grandmother?" History, Pseudo-History, and Genre in *Doctor Who*', in *Time and Relative Dissertations in Space: Critical Perspectives on Doctor Who*, ed. David Butler (Manchester: Manchester University Press, 2007), 56–7.

29 Hills, *Triumph*, 7; see also David Butler, 'How to Pilot a TARDIS: Audiences, Science Fiction and the Fantastic in *Doctor Who*', in *Time and Relative Dissertations in Space: Critical Perspectives on Doctor Who*, ed. David Butler (Manchester: Manchester University Press, 2007), 20.

30 Tulloch and Alvarado, *The Unfolding Text,* 5.

31 Jason Mittell, *Genre and Television: From Cop Shows to Cartoons in American Culture* (New York: Routledge, 2004), 7.

32 Davies, *Writers*, 150.

33 Murray, 'Talons', 219.

34 Gareth Roberts, 'Robert Holmes', *Doctor Who Magazine Special Edition #5* (2003): 55.

35 Hills, 'Gothic', 3; Hills, *Triumph*.

36 Charles, 'Crack'.

37 Paul Booth, *Time on TV: Temporal Displacement and Mashup Television* (New York: Peter Lang, 2012), 155.

38 Andrew Tudor, 'Genre', in *Film Genre Reader IV*, ed. Barry Keith Grant (Austin: University of Texas Press, 2012), 5.

39 Mittell, *Genre,* 11–12.

40 Rolinson, '"*Who* Done It"', 182–3; see also Hills, 'Gothic', 7.

41 Britton, *TARDISbound*, 5; Pat Harrigan and Noah Wardrip-Fruin, 'Introduction', in *Third Person: Authoring and Exploring Vast Narratives*, ed. Pat Harrigan and Noah Wardrip-Fruin (Cambridge: The MIT Press, 2009), 2.

42 David Butler, 'Introduction', in *Time and Relative Dissertations in Space*, ed. David Butler (Manchester: Manchester University Press, 2007), 8.

43 Hills, *Triumph,* 8.

44 See Butler, 'Introduction', 7; Elizabeth Sandifer, *TARDIS Eruditorum – An Unauthorized Critical History of* Doctor Who *Volume 1: William Hartnell* (USA: CreateSpace, 2011).

45 John Frow, *Cultural Studies and Cultural Value* (Oxford: Clarendon, 1995), 145.

46 Hills, *Fan Cultures*, 46.

47 Derecho, 'Archontic'.

48 Derecho, 'Archontic', 64.

49 See Paul Booth, *Digital Fandom 2.0: New Media Studies* (New York: Peter Lang, 2016).

50 Tulloch and Alvarado, *The Unfolding Text,* 5–6.

51 Jacques Derrida, *Archive Fever*, trans. Eric Prenowitz (Chicago: University of Chicago Press, 1996), 17.

52 Britton, *TARDISbound,* 23.

53 McKee, '"Which Is the Best *Doctor Who* Story?" A Case Study in Value Judgments Outside the Academy'.

54 Lance Parkin and Lars Pearson, *AHistory: An Unauthorized History of the Doctor Who Universe*, 3rd ed. (Des Moines: Mad Norwegian, 2012).

55 Lance Parkin, 'Truths Universally Acknowledged: How the "Rules" of *Doctor Who* Affect the Writing', in *Third Person: Authoring and Exploring Vast Narratives*, ed. Pat Harrigan and Noah Wardrip-Fruin (Cambridge, MA: The MIT Press, 2009), 13–24.

56 Hills, *Triumph,* 6–7.

57 Gillatt, 'Fan Gene', 13–14.

58 Davies, *Writers,* 627.

59 Derrida, *Archive,* 68.

60 Ibid., 14.

61 Jones, 'Life in the Hiatus'.

62 Alec Charles, 'The Ideology of Anachronism: Television, History and the Nature of Time', in *Time and Relative Dissertations in Space: Critical Perspectives on Doctor Who*, ed. David Butler (Manchester: Manchester University Press, 2007), 111.

63 Booth, *Digital,* 109.

64 Britton, *TARDISbound*, 26.

65 Matt Hills, 'Absent Epic, Implied Story Arcs, and Variation on a Narrative Theme: *Doctor Who* (2005–2008) as Cult/Mainstream Television', in *Third Person: Authoring and Exploring Vast Narratives*, ed. Pat Harrigan and Noah Wardrip-Fruin (Cambridge: The MIT Press, 2009), 334.

66 Hills, 'Gothic'; Hills, *Triumph*.

67 Leora Hadas and Limor Shifman, 'Keeping the Elite Powerless: Fan-Producer Relations in the "Nu Who" (and New YOU) Era', *Critical Studies in Media Communication* 30, no. 4 (2012): 10.

Case Study 3A

1 Bob Baker, 'Going Solo', *Nightmare of Eden DVD* documentary, London: BBC, 2012.

2 See 'Nightmare of Eden', *Wikipedia,* https://en.wikipedia.org/wiki/Nightmare_of_Eden, 2018.

3 Baker, 'Going Solo'.

4 See Chapter 2 and our discussion of rankings in *Doctor Who Magazine*.

5 Tulloch and Alvarado, *The Unfolding Text*, 154.

6 The question mark is part of his name.

7 Robert Smith?, 'Williams' Lib', in *Time Unincorporated: The Doctor Who Fanzine Archives, Vol. 2: Writings on the Classic Series*, ed. Graeme Burk and Robert Smith? (Des Moines: Mad Norwegian, 2010), 159.

8 Smith?, 'Williams' Lib', 160–1.

9 Mike Morris, '10 Things I Want to Say about the Graham Williams Era (Taking in "Why Various Other Shows Are Rubbish" on the Way)', in *Time Unincorporated: The Doctor Who Fanzine Archives, Vol. 2: Writings on* *the Classic Series*, ed. Graeme Burk and Robert Smith? (Des Moines: Mad Norwegian, 2010), 112-14.

10 Baker, 'Going Solo'.

11 *'Nightmare of Eden'*, n.d., http://www.androzani.com/eden.shtml, accessed 15 January 2019.

12 *'Nightmare of Eden'*.

13 Well, I'm sure some people would.

14 Alan McKee, 'Why Is "City of Death" the Best *Doctor Who* Story?' in *Time and Relative Dissertations in Space*, ed. David Butler (Manchester: Manchester University Press, 2007).

15 Paul Cornell, Martin Day, and Keith Topping, *The Discontinuity Guide* (London: Virgin, 1995), 245.

Case Study 3B

1 Ken Griffin, 'Insufficient Evidence: Evaluating Dr Who's Lost Adventures', *Science Fiction Film and Television* 7, no. 2 (2014): 264.

2 The Reaction Index was a statistical method used by the BBC to measure viewer sentiment about a particular text; audiences were polled on their feelings about an episode, the results of which were then averaged to find the general appreciation.

3 BBC Caversham, Audience Research Report, 'The Meddling Monk', VR/65/371 (12 August 1965). The authors wish to thank Tom Hercock of the Written Archives Centre for his assistance in locating these reports.

4 BBC Caversham.

5 Anon, 'Living in the Past', *Doctor Who Magazine #56* (September 1981), 27.

6 Writing in 2008, Paul Lee speculated that copies of individual episodes of *The Time Meddler* were known about within fandom prior to the return of overseas copies in 1984; See, Paul Lee 'Missing without Trace', *Whotopia* 14 (2008), 9. Elsewhere, Lee claims the discoverer of these episodes was Ian Levine, and that they were located in 1982 (http://www.paullee.com/drwho/missingwithouttrace.html, accessed 1 November 2018).

7 The serial was not novelized until 1987.

8 Richard Marson, 'Comedy in *Doctor Who*', *Doctor Who Magazine #104* (1985): 22.

9 *An Adventure in Time and Space* 19 (1986): 6.

10 See the collection of highly admiring fan reviews at http://www.pagefillers.com/dwrg/timeme.htm (last accessed 2 November 2018), originally uploaded between 1998 and 2012. Praise for *The Time Meddler* was not uniform, however. Graham Howard's 1993 review of a recent New Zealand repeat sounded a note of qualification; the serial offered 'quite an entertaining tale', but was also 'at times somewhat ponderous', and the story was unfavourably compared with *Day of the Daleks*, the Jon Pertwee serial that *The Time Meddler* was scheduled to replace. *Time Space Visualiser* 33 (April 1993); archived copy at http://doctorwho.org.nz/archive/tsv33/thetimemeddler.html, accessed 2 November 2018.

11 Of the four Hartnell serials placed higher, three were the perennially popular Dalek stories; the other, *The Aztecs* (1964), placed 61st.

12 For commentary, see the untitled article by Craig Owen Jones, *Panic Moon* 9 (May 2014): 29–31.

13 Burk and Smith?, *Who's 50*, 373.

14 Emily Cook, 'London 1965', *Doctor Who Magazine #527* (August 2018): 28–9.

Dialogue 3C

1 Hills, 'Dispersible Television Text'.

2 Lynne M. Thomas, 'Build High for Happiness!', in *Chicks Unravel Time*, ed. Deborah Stanish and L.M. Myles (Des Moines, IA: Mad Norwegian Press, 2012), 173.

3 Thomas, 'Build High for Happiness!'

4 Wood, *About Time 6*, 201–2.

5 Tulloch and Alvarado, *The Unfolding Text*, 249.

Chapter 4

1 See Paul Booth and Peter Kelly, 'The Changing Faces of *Doctor Who* Fandom: New Fans, New Technologies, Old Practices?' *Participations* 10, no. 1 (2013): 56–72.

2 For the exceptionally caustic response of fans of the 1970s original version of *Battlestar Galactica* to the re-imagining of the show in 2003, see Ryan Britt, 'How Battlestar Galactica Barely Survived Toxic Fandom', *Den of Geek*, 30 August 2018, www.denofgeek.com/us/tv/battlestar-galactica/275995/how-battlestar-galactica-barely-survived-toxic-fandom, accessed 5 November 2018.

3 Booy, *Love and Monsters*, 7.

4 Mark Jefferies and Nicola Methven, *Daily Mirror*, '*Doctor Who* Fans Boycott Official Magazine over Young Age of New Reviewer Team', 7 May 2018, https://www.mirror.co.uk/tv/doctor-who-fans-boycott-official-12496989, accessed 4 November 2018.

5 Maria Kalotichou, 'Things Aren't What They Used to Be …', www.bigblueboxpodcast.co.uk/things-arent-what-they-used-to-be/, 30 May 2018, accessed 5 November 2018.

6 Kara Dennison, 'Time Team vs. the Classics', 7 May 2018, http://karadennison.blogspot.com/2018/05/doctor-who-time-team-vs-classics.html, accessed 5 November 2018.

7 Dennison suggests, however, that this comment may have been tongue-in-cheek.

8 Booy, *Love and Monsters*, 7.

9 Both of the current authors have previously quoted it in academic publications.

10 Boym, *The Future of Nostalgia*; Christina Goulding, 'An Exploratory Study of Age Related Vicarious Nostalgia and Aesthetic Consumption', *Advances in Consumer Research* 29 (2002): 542–46.

11 Chapman, *Inside the TARDIS*, 290–1.

12 Malcolm Hulke and Terrance Dicks, *The Making of Doctor Who* (London: Target, 1972).

13 *DWM #51* (April 1981): 5.

14 Van Wyck Brooks, 'On Creating a Usable Past', *The Dial* LXIV (1918): 341.

15 The 'one day' speech, for example, formed the centrepiece to the cold opening of *Remembrance of the Daleks* (1988), and also featured in *The Five Doctors* (1983) and *An Adventure in Space and Time* (2013).

16 Jason Mittell, *Complex TV: The Poetics of Contemporary Television Storytelling* (New York: New York University Press, 2006), 43.

17 Andrew Blair, 'Doctor Who, Twitch, and Why Are We Surprised Younger Viewers Love Classic Who?', 5 June 2018, http://cultbox.co.uk/features/doctor-who-twitch-and-why-are-we-surprised-younger-viewers-love-classic-who, accessed 9 November 2018.

Case Study 4A

1 Danny Nicol, *Doctor Who: A British Alien?* (Basingstoke, UK: Palgrave, 2018), 52.

2 In the audio release of this mostly missing serial (released in the 1990s), it is contrived that Peter Purves' commentary is heard over the offending line.

3 Stagism is the belief that people of different races/cultural backgrounds 'develop' at a different pace from each other, and thus non-European peoples were at a more 'primitive' stage in their development (see Lindy A. Orthia, 'Savages, Science, Stagism and the Naturalized Ascendancy of the Not-We in *Doctor Who*', in *Doctor Who and Race*, ed. Lindy A. Orthia (Bristol, UK: Intellect, 2013), 272).

4 Lindy A. Orthia, '"Sociopathetic Abscess" or "Yawning Chasm"? The Absent Postcolonial Transition in *Doctor Who*', *The Journal of Commonwealth Literature* 45 (2010): 213–14.

5 The serial placed fourth in the Mighty 200 fan poll of 2009, and sixth in the fiftieth anniversary poll conducted by *DWM* in early 2014.

6 Kate Orman, '"One of Us Is Yellow": Doctor Fu Manchu and *The Talons of Weng-Chiang*', in *Doctor Who and Race*, ed. Lindy A. Orthia (Bristol, UK: Intellect, 2013), 85.

7 Possibly a moniker rather than a real name; a Lynda Day appears as a character in Steven Moffat's first television hit, the ITV drama *Press Gang* (1989–93), played by Julia Sawalha.

8 Lynda Day, comment on 'Injury, Insult and *The Talons of Weng-Chiang* (1977)', blog by Johnny Spandrell, 15 November 2015, https://randomwhoness. com/2015/11/14/injury-insult-and-the-talons-of-weng-chiang-1977/, accessed 3 November 2018.

9 Gavin Schaffer, '"Till Death Us Do Part" and the BBC: Racial Politics and the British Working Classes 1965–75', *Journal of Contemporary History* 45 (2010): 459–61.

10 *Love Thy Neighbour* (ITV, 1972–76) centred on the antagonisms created in a white household when a black family moves in next door. *Curry and Chips* (ITV, 1969) starred Irish actor Spike Milligan in brownface as a Pakistani immigrant; despite achieving high ratings, it was cancelled after one series. The peculiar racial politics of the latter are discussed at length by Sarita Malik, *Representing Black Britain: Black and Asian Images on Television* (London: Sage, 2002), 95.

11 Louis Mahoney, 'Racist Beliefs "Endemic" amongst White Population', *The Stage*, 5 October 1975, 10.

12 Schaffer, '"Till Death Us Do Part" and the BBC', 470.

13 *Liverpool Echo*, 15 February 1982, 2–3.

14 Including as far afield as America; see, for example, *The Daily Illini*, 18 January 1975, 13.

15 Orman, 'One of Us Is Yellow', 85.

16 Tulloch and Alvarado, *The Unfolding Text*, 30.

17 Nicol, *A British Alien?* 54.

18 Jan Johnson-Smith, *American Science Fiction TV: Star Trek, Stargate, and Beyond* (London, UK: I.B. Tauris, 2005), 82.

Case Study 4B

1 Alan Barnes, 'Editor's Note', *Doctor Who Magazine #295* (20 September 2000): 6.

2 Gary Gillatt, 'The Twin Dilemma', *Doctor Who Magazine #413* (14 October 2009): 59–60.

3 Miles and Wood, *About Time 5*, 320.

4 Stuart, 'Doctor Who – The Twin Dilemma Review (or 'In the Immortal Words of Krusty the Klown "What the Hell Was That?")', 30 April 2013, https:// stuartreviewsstuff.wordpress.com/2013/04/30/doctor-who-the-twin-dilemma-review-or-in-the-immortal-words-of-krusty-the-klown-what-the-hell-was-that/

5 Elizabeth Sandifer, 'Does It Offend You? (The Twin Dilemma)', *TARDIS Eruditorum Blog*, May 2012, http://www.eruditorumpress.com/blog/does-it-offend-you-the-twin-dilemma/, accessed 8 November 2018.

6 Christopher Bahn, 'Doctor Who (Classic): "The Twin Dilemma"', 10 July 2011, https://tv.avclub.com/doctor-who-classic-the-twin-dilemma-1798168968, accessed 8 November 2018.

7 Booy, *Love and Monsters*, 113–18.

8 As discussed in David J. Howe, Mark Stammers, and Stephen James Walker, *The Handbook: The Unofficial and Unauthorised Guide to the Production of Doctor Who* (UK: Telos, 2005), 640–2.

9 The interview originally appeared in *Starlog #97,* 1986, but has been reprinted as 'Eric Saward (1986)', *Dr Who Interviews*, 6 August 2009, https://drwhointerviews.wordpress.com/2009/08/06/eric-saward-1986/, accessed 20 November 2018.

10 He is also the only person to have directed both Classic and New *Who* episodes, at least as of 2019.

11 Miles and Wood, *About Time 5,* 63.

12 Muir, *Critical History*, 345.

13 Miles and Wood, *About Time 5,* 320.

14 Miles and Wood, *About Time 5,* 307.

15 Gillatt, 'The Twin Dilemma', 59 (*my emphasis*).

Dialogue 4C

1 Owen Jones, 'Life in the Hiatus'.

2 We refrain from calling it a 'webisode', as it was viewable on terrestrial television via the red button service for a week after its release online.

3 Beware the time scoop!

4 http://missingepisodes.proboards.com/thread/12464/dimensions-time-footage, accessed 29 November 2018.

5 http://missingepisodes.proboards.com/thread/12575/master-tape-dimensions-time-wiped, accessed 29 November 2018.

6 As an insert for the 1993 Children in Need BBC telethon, all the actors involved waived a fee, but as a result, BBC Enterprises undertook never to release the episodes for commercial gain.

Conclusion

1 He also links this to Henry Jenkins' discussion of *The Velveteen Rabbit* and the way that *love* can bring value to objects (*Textual Poachers*).

2 It's a sweet moment.

3 See Karin Hellekson, 'A Fannish Field of Value: Online Fan Gift Culture', *Cinema Journal* 48, no. 4 (2009): 113–18; Lewis Hyde, *The Gift: Creativity and the Artist in the Modern World* (New York: Vintage, 2007).

4 Paul Booth, *Digital Fandom 2.0: New Media Studies* (New York: Peter Lang, 2016).

5 C. Lee Harrington and Denise Bielby, 'A Life Course Perspective on Fandom', *International Journal of Cultural Studies* 13, no. 5 (2010): 429–50.

6 Henry Jenkins, 'Acafandom and Beyond: Week Two, Part One (Henry Jenkins, Erica Rand, and Karen Hellekson)', *Confessions of an Aca-Fan*, 20 June 2011, http://henryjenkins.org/blog/2011/06/acafandom_and_beyond_week_two.html, accessed 5 November 2018); Hills, *Fan Cultures*.

7 Hills, *Fan Cultures,* 11–12.

8 Katherine Larsen and Lynn Zubernis, *Fangasm* (Iowa City, IA: University of Iowa Press, 2013), 81.

9 Kelli Marshall, 'I'm an Academic, and I Run a Fan Site', *ChronicleVitae*, 11 February 2016, https://chroniclevitae.com/news/1286-i-m-an-academic-and-i-run-a-fan-site, accessed 8 November 2018.

10 See Sean Ahern, '"We FBA Now": Community Building and the Furry Basketball Association', in *Popular Culture in the Twenty-First Century*, ed. Myc Wiatrowski and Cory Barker (Newcastle, UK: Cambridge Scholars Press, 2013), 83 for an example.

11 Hills, *Fan Cultures*.

12 Hills, *Triumph*, 9.

13 Although given the structural inequalities in the academic system, this is closer to the reality of academia than we would like.

14 Of course, these are just specific examples of specific moments – one could easily point to 1970's politics, 1980's feminism, or 2016's racial diversity in media as key comparisons. Or others ….

15 See Piers Britton, *TARDISbound* (London: I.B. Tauris, 2012).

16 Although, of course, they will always exist in one form or another.

17 See Hill *et al.*, *Red White and Who*.

18 See Andrew O'Day, ed. *Doctor Who – The Eleventh Hour: A Critical Celebration of the Matt Smith and Steven Moffat Era* (London: I.B. Tauris, 2014).

19 Hills, *Triumph*, 9.

20 Let us know, future people of Earth! Are you looking forward to the seventy-fifth anniversary of *Doctor Who*?

Bibliography

'A New Face for Dr Who'. *Sydney Morning Herald*, 26 April 1982. http://cuttingsarchive.org/index.php/A_new_face_for_%27Dr_Who%27. Accessed 19 March 2018.

'Appreciation Index'. *Wikipedia*, 2018. https://en.wikipedia.org/wiki/Appreciation_Index. Accessed 8 November 2018.

'Doctor Who 50th – The Curator/Future Doctor (Reaction Mashup), Part 4 of 5'. https://www.youtube.com/watch?v=B2oSM4cU-_s. Accessed 22 October 2018.

'Doctor Who Magazine'. *Wikipedia*, 2018. https://en.wikipedia.org/wiki/Doctor_Who_Magazine. Accessed 8 November 2018.

'Dr Who Companion Wants to Be Role Model'. *Sarasota Herald Tribute*, 26 May 1987. http://cuttingsarchive.org/index.php/Names_in_the_News,_May_25,_1987. Accessed 19 March 2018.

'Eric Saward (1986)'. *Dr Who Interviews*, 6 August 2009. https://drwhointerviews.wordpress.com/2009/08/06/eric-saward-1986/. Accessed 20 November 2018.

'I'm Bossy Enough to Take on Two Doctors!'. *Daily Express*, 28 February 1981. http://cuttingsarchive.org/index.php/I%27m_bossy_enough_to_take_on_two_doctors! Accessed 20 March 2018.

'Nightmare of Eden'. *Wikipedia*, 2018. https://en.wikipedia.org/wiki/Nightmare_of_Eden. Accessed 22 October 2018.

Ahern, Sean. '"We FBA Now": Community Building and the Furry Basketball Association'. In *Popular Culture in the Twenty-First Century*, edited by Myc Wiatrowski and Cory Barker, 82–92. Newcastle: Cambridge Scholars Press, 2013.

An Adventure in Time and Space 19 (1986), 6.

Anon. *Huddersfield Daily Examiner,* 7 December 1963. Retrieved from Grapham Kibble-White Twitter at https://twitter.com/grahamkw/status/935527337898233856.

Anon. 'Living in the Past'. *Doctor Who Magazine #56*, September 1981.

Bahn, Christopher. 'Doctor Who (Classic): "The Twin Dilemma"', 10 July 2011. https://tv.avclub.com/doctor-who-classic-the-twin-dilemma-1798168968. Accessed 8 November 2018.

Baker, Bob. 'Going Solo'. *Nightmare of Eden DVD* documentary. London: BBC, 2012.

Baker, Colin. Interview with Benjamin Cook. *Doctor Who Magazine #322*, 16 October 2002.

Barnes, Alan. 'Editor's Note'. *Doctor Who Magazine #295*, 20 September 2000, 6.

Barron, Lee. 'Intergalactic Girlpower: The Gender Politics of Companionship in 21st Century Doctor Who'. In *Ruminations, Peregrinations, and Regenerations: A Critical Approach to Doctor Who*, edited by Chris Hansen, 130–49. Newcastle: Cambridge Scholars Press, 2010.

Barron, Lee. 'Proto-Electronica vs. Martial Marches: *Doctor Who, Stingray, Thunderbirds* and the Music of 1960s British SF Television'. *Science Fiction Film and Television* 3, no. 2 (2010): 239–52.

BBC Caversham. Audience Research Report, 'The Meddling Monk', VR/65/371. 12 August 1965.

Beaty, Bart, and Benjamin Woo. *The Greatest Commit Book of All Time*. London: Palgrave, 2016.

Bignell, Jonathan. 'Exemplarity, Pedagogy and Television History'. *New Review of Film and Television Studies* 3, no. 1 (2005): 15–32.

Bignell, Jonathan. 'The Child as Addressee, Viewer and Consumer in Mid-1960s *Doctor Who*'. In *Time and Relative Dissertations in Space: Critical Perspectives on Doctor Who*, edited by David Butler, 43–55. Manchester: Manchester University Press, 2007.

Bishop, Vanessa. 'Review: *Tomb of the Cybermen*'. *Doctor Who Magazine #313*, February 2002.

Blair, Andrew. 'Doctor Who, Twitch, and Why Are We Surprised Younger Viewers Love Classic Who?', 5 June 2018. http://cultbox.co.uk/features/doctor-who-twitch-and-why-are-we-surprised-younger-viewers-love-classic-who. Accessed 9 November 2018.

Booth, Paul. *Digital Fandom 2.0: New Media Studies*. New York: Peter Lang, 2016.

Booth, Paul. 'Fans' List-Making: Memory, Influence, and Argument in the "Event" of Fandom'. *MATRIZes* 9, no. 2 (2015): 85–107.

Booth, Paul. *Playing Fans: Negotiating Fandom and Media in the Digital Age*. Iowa City, IA: University of Iowa Press, 2015.

Booth, Paul. *Time on TV: Temporal Displacement and Mashup Television*. New York: Peter Lang, 2012.

Booth, Paul, and Jef Burnham. 'Who Are We? Re-Envisioning the Doctor in the 21st Century'. In *Remake Television: Reboot, Re-use, Recycle,* edited by Carlen Lavigne, 203–20. Lanham, MD: Lexington Books, 2014.

Booth, Paul, and Peter Kelly. 'The Changing Faces of *Doctor Who* Fandom: New Fans, New Technologies, Old Practices?' *Participations* 10, no. 1 (2013): 56–72.

Booy, Miles. *Love and Monsters: The Doctor Who Experience 1979–Present*. London: I.B. Tauris, 2012.

Boym, Svetlana. *The Future of Nostalgia*. New York: Basic Books, 2001.

Briggs, Nicholas. 'Letters'. *Vortex – The Magazine of Big Finish*, 2014. https://www.bigfinish.com/vortex/v/60

Briggs, Nick. 'The Real McCoy: Part Two'. *Doctor Who Magazine #217*, 26 September 1994.

Britt, Ryan. 'Genre in the Mainstream: *The New Yorker*'s Science Fiction Issue'. Tor.com, 31 May 2012. https://www.tor.com/2012/05/31/genre-in-the-mainstream-the-science-fiction-issue-of-the-new-yorker/. Accessed 24 November 2018.

Britt, Ryan. 'How Battlestar Galactica Barely Survived Toxic Fandom'. *Den of Geek*, 30 August 2018. www.denofgeek.com/us/tv/battlestar-galactica/275995/how-battlestar-galactica-barely-survived-toxic-fandom. Accessed 5 November 2018.

Britton, Piers. *TARDISBound: Navigating the Universes of Doctor Who*. London: I.B. Tauris, 2011.

Brooks, Van Wyck. 'On Creating a Usable Past'. *The Dial* LXIV (1918): 337–41.

Burk, Graeme, and Robert Smith?. *Who's 50: The 50 Doctor Who Stories to Watch before You Die – An Unofficial Companion*. Toronto: ECW Press, 2013.

Butler, David. 'How to Pilot a TARDIS: Audiences, Science Fiction and the Fantastic in *Doctor Who*'. In *Time and Relative Dissertations in Space: Critical Perspectives on Doctor Who*, edited by David Butler, 19–42. Manchester: Manchester University Press, 2007.

Butler, David. 'Introduction'. In *Time and Relative Dissertations in Space*, edited by David Butler, 1–15. Manchester: Manchester University Press, 2007.

Camford, Vic. 'If You Tolerate This Your Children Will Be Next'. *Doctor Who Magazine #284*, 17 November 1999.

Campbell, Mark. *Doctor Who: The Complete Guide*. Harpenden: Pocketguide, 2007.

Canberra Times. 20 May 1982.

Chapman, James. *Inside the TARDIS: The Worlds of Doctor Who*. London: I.B. Tauris, 2006.

Charles, Alec. 'The Crack of Doom: The Uncanny Echoes of Steven Moffat's *Doctor Who*'. *Science Fiction Film and Television* 4, no. 1 (2011): 1–23.

Charles, Alec. 'The Ideology of Anachronism: Television, History and the Nature of Time'. In *Time and Relative Dissertations in Space: Critical Perspectives on Doctor Who*, edited by David Butler, 108–22. Manchester: Manchester University Press, 2007.

Cherry, Brigid. 'Squee, Retcon, Fanwank, and the Not-We: Computer-Mediated Discourse and the Online Audience for NuWho'. In *Ruminations, Peregrinations, and Regenerations: A Critical Approach to* Doctor Who, edited by Chris Hansen, 209–32. Newcastle: Cambridge Scholars Press, 2010.

Cook, Emily. 'London 1965'. *Doctor Who Magazine #527*, August 2018.

Cornell, Paul, Martin Day, and Keith Topping. *The Discontinuity Guide*. London: Virgin, 1995.

Cranny-Francis, Anne, and John Tulloch. 'Vaster than Empire(s), and More Slow: The Politics and Economics of Embodiment in *Doctor Who'*. In *Third Person: Authoring and Exploring Vast Narratives*, edited by Pat Harrigan and Noah Wardrip-Fruin, 343–56. Cambridge: The MIT Press, 2009.

Davies, Russell T, with Benjamin Cook. *The Writer's Tale: The Final Chapter*. London: BBC, 2010.

Day, Lyndia. Comment on 'Injury, Insult and *The Talons of Weng-Chiang* (1977)'. Blog by Johnny Spandrell, 15 November 2015. https://randomwhoness.com/2015/11/14/injury-insult-and-the-talons-of-weng-chiang-1977/. Accessed 3 November 2018.

Dennison, Kara. 'Time Team vs. the Classics', 7 May 2018. http://karadennison.blogspot.com/2018/05/doctor-who-time-team-vs-classics.html. Accessed 5 November 2018.

Derecho, Abigail. 'Archontic Literature: A Definition, a History, and Several Theories of Fan Fiction'. In *Fan Fiction and Fan Communities in the Age of the Internet*, edited by Karen Hellekson and Kristina Busse, 61–78. Jefferson: McFarland, 2006.

Derrida, Jacques. *Archive Fever*, translated by Eric Prenowitz. Chicago: University of Chicago Press, 1996.

Doctor Who Magazine #51, April 1981.

Doctor Who Magazine #62, March 1982.

Doctor Who Magazine #100, May 1985.

Doctor Who Magazine #150, July 1989.

Doctor Who Magazine #160, May 1990.

Doctor Who Magazine #265, 7 May 1998.

Doctor Who Magazine #413, 14 October 2009.

Doctor Who Magazine #474, July 2014.

Duncombe, Stephen. *Notes from the Underground: Zines and the Politics of Alternative Culture*. London: Verso, 1997.

Foucault, Michel. *The Archaeology of Knowledge*, translated by A.M. Sheridan Smith. New York: Pantheon, 1972.

Frankel, Valerie Estelle. *Women in Doctor Who: Damsels, Feminists and Monsters*. Jefferson, NC: McFarland, 2018.

Freund, Katharina. '"We're Making Our Own Happy Ending": The *Doctor Who* Fan Vidding Community'. In *Doctor Who: Fan Phenomena*, edited by Paul Booth, 96–105. Bristol: Intellect, 2013.

Frow, John. *Cultural Studies and Cultural Value*. Oxford: Clarendon, 1995.

Geraghty, Lincoln. *Cult Collectors: Nostalgia, Fandom and Collecting Popular Culture*. London: Routledge, 2014.

Giles, David Boarder, and Amy Peloff. '"There's Nothing Only about Being a Girl": Learning to "Play" the Doctor's Companion'. In *Who Travels with the Doctor? Essays on the Companions of Doctor Who*, edited by Gilliam I. Leitch, and Sherry Ginn, 52–68. Jefferson, NC: McFarland, 2016.

Gillatt, Gary. 'The Fan Gene: Part One: Defining the Indefinable'. *Doctor Who Magazine* #326, 5 February 2003.

Gillatt, Gary. 'The Twin Dilemma'. *Doctor Who Magazine #413*, 14 October 2009.

Goulding, Christina. 'An Exploratory Study of Age Related Vicarious Nostalgia and Aesthetic Consumption'. *Advances in Consumer Research* 29 (2002): 542–6.

Griffin, Ken. 'Insufficient Evidence: Evaluating Dr Who's Lost Adventures'. *Science Fiction Film and Television* 7, no. 2 (2014): 257–64.

Griffiths, Peter. 'The Mighty 200'. *Doctor Who Magazine #413*, 14 October 2009.

Hadas, Leora, and Limor Shifman. 'Keeping the Elite Powerless: Fan-Producer Relations in the 'Nu Who' (and New YOU) Era'. *Critical Studies in Media Communication* 30, no. 4 (2012): 1–17.

Haining, Peter. *Doctor Who: A Celebration*. London: WH Allen, 1983.

Harrigan, Pat, and Noah Wardrip-Fruin. 'Introduction'. In *Third Person: Authoring and Exploring Vast Narratives*, edited by Pat Harrigan and Noah Wardrip-Fruin, 1–9. Cambridge: The MIT Press, 2009.

Harrington, C. Lee, and Denise Bielby. 'A Life Course Perspective on Fandom'. *International Journal of Cultural Studies* 13, no. 5 (2010): 429–50.

Haslett, Michael. 'Swap Shop'. *Doctor Who Magazine #310*, 14 November 2001.

Hellekson, Karen. '"Doctor Who Unbound", the Alternate History and the Fannish Text'. In *Fan Phenomena: Doctor Who*, edited by Paul Booth, 128–35. Bristol: Intellect, 2013.

Hellekson, Karin. 'A Fannish Field of Value: Online Fan Gift Culture'. *Cinema Journal* 48, no. 4 (2009): 113–18.

Hewett, Richard. 'Who Is Matt Smith? Performing the Doctor'. In *Doctor Who: The Eleventh Hour*, edited by Andrew O'Day, 13–30. London: I.B. Tauris, 2014.

Hill, Steven Warren, Jennifer Adams Kelley, Nicholas Seidler, and Robert Warnock with Janine Fennick and John Lavalie. *Red White and Who: The Story of Doctor Who in America*. Illinois: ATB Publishing, 2017.

Hills, Matt. 'Absent Epic, Implied Story Arcs, and Variation on a Narrative Theme: *Doctor Who* (2005–2008) as Cult/Mainstream Television'. In *Third Person: Authoring and Exploring Vast Narratives*, edited by Pat Harrigan and Noah Wardrip-Fruin, 333–42. Cambridge: The MIT Press, 2009.

Hills, Matt. 'Defining Cult TV; Texts, Inter-Texts and Fan Audiences'. In *The Television Studies Reader*, edited by Robert Allen and Annette Hills, 509–23. London: Routledge, 2004.

Hills, Matt. 'The Dispersible Television Text: Theorising Moments of the New *Doctor Who*'. *Science Fiction Film and Television* 1, no. 1 (2008): 25–44.

Hills, Matt. '*Doctor Who*'s Textual Commemorators: Fandom, Collective Memory and the Self-Commodification of Fanfac'. *Journal of Fandom Studies* 2, no. 1 (2014): 31–51.

Hills, Matt. *Doctor Who: The Unfolding Event – Marketing, Merchandising and Mediatizing a Brand Anniversary*. Houndmills: Palgrave, 2015.

Hills, Matt. *Fan Cultures*. London: Routledge, 2002.

Hills, Matt. 'Foreword'. In *Fan Phenomena: Doctor Who*, edited by Paul Booth, 5–9. Bristol: Intellect, 2013.

Hills, Matt. '"Gothic" Body Parts in a "Postmodern" Body of Work? The Hinchcliffe/Holmes Era of *Doctor Who* (1975–77)'. *Intensities: The Journal of Cult Media* 4 (2007). http://intensitiescultmedia.files.wordpress.com/2012/12/hills-gothic-body-parts-in-postmodern-body-of-work.pdf, accessed 15 January 2019.

Hills, Matt. 'Televisuality without Television? The Big Finish Audios and Discourses of "Tele-Centric" *Doctor Who*'. In *Time and Relative Dissertations in Space*, edited by David Butler, 280–95. Manchester: Manchester University Press, 2007.

Hills, Matt. *Triumph of a Time Lord: Regenerating Doctor Who in the Twenty-First Century*. London: I.B. Tauris, 2010.

Howe, David J., and Mark Stammers. *Doctor Who: Companions*. London: Virgin, 1995.

Howe, David J., Mark Stammers, and Stephen James Walker. *Doctor Who: The Eighties*. London: London Bridge, 1996.

Howe, David J., Mark Stammers, and Stephen James Walker. *The Handbook: The Unofficial and Unauthorised Guide to the Production of Doctor Who*. Canterbury: Telos, 2005.

Hulke, Malcolm, and Terrance Dicks. *The Making of Doctor Who*. London: Target, 1972.

Hyde, Lewis. *The Gift: Creativity and the Artist in the Modern World*. New York: Vintage, 2007.

Jameson, Fredric. *Postmodernism, or, the Cultural Logic of Late Capitalism*. Durham, NC: Duke University Press, 1992.

Jefferies, Mark, and Nicola Methven. 'Doctor Who Fans Boycott Official Magazine over Young Age of New Reviewer Team'. *Daily Mirror*, 7 May 2018. https://www.mirror.co.uk/tv/doctor-who-fans-boycott-official-12496989. Accessed 4 November 2018.

Jenkins, Henry. 'Acafandom and Beyond: Week Two, Part One (Henry Jenkins, Erica Rand, and Karen Hellekson)'. *Confessions of an Aca-Fan*, 20 June 2011. http://henryjenkins.org/blog/2011/06/acafandom_and_beyond_week_two.html. Accessed 5 November 2018.

Jenkins, Henry. *Textual Poachers: Television Fans and Participatory Culture*, 2nd ed. New York: Routledge, 2012.

Johnson-Smith, Jan. *American Science Fiction TV: Star Trek, Stargate, and Beyond*. London, UK: I.B. Tauris, 2005.

Jones, Craig Owen. 'Custodial Narration in *Doctor Who* – Or Why 'The Night of the Doctor' Is the Most Important Episode You'll Ever See'. In *New Worlds, Terrifying Monsters, Impossible Things: Exploring the Contents and Contexts of Doctor Who*, edited by Erin Giannini, np. Chicago, IL: PopMatters, 2016.

Jones, Craig Owen. 'Life in the Hiatus: New *Doctor Who* Fans, 1989–2005'. In *Fan Phenomena: Doctor Who*, edited by Paul Booth, 39–48. Bristol: Intellect, 2013.

Jones, Craig Owen. *Panic Moon* 9, May 2014: 29–31.

Jowett, Lorna. *Dancing with the Doctor: Dimensions of Gender in the* Doctor Who *Universe*. London: I.B. Tauris, 2017.

Kalotichou, Maria. 'Things Aren't What They Used to Be …', 30 May 2018. www.bigblueboxpodcast.co.uk/things-arent-what-they-used-to-be/. Accessed 5 November 2018.

Kilburn, Matthew. 'Was There a Hinchcliffe Era?'. In *Time Unincorporated 2: Writings about the Classic Series*, edited by Graeme Burk and Robert Smith?, 167–74. Des Moines: Mad Norwegian, 2010.

Kornberger, Martin. *Brand Society: How Brands Transform Management and Lifestyle*. Cambridge: Cambridge University Press, 2010.

Larsen, Katherine, and Lynn Zubernis. *Fangasm*. Iowa City, IA: University of Iowa Press, 2013.

Lee, Paul. 'Missing without Trace'. *Whotopia* 14 (2008).

Levin, Ian. Twitter, 16 July 2017. Tweet archived at https://www.bleedingcool.com/2017/07/16/ian-levine-jodie-whittaker-doctor-who-hi-nrg-song/. Accessed 8 November 2018.

Lindlof, Thomas R., Kelly Coyle, and Debra Grodin. 'Is There a Text in This Audience? Science Fiction and Interpretive Schism'. In *Theorizing Fandom: Fans, Subculture and Identity*, edited by Cheryl Harris and Alison Alexander, 219–47. Cresskill: Hampton, 1998.

Liverpool Echo, 15 February 1982, 2–3.

Lutz, Tom. *Crying: The Natural and Cultural History of Tears*. New York: W. W. Norton, 1999.

MacDonald, Philip. 'Sign 'O' the Times'. *Doctor Who Magazine Special Edition #10: The Complete Seventh Doctor*, 13 April 2005.

MacDowell, James, and James Zborowski. 'The Aesthetics of "So Bad It's Good": Value, Intention, and *The Room*'. *Intensities: The Journal of Cult Media* 6 (2013): 1–30.

Mahoney, Louis. 'Racist Beliefs "Endemic" amongst White Population'. *The Stage*, 5 October 1975.

Malik, Sarita. *Representing Black Britain: Black and Asian Images on Television*. London: Sage, 2002.

Marshall, Kelli. 'I'm an Academic, and I Run a Fan Site'. *ChronicleVitae*, 11 February 2016. https://chroniclevitae.com/news/1286-i-m-an-academic-and-i-run-a-fan-site. Accessed 8 November 2018.

Marson, Richard. 'Comedy in *Doctor Who*'. *Doctor Who Magazine #104*, September 1985, 20–3.

Marson, Richard. *JN-T: The Life and Scandalous Times of John Nathan-Turner*. London: Miwk Publishing, 2013.

Martin, Dan. 'Doctor Who Recap: Series 37, Episode 7 –Kerblam!'. *The Guardian*, 18 November 2018. https://www.theguardian.com/tv-and-radio/2018/nov/18/doctor-who-recap-series-37-episode-7-kerblam. Accessed 29 November 2018.

McKee, Alan. 'Which Is the Best *Doctor Who* Story? A Case Study in Value Judgments outside the Academy'. *Intensities: The Journal of Cult Media* 1, no. 1 (2001). https://intensitiescultmedia.files.wordpress.com/2012/12/mckee.pdf.

McKee, Alan. 'Why Is "City of Death" the Best *Doctor Who* Story?' In *Time and Relative Dissertations in Space: Critical Perspectives on Doctor Who*, edited by David Butler, 233–45. Manchester: Manchester University Press, 2007.

Miles, Lawrence, and Tat Wood. *About Time 5: The Unauthorized Guide to Doctor Who 1980–1984, Seasons 18 to 21*. Des Moines: Mad Norwegian Press, 2004.

Mittell, Jason. *Complex TV: The Poetics of Contemporary Television Storytelling*. New York: New York University Press, 2006.

Mittell, Jason. *Genre and Television: From Cop Shows to Cartoons in American Culture*. New York: Routledge, 2004.

Moffat, Steven. Introduction to *Earthshock. The Doctors Revisited vol. 2*. New York: BBC America DVD, 2013.

Moffat, Steven. Introduction to *Remembrance of the Daleks. The Doctors Revisited vol. 2*. New York: BBC America DVD, 2013.

Moffat, Steven. Introduction to *The Aztecs. The Doctors Revisited vol. 1*. New York: BBC America DVD, 2013.

Moffat, Steven. Introduction to *The Pyramids of Mars. The Doctors Revisited vol. 2*. New York: BBC America DVD, 2013.

Moffat, Steven. Introduction to *The TV Movie. The Doctors Revisited vol. 2*. New York: BBC America DVD, 2013.

Moffat, Steven. Introduction to *Tomb of the Cybermen. The Doctors Revisited vol. 1*. New York: BBC America DVD, 2013.

Moffat, Steven. 'The Time Is Now! The DWM Interview: Steven Moffat'. *Doctor Who Magazine #418*, 3 March 2010.

Mooney, Darren. 'Doctor Who: Paradise Towers (Review)'. *The M0vie Blog*, 2 July 2013. https://them0vieblog.com/2013/07/02/doctor-who-paradise-towers-review/. Accessed 25 November 2018.

Morris, Dylan. 'Britain as Fantasy: New Series Doctor Who in Young American Nerd Culture'. In *Fan Phenomena: Doctor Who*, edited by Paul Booth, 50–61. Bristol: Intellect, 2013.

Morris, Mike. '10 Official Writers' Guidelines for the Pertwee Era'. In *Time Unincorporated: The Doctor Who Fanzine Archives, Vol. 2: Writings on the Classic Series*, edited by Graeme Burk and Robert Smith?, 112–14. Des Moines: Mad Norwegian, 2010.

Morris, Mike. '10 Things I Want to Say about the Graham Williams Era (Taking in "Why Various Other Shows Are Rubbish" on the Way)'. In *Time Unincorporated: The Doctor Who Fanzine Archives, Vol. 2: Writings on the Classic Series*, edited by Graeme Burk and Robert Smith?, 177–84. Des Moines: Mad Norwegian, 2010.

Muir, John Kenneth. *A Critical History of Doctor Who in Television*. Jefferson, NC: McFarland, 1999.

Mumby, Daniel. 'BLOG SPOT #24: ChiqueGeeks'. *Mumby at the Movies*, 14 May 2014. http://mumbyatthemovies.blogspot.com/2014/05/blog-spot-24-chiquegeeks.html. Accessed 22 October 2018.

Murray, Andy. 'The Talons of Robert Holmes'. In *Time and Relative Dissertations in Space: Critical Perspectives on Doctor Who*, edited by David Butler, 217–32. Manchester: Manchester University Press, 2007.

Murray, Simone. 'Brand Loyalties: Rethinking Content within Global Corporate Media'. *Media, Culture & Society* 27, no. 3 (2005): 415–35.

Nathan-Turner, John. *Doctor Who: The Companions*. London: Piccadilly Press, 1986.

Newman, Kim. *Doctor Who: A Critical Reading of the Series*. London: BFI, 2005.

Nicol, Danny. *Doctor Who: A British Alien?* Basingstoke: Palgrave, 2018.

O'Day, Andrew, ed. *Doctor Who – The Eleventh Hour: A Critical Celebration of the Matt Smith and Steven Moffat Era*. London: I.B. Tauris, 2014.

O'Day, Andrew. 'Event TV: Fan Consumption of Televised *Doctor Who* in Britain (1963–Present)'. In *Doctor Who in Time and Space*, edited by Gillian Leitch, 7–24. Jefferson: McFarland, 2013.

O'Mahoney, Daniel. '"Now How Is That Wolf Able to Impersonate a Grandmother?" History, Pseudo-History, and Genre in *Doctor Who*'. In *Time and Relative Dissertations in Space: Critical Perspectives on Doctor Who*, edited by David Butler, 56–67. Manchester: Manchester University Press, 2007.

Orman, Kate. '"One of Us Is Yellow": Doctor Fu Manchu and *The Talons of Weng-Chiang*'. In *Doctor Who and Race*, edited by Lindy A. Orthia, 83–100. Bristol: Intellect, 2013.

Orthia, Lindy A. 'Savages, Science, Stagism and the Naturalized Ascendancy of the Not-We in *Doctor Who*'. In *Doctor Who and Race*, edited by Lindy A. Orthia, 269–88. Bristol: Intellect, 2013.

Orthia, Lindy A. '"Sociopathetic Abscess" or "Yawning Chasm"? The Absent Postcolonial Transition in *Doctor Who*'. *The Journal of Commonwealth Literature* 45 (2010): 207–25.

Orthia, Lindy. 'A Very Good Googly - Race in Four to Doomsday'. https://doctorwhoandrace.com/2013/05/23/a-very-good-googly-race-in-four-todoomsday/, 23 May 2013. Accessed 8 November 2018.

Owen, Dave. '*Talons of Weng-Chiang*'. *Doctor Who Magazine Special Edition #6: We Doctor Who*, 2003.

Parkin, Lance. 'Truths Universally Acknowledged: How the "Rules" of *Doctor Who* Affect the Writing'. In *Third Person: Authoring and Exploring Vast Narratives*, edited by Pat Harrigan and Noah Wardrip-Fruin, 13–24. Cambridge, MA: The MIT Press, 2009.

Parkin, Lance, and Lars Pearson. *AHistory: An Unauthorized History of the Doctor Who Universe*, 3rd ed. Des Moines: Mad Norwegian, 2012.

Roberts, Gareth. 'Robert Holmes'. *Doctor Who Magazine Special Edition #5*, 31 December 2003.

Roberts, Gareth. 'Same Old Story?' *Doctor Who Magazine #332*, 23 July 2003.

Rolinson, Dave. '"*Who* Done It": Discourses of Authorship during the John Nathan-Turner Era'. In *Time and Relative Dissertations in Space: Critical Perspectives on Doctor Who*, edited by David Butler, 176–89. Manchester: Manchester University Press, 2007.

Russell, Gary. 'Off the Shelf: *Genesis of the Daleks*'. *Doctor Who Magazine #179*, 30 October 1991.

Russell, Gary. 'Off the Shelf: *The Krotons*'. *Doctor Who Magazine #171*, 13 March 1991.

Sandifer, Elizabeth. 'Does It Offend You? (The Twin Dilemma)'. *TARDIS Eruditorum*, May 2012. http://www.eruditorumpress.com/blog/does-it-offend-you-the-twin-dilemma/. Accessed 8 November 2018.

Sandifer, Elizabeth. *TARDIS Eruditorum – An Unauthorized Critical History of Doctor Who Volume 1: William Hartnell*. USA: CreateSpace, 2011.

Sarachan, Jeremy. 'Doctor Who Fan Videos, YouTube, and the Public Sphere'. In *Ruminations, Peregrinations, and Regenerations: A Critical Approach to Doctor Who*, edited by Chris Hansen, 249–61. Newcastle: Cambridge Scholars Press, 2010.

Schaffer, Gavin. '"Till Death Us Do Part" and the BBC: Racial Politics and the British Working Classes 1965–75'. *Journal of Contemporary History* 45 (2010): 454–77.

Schwartz, Barry. *The Paradox of Choice*. New York: HarperCollins, 2004.

Scott, Suzanne. 'Who's Steering the Mothership? The Role of the Fanboy Auteur in Transmedia Storytelling'. In *The Participatory Cultures Handbook*, edited by Aaron Delwiche and Jennifer Jacobs Henderson, 43–52. New York: Routledge, 2013.

Semper 10, November 1985.

Smith?, Robert. 'Williams' Lib'. In *Time Unincorporated: The Doctor Who Fanzine Archives, Vol. 2: Writings on the Classic Series*, edited by Graeme Burk and Robert Smith?, 159–63. Des Moines: Mad Norwegian, 2010.

Sontag, Susan. 'Notes on "Camp"'. 1964. https://faculty.georgetown.edu/irvinem/theory/Sontag-NotesOnCamp-1964.html. Accessed 24 November 2018. Originally published as 'Notes on "Camp"'. *Partisan Review* 31, no. 4 (1964): 515–30.

Stein, Louisa Ellen. *Millennial Fandom: Television Audiences in the Transmedia Age*. Iowa City, IA: University of Iowa Press, 2015.

Steward, Tom. 'Author Who? Masterplanners, Scribermen, and the Script Doctors: The Producers, Writers and Script Editors of *Doctor Who*'. In *Ruminations, Peregrination, and Regenerations: A Critical Approach to*

Doctor Who, edited by Chris Hansen, 312–27. Newcastle: Cambridge Scholars, 2010.

Stuart. 'Doctor Who – The Twin Dilemma Review (or 'In the Immortal Words of Krusty the Klown "What the Hell Was That?")', 30 April. https://stuartreviewsstuff.wordpress.com/2013/04/30/doctor-who-the-twin-dilemma-review-or-in-the-immortal-words-of-krusty-the-klown-what-the-hell-was-that/. Accessed 8 November 2018.

The Age (Melbourne). 9 September 1982.

The Age (Melbourne). 23 September 1982.

The Daily Illini, 18 January 1975.

Thomas, Lynne M. 'Build High for Happiness!'. In *Chicks Unravel Time*, edited by Deborah Stanish and L.M. Myles, 173–79. Des Moines, IA: Mad Norwegian Press, 2012.

Tudor, Andrew. 'Genre'. In *Film Genre Reader IV*, edited by Barry Keith Grant, 3–11. Austin: University of Texas Press, 2012.

Tulloch, John, and Manual Alvarado. *Doctor Who: 88 Unfolding Text*. New York: St. Martin's, 1984.

Vale, Vicky, ed. *Vol 1. Zines!* San Francisco, CA: V/ Search, 1996.

Walker, Stephen James. 'The Web Planet'. *Doctor Who Magazine Special Edition #7 – The Complete First Doctor*, 2004.

Wallace, Richard. '"But Doctor?" – A Feminist Perspective of *Doctor Who*'. In *Ruminations, Peregrinations, and Regenerations: A Critical Approach to Doctor Who*, edited by Chris Hansen, 102–16. Newcastle: Cambridge Scholars Press, 2010.

Webb, Diana. *Pilgrims and Pilgrimage in the Medieval West*. London: Bloomsbury, 2001.

Wertham, Fredric. *The World of Fanzines*. Carbondale, IL: SIU Press, 1973.

White, Hayden. *The Content of the Form: Narrative Discourse and Historical Representation*. Baltimore: The Johns Hopkins University Press, 1987.

Williams, Linda. *Hard Core: Power, Pleasure, and the Frenzy of the Visible*. Berkeley, CA: University of California Press, 1999.

Williams, Rebecca. *Post-Object Fandom: Television, Identity and Self-Narrative*. New York: Bloomsbury, 2015.

Wilson, Anna. 'The Role of Affect in Fan Fiction'. In *The Classical Canon and/ as Transformative Work*, edited by Ika Willis. Special issue, *Transformative Works and Cultures* 21 (2016). http://dx.doi.org/10.3983/twc.2016.0684. Accessed 22 October 2018.

Woo, Benjamin. 'Understanding Understandings of Comics: Reading and Collecting as Media-Oriented Practices'. *Participations: Journal of Audience and Reception Studies* 9, no. 2 (2012): 180–99. http://www.participations.org/volume%209/issue%202/12%20Woo.pdf, accessed 15 January 2019.

Wood, Tat, and Lawrence Miles. *About Time 2: The Unauthorized Guide to Doctor Who 1966–1969, Seasons 4 to 6*. Des Moines: Mad Norwegian, 2006.

Wood, Tat. *About Time 6: The Unauthorized Guide to Doctor Who 1985–1989, Seasons 22 to 26, The TV Movie*. Des Moines: Mad Norwegian, 2007.

Wood, Tat. 'How to Make Fans (and Influence People!)'. *Doctor Who Magazine #320*, 21 August 2002.

Index

Index of Names

Index of Media